Praise for Louis Begley and the Jack Dana Thrillers

KILL AND BE KILLED

"[This] is delightfully sop
Begley's 1996 novel *About S...*
for two more novels. Jack D...

"[A] gripping thriller filled with tension, danger, and the unknown; and written in such graceful prose, it deserves to be called a literary thriller."　　　　　—*The Huffington Post*

"[An] intriguing follow-up to *Killer, Come Hither* ... Fans of Lee Child's Jack Reacher should enjoy Jack Dana's adventures."　　　　　—*Publishers Weekly*

"Lovers of New York will enjoy the scenes of the city wonderfully portrayed by Begley. The characters are interesting and the lines between good and evil clearly marked. We know Jack will win, but occasionally he needs a little luck and help. Seeing the rich and famous get their comeuppance can be a guilty pleasure. While it appears that Jack has accomplished avenging the murders of his friends, one wonders if there are more of these adventures in Begley's repertoire."　　　　　—*Bookreporter*

"*Kill and Be Killed* is a humdinger. The final confrontation between Jack and Abner Brown is unforgettable."
　　　　　—*The Southampton Press*

"Admirers of the City will love the scenes in this book! The location is fabulous and the details are perfectly written to make the reader feel as if they're right by Jack's side the whole time. A continuation of book one, *Killer, Come Hither,* the main characters are interesting, both good and evil, and the author has added some new, menacing ones to the fire."
— *Suspense Magazine*

KILLER, COME HITHER

"A stealthy, page-turning thriller . . . All admirers of crisp prose and taut plotlines will gladly follow Jack on his deadly quest to circumvent the law."
— *Booklist*

"Louis Begley's award-winning fiction usually takes on bad behavior among the well-bred and prosperous. *Killer, Come Hither* ratchets up the intrigue—and the evil."
— *The Wall Street Journal*

"Begley writes clean, crisp, graceful prose, the kind that's always rare and ever a blessing."
— *The Washington Post*

"*Killer, Come Hither* beckons."
— *Vanity Fair*

"Combines unexpected plot twists and narrative tension with Begley's trademark elegant prose."
— *Shelf Awareness*

FICTION

Kill and Be Killed

Killer, Come Hither

Memories of a Marriage

Schmidt Steps Back

Matters of Honor

Shipwreck

Schmidt Delivered

Mistler's Exit

About Schmidt

As Max Saw It

The Man Who Was Late

Wartime Lies

NONFICTION

Why the Dreyfus Affair Matters

Franz Kafka: The Tremendous World I Have Inside My Head

KILL AND BE KILLED

Kill and Be Killed

A novel

LOUIS BEGLEY

BALLANTINE BOOKS

NEW YORK

2017 Ballantine Books Trade Paperback Edition

Copyright © 2016 by Louis Begley 2007 Revocable Trust
Reading group guide copyright © 2017 by Penguin Random
House LLC

Published in the United States by Ballantine Books, an imprint of
Random House, a division of Penguin Random House LLC, New
York.

BALLANTINE and the HOUSE colophon are registered trademarks
of Penguin Random House LLC.
RANDOM HOUSE READER'S CIRCLE & Design is a registered
trademark of Penguin Random House LLC.

Originally published in hardcover in the United States by Nan A.
Talese, an imprint of the Knopf Doubleday Publishing Group, a
division of Penguin Random House LLC, in 2016.

ISBN 978-1-101-96482-8
Ebook ISBN 978-0-385-54072-8

Printed in the United States of America on acid-free paper

randomhousebooks.com
randomhousereaderscircle.com

9 8 7 6 5 4 3 2 1

Book design by Peter A. Andersen

For Anka and Adam,

my first responder readers

KILL AND BE KILLED

I

Solitude, the charm of Torcello, the island in the Lagoon of Venice on which I had taken refuge after I left New York City, almost daily contemplation in the basilica of the great mosaic of the Last Judgment, and, above all, time had done their work. The wound caused by Kerry's leaving me closed, but a blush of shame still came over my face when I recalled her parting words: I can't stand the way you smell when you touch me, you smell of blood. But the wound and the hurt were slowly becoming an attenuated memory, like the recollection of my beautiful mother's struggle with cancer and her long agony. For all the sorrow, I remained unable to muster any remorse for the way I killed Slobo. Yes, I had watched him bleed, and yes, I had made sure, before I called 911, that he had bled enough for the chances of his being alive and receiving a transfusion when the ambulance brought him from Sag Harbor to the hospital in Southampton to be nil. But the son of a bitch had tortured and killed my beloved uncle Harry, and tortured and killed his beautiful cat, whom I also loved. Was I to hand over that contract killer, wanted by Interpol and who knows how many other police forces, to the Suffolk County D.A. so he could plea-bargain his way to a twelve-, fifteen-year sentence? Never. I'd made no secret of my intention to kill Slobo. A tough, bright, big-time litigator like Kerry, with prosecutorial experience, should have found a way to let me know that if I didn't play the game according to Hoyle she'd dump me, that self-defense, to which she allowed I was entitled in a confrontation with Slobo, meant only what New York law provided, using no more force than a reasonable man would think was reasonably needed. How was I to understand this new—it had to be new—squeamishness and sanctimony? I smelled of blood! Where was her fine olfactory sense when we first made love, and went on making love fervently, every night except when she had to be away for client meetings and when I went out of town twice, once to seek advice from my best friend, Scott Prentice, now working for the Agency in Langley, Virginia, and once to beard Abner Brown, the right-wing mogul and devil incarnate who'd sent Slobo on his murderous errand. Had she not smelled during those nights the blood of the men I'd killed in Iraq and Afghanistan, some of them in hand-to-hand combat? Or did her fine legal sense tell her that every killing by a Marine Corps Infantry officer and Force Recon platoon commander fighting the Global War on Terror is justified? I would stop these silent rants, realizing that they hurt me even more than Kerry's rejection. The other side of that coin, the inescapable truth, was that, however much I fumed, I loved her no less than before.

I emailed her soon after arriving on Torcello, describing—since I knew she'd never seen it—the island's eerie waterlogged landscape, the glories of the basilica, the refined rustic pleasures offered by the *locanda* at which I stayed, and screwed up my courage to add that I would be deliriously happy if she came to visit. Her answer was perhaps three lines long. It told me she was glad I had gone to a place so much to my taste and ignored the invitation to join me. I am embarrassed to say that I persevered. Not to the point, it would seem, of becoming enough of a nuisance for her to block my emails, but writing often enough about my daily life to get her to understand that she was very present in my thoughts. I wanted to avoid the impression that I dashed off notes to her when, like all professional writers who work on a computer, I needed a break and felt the urgent need to Google such red-hot subjects as Cabo Verde or the year in which Mother's Day was first celebrated, or to send long-overdue emails to friends dwelling in the suburbs of my affection. Most of those messages remained unanswered.

I am a novelist. A large part of my first book, about the two wars I'd been to, in Iraq and Afghanistan, I wrote at the Walter Reed Army Medical Center, where surgeons repaired damage a sniper in Sangin had done to my pelvis. More novels followed. On Torcello, I began a book relating the story of Uncle Harry's murder and the vengeance I exacted. Working on it made it impossible not to think about Kerry, not only because she was my girl during that time but also because she had been Harry's protégée and his partner at the law firm and had led me to grasp why Abner Brown decided he had to get Harry out of the way. Turning those events over in my mind, I wrote to her again, at much greater length, explaining more lucidly, I hoped, than when I had argued with her face-to-face why she should accept that Slobo had amply deserved to be killed as I had killed him, that what had been done could not be undone, and that we should not sacrifice our love to the chimera of legality. Her one-sentence answer came swiftly. It's no use writing, Jack, she wrote, I've moved on. She signed "Kerry"—without a closing. No "Love" or "Be well" or "Regards"—but perhaps that was better. Loveless love and empty words might have stung more. But I was left with a tormenting question. What did she mean? Was she telling me that she had someone else and the rights and wrongs of her dismissing me on account of Slobo had become moot? Could she possibly mean that she had lost interest in Abner Brown and his empire of crime and no longer cared whether the road map for prosecutors Harry had prepared and that we handed over to the U.S. attorney ever landed him in jail? That couldn't be. I followed avidly the proceedings brought against Abner's companies by the SEC, the EPA, the IRS, and the Justice Department whenever they were reported in the press I read online. Simon Lathrop, a senior partner in Harry's old firm, Jones & Whetstone, and Harry's best friend going way back to Harvard Law School, emailed me with information appearing in specialized legal and business publications and gossip he picked up. Although Abner Brown himself was not yet under direct attack, his companies were besieged, and the government wasn't sparing its ammunition. How could she have lost interest? That left a hypothesis that I thought was wildly optimistic but was unwilling to abandon. She was telling me through this message, so curt and brusque because she was too proud to admit she had changed her mind, that she was ready to let the past be the past. Only

I would have to plead my case in person. The U.S. government had been shut down for three days, since Tuesday, and no one could predict how long the shutdown would continue, but air traffic controllers remained on the job, keeping—one hoped—their eyes on those computer screens. It was time to take Kerry in my arms, to inhale the head-spinning mixture of soap and fresh sweat that wet her armpits as soon as she was aroused. I had voted by absentee ballot for Obama and was elated by his victory. Ever since, it had seemed to me that the country that had made so decisively the right decision had gone mad. How many times had the House Republicans voted to repeal Obamacare? Twenty-five? Thirty? Was there any measure that carried the country's work forward around which they would coalesce? I didn't think that going home would give me a clearer picture, but I was returning for the most important affair of my life, to win Kerry back and not out of some half-baked sense of civic duty. I had given seven years of my life to unstinting service on the battlefield. *Basta così!* Those that remained would be devoted to my books and loving Kerry. I bought a seat on a direct flight from Venice's Marco Polo to JFK for the following Tuesday and alerted to my arrival Harry's housekeeper, Jeanette, who had been with him for decades and had agreed to stay and work for me.

As flies to wanton boys are we to the gods; they kill us for their sport. Early October may be the most agreeable season in Venice and on Torcello. The air is mild. The rare tourists are apt to be serious people, interested in architecture and art. They speak in low voices. On Sunday I was having what I thought of as my farewell lunch of pasta *frutti di mare* and a Friuli white wine in the garden of my *locanda* when my cell phone rang. It was pure chance that I had turned it on and put it in the pocket of my jacket. Most of the time I left it on the worktable in my room. The reception was spotty, no one telephoned me, and I used my cell phone, if at all, to check on email when I was away from the *locanda*. My heart leaped with excitement when I saw in the caller-ID window Simon Lathrop's name. I was sure he was calling because there had been an important development in the government litigation against Abner Brown's companies. Still, calling on Sunday . . . As soon as I heard his voice, quavering and weak, I knew I was wrong. This wasn't about litigation.

Jack, he said, it's a tragedy.

He seemed unable to continue, so I urged him. What happened, Simon, what is the matter?

Kerry. He got out the word with difficulty. She died on Friday night. In a hotel room in Chelsea. Of an overdose. She'd been at some club down there. A place called Le Raton. Then she checked into this hotel and did it. The chambermaid found her on Saturday morning. There'll probably be something in the *Times* online Breaking News. I wanted to be sure I got to you before you read it. Such a tragedy!

But she didn't use drugs when we were together, I told him. It wasn't a long time, but except when she was at the office I was with her practically every evening, every night. There was no hint of anything of the sort. How is it possible? How can such a thing be?

I realized I was pleading with him, as though he had the power to change what had happened.

There was a long silence, and I thought the call had been dropped. But he spoke again.

Jack, he said, things aren't always as they seem. Rob Mooney, that's the firm's new chairman, has asked me to ride herd on this, and I've been talking to the D.A.—he's a good fellow and I know him well from a City Bar committee I chaired—and to the people he's put in charge of the case. It seems she was a known user at that club. Cocaine and something they call MDMA or E. That Friday night she checked into the hotel alone, paying in advance with a credit card. She was found naked. No signs of struggle, no sign of robbery, her wallet was undisturbed, the door wasn't forced. She'd injected the stuff into a vein on her arm. Analysis of the syringe showed traces of cocaine, MDMA and impurities often associated with it, and heroin. Apparently a deadly cocktail. She'd been drinking, but the alcohol content in her stomach wasn't in excess of whatever norm they use. The point is she wasn't drunk out of her mind. Anyway not too drunk to hit the vein on the first try. They looked for fingerprints, of course. There were her fingerprints everywhere, including on the syringe and the glass in which she mixed the stuff. No other fresh prints. Now you know everything I know. The D.A. thinks it's an open-and-shut case. Suicide or accident.

Simon, I said, forcing myself to speak, it's a question I have to ask, but here it is. Had she had sex?

Unclear, dear boy, unclear. As they put it, the condition of the organs was consistent with sex. Vigorous though not necessarily violent sex. They couldn't determine when the sex would have taken place. No semen was found.

It was my turn to fall silent. I was weeping. As soon as I controlled myself I told Simon I'd made arrangements to be back in the city on Tuesday on a direct flight from Venice. There was some chance that I could catch a plane to Rome or Paris that would get to JFK early on Monday. If I did that, would I be in time for the funeral?

There won't be one, Jack. She left her body to New York–Presbyterian with instructions that what remained after the organs had been harvested be cremated. Frankly I don't know—and haven't had time to find out—if they can use organs in a case like this, but I'm sure they'll try, and they'll surely honor her wishes and go ahead with the cremation. After consulting some of the seniors, we decided, Rob and I, that we would put a short and dignified obituary notice in the *Times,* but we would not hold a memorial service. In the circumstances we think it would be unseemly.

As I listened to Simon drone on so reasonably I realized that I was beginning to feel sick. The waiter had taken away my plate with the uneaten pasta but had left my wineglass. I raised it to my lips and sipped very slowly.

Are the parents still alive? I asked when I thought he had finished. Are there any other relatives?

I believe that the father died a few months ago. The mother is alive. She may be in some sort of retirement community. That Jewish lawyer you use has Kerry's will and is her executor. He'll be on top of all that.

Yes, I muttered. Moses. Moses Cohen. It was Kerry who suggested I turn to him. Perhaps I'll give him a call.

And then I recognized with a start something that had become obvious.

Simon, I said, I'm going to cancel my flight to New York. Whatever else I may have been telling myself, the real reason I wanted to return was to win back my poor Kerry. Now there's no point. I won't stay here forever, but I can work here pretty well. The time to return will come, but not now. I can't go back now.

I understand, Simon answered. Perhaps Jennie and I will first see you in Venice. We too need to get away.

Just as we were going to hang up, a question occurred to me.

You've stayed in touch with her, right? What was she like during the last months? Was she functioning at the office? Getting her work done?

That's the strangest thing, Simon replied. There was no change in her. She was doing a brilliant job on a major litigation for Western Industries. The word about an injunction she'd gotten against a competitor in an unfair advertising action had gotten around, and she was asked by a major new client to review a litigation it's planning to bring. It will be hard to reassign her work and keep the clients satisfied. But I gather that high-performing people can keep cocaine use under control. Something went desperately wrong on Friday night. She made a gross mistake.

I was awake until well past two during the night that followed, reliving every moment I had spent with Kerry. How could I have been so obtuse and failed to notice signs of drug use, perhaps addiction? She was such a straight arrow, so much the all-American girl. A former federal prosecutor, for Christ's sake! How could I have suspected that concealed behind the façade were Mollies, cocaine, and even heroin? If she was addicted, how did she manage to stay off that stuff while I was there? What depths of unhappiness had she hidden from me—and from Harry and the other Jones & Whetstone partners who took her into the firm a year ahead of schedule? By what miracle had it been possible for her to shoulder the weight of a young litigating partner's responsibilities? I didn't know the answer to those questions. Instead, my own insomnia reminded me of our first night together, when I had lain awake for what seemed like hours, savoring the soundness of her sleep. The memory brought to my consciousness another one, which was perhaps less innocent, of looking for dental floss in her bathroom and, having opened a medicine cabinet that turned out not to hold the floss, coming upon a comically long row of amber vials that held pills of various shapes and colors. Somebody is unable to throw away any medicine the doctor prescribes—I chuckled—just like my mother! Indeed my lovely mother had never separated herself from the expired antibiotics, cough remedies, and allergy pills that had turned her bathroom shelves into something resembling a dispensary. That amusing trait, which had enchanted me—just as did Kerry's serving hors d'oeuvres exactly the way my mother might have done—now seemed to me a potential warning I had ignored. Of course, I had not examined those vials. But now it seemed to me not unlikely that they held, instead of just antacids, antihistamines, and leftover amoxicillin, also Prozac, Zoloft, and Xanax and a junkie's hoard of Klonopin, Ativan & Co., as well as, of course, Ambien, Halcion, and, if she could find someone to prescribe or sell it, Seconal. I cursed my stupid good manners. If I'd seen Prozac or Zoloft I might at least have understood that she was in treatment for depression, that she was vulnerable. I might have made a connection between them and her strange, overwrought confession of guilt feelings and cowardice. Culpable cowardice? Because the need to pay the facility where her demented father was hospitalized made her afraid of antagonizing the management of her law firm? Nothing could be more natural, or easier to understand, than her sense that she mustn't put at risk her future at that place and her ability to earn a large income. Instead, all I saw before me was a superwoman who also happened to be the best lover I'd ever had.

In the morning it rained heavily, water coming down straight as it often does in the Venice Lagoon. I stayed in my room after breakfast and opened my laptop. Habit is a powerful force. It overcame my misery. I wrote steadily until almost one and found I had produced my normal quota of thirteen-hundred-and-some usable words. Feeling that I needed a drink, I went down to the combination bar and restaurant, got the bartender to make me a dry gin martini, and had lunch. I lingered and was having my third espresso when the chambermaid brought me a letter addressed in typed capital letters to Jack Dana. It had been posted on Saturday in Venice. Inside was a sheet of white paper in the center of which was a large black spot. No writing, just that spot. Someone has been reading *Treasure Island,* I said to myself, and knows that I will know the meaning of this sign. It was a disturbing thought, especially since the message came from Venice, where my only friends and acquaintances were a New York plastic surgeon and his wife, who had a house on the

Dorsoduro but had left for New York some ten days earlier, an Italian winemaker and his French wife, both of whom I considered particularly well disposed toward me, a restaurant owner called Signor Ernesto, who served the best hamburger in the world in his tiny establishment on the Calle degli Assassini, and the people at a gym in Dorsoduro, where I went two or three times a week to work with a trainer astonishingly like my New York trainer, Wolf. We did kickboxing and some Krav Maga together, and he'd brought me to a level that he thought qualified me to become an instructor. It was inconceivable that any of them would have played this tasteless joke. I really could think of no other Venetians who knew both my name and my address on Torcello. That left, of course, the possibility that the black spot had been sent by the manager of the *locanda* or someone on his staff, but I was a generous tipper, made no trouble, and saw no reason to doubt that my relations with them all were pleasant and amicable. I folded the sheet and put it back in the envelope, taking care not to rub off such fingerprints as there might be. We would see what happened next.

When I went back to my room for the nap that was to precede another work session—since it was too wet to go out, I thought I might as well push ahead—I first read the online edition of the *Times*. Just as Simon had predicted, I found a small news item about Kerry. It gave less detail than Simon's account but had the effect on me of a punch to the gut.

I found, however, that I could neither sleep nor work. The rain having turned into a drizzle, I put on my running shoes and clothes and set out on the daily run I'd skipped that morning. Five miles, which on that small island required inventive itineraries and a lot of cross-country running. I especially valued the latter. Once you've been a U.S. Marine Force Recon officer you want to stay as close to fighting trim as possible short of returning to active service, which was a move I hadn't contemplated and one that was in any event foreclosed by my injuries. I came back sad but able to work and wrote until nearly half past nine, which gave me just enough time to shower and dress and order my dinner before the kitchen closed.

The next day, Tuesday, the sky was of the clearest blue. Since I had produced twice my daily quota the day before, I shortened my morning writing time, took the vaporetto to Venice, and had lunch at Signor Ernesto's. He was full of concern about the Hilton Molino Stucky, a three-hundred-seventy-plus-room hotel that had risen on the Giudecca out of the shell of a long-abandoned but gorgeous flour mill. How many more tourists can we accommodate during the high season? he moaned. Or the ships that will bring them? No respectable business needs them! It was very clear that he did not. His restaurant was full of locals from the Fenice neighborhood—antique-shop owners, real estate and insurance agents, the neighborhood pharmacist, and a couple of lawyers, all of them men wearing suits and neckties—and one or two well-behaved foreigners like me. Ernesto had a gift for inclusion and exclusion. If he liked the cut of your jib, he would rearrange the ingeniously crafted tables so as to be able to seat you. If he didn't, every empty table was reserved. Sorry, I can't help you. *Non c'è niente da fare.* Ernesto came over to my table, as he often did, ready to talk about American politics. I invited him to sit down and poured him a glass of the excellent wine he'd recommended. *Un vino stupendo,* he had said, *stupendo,* and, as always, it deserved the praise. After I'd explained in my usual mix of Italian and English the operation of the debt ceiling and the need for Congress to raise it, and he'd shaken his head once more in disbelief, I asked him just what kind of person—I made clear that I was speaking about Venetians—would, in his opinion, be apt to send me by mail to my *locanda* on Torcello a threatening message. Some anti-American nut, right or left wing? A waiter who thought I hadn't tipped him adequately? I added I was pretty sure that as a rule I over-tipped. A practical joker? Ernesto shook his head and said it was impossible. You're a gentleman, he said, who is liked and respected here. Anyway, stupid messages aren't a Venetian trick.

The weather continued to be beautiful. On Thursday, I had lunch again in the garden of my *locanda.* Sorrow for Kerry had become a constant ache that kept me company from the moment I woke to when I finally fell asleep. It visited me in my dreams, resembling most nearly the dull pain—seven on a scale from one to ten, I would estimate for the pain-management specialist—that plagued me for months after Walter Reed surgeons had repaired my pelvis. I knew the hurt and had carried on with occasional help from Percocet, and I carried on now on Torcello, working steadily, taking my noonday meals in the garden if the sun shone as it did the next day, Friday, exactly one week after Kerry died, plotting in my head the structure of the next chapter. The great difference was that there were no remedies for the present ache and that, deep inside, I didn't wish for relief, lest it signal the slackening of my love.

I finished my half bottle of wine and may have been about to doze off at table—something that occasionally happened to me—when the chambermaid's *Scusi, signore* roused me. She had brought a letter. Like the first, it was addressed to me in solid capital letters and was postmarked Venice with the previous day's date. I slit the envelope with great care and extracted the single sheet it contained. But this time, instead of the black spot, there was an explicit though brief verbal message written out also in solid capital letters: YOU'RE NEXT, FUCKHEAD! I took a deep breath, attracted the attention of the waiter lounging against the balustrade of the veranda, and asked him for an espresso *chiuso,* as concentrated as possible, and a glass of an old Barolo grappa. The identity of the scribe who had set down those words on paper was of secondary interest to me. That the diction was Abner Brown's, I had no doubt. He had dictated them. The thought and the intention were equally familiar. He had tried to have me killed after I discovered that my uncle's suicide was in fact murder, that he had been forced to hang himself by a hit man Brown had sent, a Serb by the name of Slobodan Milić. I killed the Serb, and when I taunted Brown, giving him the news over the telephone, he called me a fuckhead— apparently a term of endearment in Abnerspeak—and gave me the long version of the threat I'd just received. I'll get you, he'd yelled. If it isn't this week or this month, don't think it won't come. I'll hunt you down like the varmint you are. The new element was my being "next." So someone had already been hunted down. I didn't think he meant Harry. For Abner that would be ancient history. The quarry he referred to was clearly Kerry, Harry's most trusted lieutenant, who had learned from Harry most of what he had discovered about the fraud and criminality that pervaded Abner Brown's businesses to the point of being inseparable from them. Harry died because Abner feared that he would expose him. Kerry would have died because she knew too much, and because Abner had probably found out, through moles at the U.S. Attorney's Office in New York or Houston, the FBI, or the Justice Department, that she had interpreted for our government the road map of Abner's criminal empire that Harry had prepared and that I had found after he died. The question to which I had no answer was, Why hadn't Kerry been murdered sooner? Why had he let her live more than a year after the road map was delivered to the authorities? Because I was now convinced that, whether or not Kerry had been snorting cocaine or downing Mollies or other junk, the overdose that killed her wasn't an accident or a suicide. She had been assassinated on Abner's order, just like Harry. If the past was a guide, the threat that I'd be next was not to be taken lightly. I'd left my Marine Corps sidearm, a Colt 1911, in the safe at my apartment in New York. But I'd brought with me, in the suitcase I checked when I took the plane for Venice, the razor-sharp switchblade I took off the mullah I killed with my father's Ka-Bar knife in the barracks in Helmand, putting it right through his neck when I saw the bastard start to pull the pin of a grenade. I went upstairs to check. The suitcase was under my bed. I got it out. The knife was exactly where I'd left it. I put it in the pocket of my jacket and resolved to keep it within reach night and day until I took the plane home. There was a new and urgent reason for going back to New York.

It was three o'clock in the afternoon on Torcello, nine in the morning on the East Coast of the United States. I called the number of Scott Prentice's office cell phone. He answered at once and, after we had exchanged brief, affectionate greetings, said he'd been meaning to call me about Kerry but hadn't had the heart to do it.

You must feel sick, he told me. When I read about her in the *Times* online last Monday I thought someone had hit me with a two-by-four.

I did, I said, and I do. I had meant to go home the next day and planned to surprise you and Susie by showing up in Alexandria unannounced, but after I'd heard about Kerry from Simon Lathrop—he called on Sunday—I just couldn't. I canceled the flight I'd booked and made no other plan. I just stayed and worked.

Then I went on to tell him about the black spot and the message I'd just received.

It's got to be Abner, I said. Abner who decided she had to go, and now has me again in his sights. But I don't understand the timing. What set him off, after all those months? It's got to be linked to something going on in the cases against his companies.

Possibly, Scott replied. I haven't kept up with them the way I should have. Another reason might be that he thought he should lie low after Slobo.

I told him I didn't think going to ground was Abner's style.

Just look at him, I continued, more than a year has passed since we went to the U.S. attorney and to you guys with the

Rosetta stone that basically cracked open his schemes, and he's still sitting pretty. In fact, he's building a state within a state in the U.S., with his super PACs and the river of contributions he directs to every right-wing project, no matter how crazy. I bet you the guy thinks he's so far above the law that none of you can touch him. Something special must be involved.

When will you get back? Scott asked.

I doubt I can manage it tomorrow, but surely within the next three or four days.

Come to see us as soon as you can, and keep me posted. Meanwhile I'll poke around and learn what can be learned. And send me by FedEx those messages. Probably they've been scrubbed of anything that might be a clue, but one never knows. I'd like to have them examined very closely.

I told Scott I'd do exactly that.

II

I said goodbye to Scott, took a deep breath, and went about organizing my departure. But not without first having a drink. I went down to the reception desk, asked the concierge to see whether I could have a business-class seat the following Tuesday on Alitalia's nonstop flight to JFK, and told him he'd find me at the bar. He appeared in no time at all to say that a seat was available. I asked him to reserve it and tell bookkeeping the date of my departure. I glanced at my watch. Four-thirty. Too late for serious work. At best, I could revise the morning's and the preceding day's production. I asked the barista for an espresso and a Barolo grappa and thought about the time I had left in Venice. I would spend some hours at the Accademia and make my way from there on foot to the Gesuiti for another long look at Titian's *Saint Lawrence on the Grill.* The walk was a long one. If there was time left after the visit, I'd take the vaporetto back to the Accademia, get in a session at the gym, say ciao to my trainer Fabrizio, and encourage him once more to give me a ring if he really came to New York in the spring. I'd also give him a present. Two hundred euros seemed about right. At some point, I must revisit the Frari basilica and feast my eyes on its great Titians—the Assumption altarpiece and the Pesaro family Madonna. And I would take leave of the aristocratic winemaker and his wife, if they were in Venice, and of course Signor Ernesto. None of this was really necessary—I could write to the Contarinis and to Ernesto and tell them I had been unexpectedly summoned to New York, and I could mail my present to Fabrizio—and I began to ask myself whether it wouldn't be smarter to get a flight tomorrow, even if it meant changing planes in Paris, Frankfurt, or London. The jobs that lay ahead were to find whoever had killed Kerry and kill him and to bring to a conclusion my unfinished business with Abner Brown. I knew I couldn't and wouldn't shirk them. And yet I made no move to accelerate my departure. A mixture of inertia, nostalgia, and foreboding held me back. Torcello and Venice had been good to me. I wanted a few days' reprieve.

Next morning I was up at a quarter of six as usual for my daily run, put on my running clothes, and slipped the switchblade and my iPhone into the pocket of my windbreaker. First I ran to the vaporetto landing, then all the way back to the basilica. Once there, I doubled back to Fondamenta dei Borgognoni and followed Sentiero Casa Andrich to its end. From there I ran south, in the general direction of Burano, keeping on my right first the uninhabited Isola dei Laghi and then Isola Mazzorbo, once a refuge from barbarian invasions, now better known for the artichokes grown on it. The stretch of dune grass and dwarf thyme and laurel that lay inland to my left was trackless. It was there that I habitually switched to a fartlek run, alternating sprints with jogging, doing squats and push-ups and jumping jacks, and adding exercises of my own invention useful for taking evasive action in an exposed terrain. I'd keep a low profile as I ran, dropping down to the ground at irregular intervals, zigzagging, and crawling. The routine was hell on my running suits, but I was sick of fatigues and anyway didn't want to acquire the reputation as a total weirdo. That concern was surely misplaced. No one was around on that part of the island at my chosen hours, and the few locals who lived on Torcello had long ago become used to foreigners' oddities.

I was about fifty yards from the shoreline, and nearing the southern tip of Torcello, when I saw out of the corner of my eye, as I got up from a crawl, a man in a ski mask rising from behind a duck blind. He held a crossbow and aimed it at me. I hit the deck not a second too soon. An arrow whizzed just above me. I waited a minute or so and showed enough of myself to offer a target—assuming the man was content to wound me. Another arrow. We played that game until he had shot ten arrows. It was time for a test. Gingerly, I raised myself to my knees. Nothing. Tough shit, kiddo, I muttered, no more arrows in your quiver. It's time to have fun. I stood up and gave him the finger. Not being sure how widely recognized it was in Italy, I followed up with the *bras d'honneur* together with the Bronx cheer. The guy seemed to be ready to play, running toward me at full speed. He'd left the crossbow behind. Instead, in his right hand he held a hunting dagger. I waited in a crouch, switchblade closed but in the palm of my right hand.

He didn't like that. Big surprise. Hadn't his bosses told him anything about me? My trainer Fabrizio had been teaching me the grossest insults in Venetian dialect. Otherwise,

I might have missed out on the meaning of the beauties he let go with when he saw I was going to fight. As it was I caught the gist of at least two: *Va in cùeo da to mare* and *Ma ti gà emoròidi in testa?* Roughly: Sodomize your mother and Have you hemorrhoids on your brain? Same to you, I cried and, in that sort of eerie quiet that descends when you're in mortal danger—sharpening your sense of humor—I made a mental note to tell Abner to clean up his own and his killers' language. It was time to get to business. The guy was shifting his dagger from hand to hand, which is standard in a knife fight, and doing a little jig meant to distract me. Then he lunged, the dagger in his right hand, going for my neck. It was a dumb move, one I had parried a hundred times in my Krav Maga sessions. I ducked under the thrust, grabbed his arm, twisted it to the point of breaking. With his other hand he went for my eyes, but it was too late. I'd opened the switchblade during his cute little dance. It was a pleasure to hear him howl as I sliced his belly open. He was wearing a sweatsuit, which gave no resistance. The guts spilled out. You don't die immediately of a stomach wound, and he continued to writhe and howl. It got on my nerves. If I'd had a gun I would have put a bullet through his head. I did the next best thing: I slit his throat.

I caught my breath when the noise stopped. In comparison with Slobo, the killer of my uncle Harry, Harry's cat, and Harry's secretary, who had tried to add me as well to his trophies, this guy wasn't ready for prime time. I wondered who he was and pulled off his ski mask. He was much younger, blond, and, unlike Slobo, had an unscarred and handsome face. Judging by his look, he too could be a Serb or Croat, but in that case why that flow of Venetian dialect filth? Perhaps that was what he'd learned first. To make sure he was good and dead I kicked him. Nothing doing. OK to search him. As I'd expected, there was nothing in his pockets, except a five-hundred-euro bill—his carfare, I snickered—and nothing in his shoes. With my cell phone, I took several photos of him, then cut a square of cloth from his sweatpants and carefully put the euros on it. On second thought, I reached for his hand, cut off his index finger, and put it also on the cloth. Tying the four corners, I made a neat bundle. Perfect material for fingerprints and DNA, I congratulated myself. As I'd also expected, there was a dinghy with an outboard motor at anchor in the narrow arm of the lagoon that separates Torcello at that point from Mazzorbo. I dragged the body over to the dinghy. My initial idea was to load the body into it and give it a good shove in the direction of Burano. I decided against doing that. It was the sort of thing that could set off a big police search for the killer. Instead, I raised the dinghy's anchor, cut the line that attached it, and wrapped the part tied to the anchor around the guy's neck, leaving less than a foot between the two. That done, I pushed the body into the water—R.I.P., kiddo!—and carried out the second part of the discarded plan. I sent the dinghy to make its way through the lagoon. The crossbow was easy to find. I threw it into the water. It was a metal job, heavier than I'd expected, and sank. I would have liked to get rid of the arrows as well, but was it worth the trouble? I didn't think so.

Back at the *locanda,* I stowed my precious bundle in the desk drawer, took a shower, dressed, and went down to breakfast. I was ravenous. By the time I'd finished, it was almost half past nine. Three-thirty in the morning, Scott's time. Never mind. If he was awake at that hour—as he often was because of calls he had to make to operatives in Europe and the Middle East—he'd answer. I went into the garden and called him. It was as though he'd been expecting me. The first words he uttered were to tell me that, as we had both expected, the examination of the two drop-dead messages I'd FedExed to him yielded nothing.

I've got bigger and worse news, I replied, and related the morning's activities.

You're out of your fucking mind, he exclaimed when I got to the part where I cut off the guy's finger.

Let's say that I was on edge, I replied. Having steel arrows shot at you from a crossbow can have that effect. To be quite serious, though, I wanted to provide the best material for getting this guy identified. I'd really like to know who he is. Another serious question. What do I do now? Go to the Italian police? I don't particularly want to. I've got a flight booked for Tuesday. Do I take it? Part of me wants to stay here, to give whoever it is who sent the guy I killed another go at me. Perhaps I could get the next candidate to talk.

Scott was silent long enough for me to wonder once again whether the call had been dropped. But he was right there, thinking.

Jack, old buddy, he said. You really are nuts. Please understand that you're in a fix. If you go to the Italian police, I'm almost certain they'll lock you up while they consider the situation. In fact, your friend's bosses may have sufficient connections to get you hauled in even now on suspicion of murder. In a couple of hours, they'll have put two and two together. You know, the guy hasn't come back, and so forth. The consulate would try to spring you, but I'm not sure they'd succeed, and I'd rather not think of you in an Italian jail, where the people who sent the hit man probably have associates. So that idea is out, and I'm glad you didn't act on some crazy desire to turn yourself in. Second, the notion that you'd wait for the replacement killer in the hope you'd get him to talk is truly bonkers. How do you know they'd give you a fighting chance? Having botched it on this try, they'd make sure the job was done. Most probably they'd get someone to shoot you. Using a high-powered rifle and a scope. You literally wouldn't know what hit you. Third, the sequence of events—day one you get the black spot, day two you get the note saying you're next in line, and day three they send a killer—tells me that Abner, if it really is he, and I'm coming to believe it is, doesn't plan to fool around. As you and I know, he has ample means to do what he wants.

Yes, I said, I think you're right.

All right, then, here is what I want you to do. Put a DO NOT DISTURB sign on your door and pack your bags. I don't want the chambermaid to walk in and see that you are about to fly the coop. When you've finished, stay put, in your room, doing whatever you want to do. Knowing you, I suppose you'll work on your book.

I guess so.

You won't have much time for it, because one of our people, an operations guy, happens to be in Venice. His name is Blaine. Not exactly an Italian name, but his mother was Italian, and he has spent years working in Italy. He'll come to get you in a launch. When he arrives at the *locanda* he'll ask for you, and when reception calls to announce him you should have him come up. He'll help you with your bags, and you'll go downstairs together, check out, get in the launch, which will be tied up right outside, and go to a hotel in Venice. The Gritti, I suppose, since we have a suite there. I suggest you tell the people at the *locanda* that you've changed your plans because of a family problem and are taking the train to Rome. I'm sure they are good people, but whoever is after you probably has an informant in the hotel. Blaine will get you a flight to New York, I hope tomorrow, and in the meantime you can hang out at the hotel. Take your meals in your room, unless Blaine thinks you can go to eat somewhere nearby, for instance Harry's Bar. In that case, he or one of his colleagues will go with you. And please, don't call friends. I don't want anyone except our people to know which flight you're taking. Information gets out, and I want to get you home safe and sound. Let's not take chances.

I thanked him. He was the best friend a man could have.

What shall I do with the package? I asked. You know, the money and the finger.

Give it to Blaine. He'll get it to me.

All right. By the way, I also took pictures of the guy. I'll email them to you. And I still have the question that bugs me. What's behind the timing? What's the rush? Why kill Kerry just then? Why is Brown in such a hurry to get me? You see what I mean.

I do. It's what we've already talked about. We don't know the reason, but we'll sure do our best to figure it out. When we do, you'll probably be on your way to having Abner locked up.

III

You have to give credit where credit is due. The CIA may have fucked up 9/11 and may be royally fucking up the drone program, so that we won't have one friend left in Afghanistan, on the Arabian Peninsula, or in Southeast Asia, but as a travel agent and concierge it can't be beat. Blaine got me checked out of the *locanda,* into the launch, across the lagoon to the Gritti landing on the Grand Canal, and into the Agency's suite with a celerity and smoothness the likes of which I had never experienced. So far as he was concerned, there was no reason we couldn't have dinner together at Harry's Bar. On the late side, if I didn't mind. My flight the next day was at noon; there'd be no need to pass security or passport control, so it would be sufficient if we left for the airport at a quarter of eleven.

That was just fine with me. We walked the two hundred yards or so to the restaurant followed by the man who had driven the launch. He took a seat at the bar, while we were shown to a table in the unfashionable back room.

I hope you don't mind, Blaine said very seriously. If you're

in the front room, you're an easy target for a shooter positioned in the *calle*. If you're here, he has to fire from the bar.
My friend Heinz would get him first.

I laughed in reply and was relieved when, after a moment of
hesitation, Blaine laughed too. He looked all-American, but
he sounded all-Italian, the latter due to the Italian mother
Scott had mentioned and to four years he had spent in Rome,
first at the American Academy and then, still in Rome, at
the Sapienza University, studying Etruscan art. Scott had
recruited him. He was unmarried and had not regretted for a
minute having succumbed to Scott's blandishments.

Why was he in Venice?

The Adriatic, he said, the Adriatic, just think of it. Venice
because of the cruise ships, Mestre and Bari because of the
freighters, have become the prime transit points for drugs—
a huge wholesale business—for valises packed with cash
leaving Italy for destinations in the Balkans, and for arms
going in both directions. Normally, this is not our concern,
but this traffic is eighty percent or more tied to financing
and provisioning international terrorism, and that is where
we come in. Some of the time we help the cops catch the
smugglers and impound the loot. In more interesting cases
we do our own thing. These fellows are even less attractive
than the guys we delivered to Guantánamo and Bagram, so
you almost never hear about them. Serb, Croat, and Albanian
rackets guys and gunmen belonging to Balkan crime families
are all over Venice and Mestre like lice. From what Scott has
told me, the fellow who tried to kill you may have come from
one of those gangs. I don't think we'll be able to identify
him. These guys are two-bit killers, part-time drug dealers,

pimps. Small-time thugs or not, the concept of avenging one of theirs is very strong. That's why Scott wanted me to take all these precautions, and by the way I agree with him one hundred percent.

I nodded and said I understood and was very grateful.

Hey, he replied, I've read your books. You're really good.

Perhaps he wanted to change the subject; perhaps he was sincere. The fact is I've never met a novelist who wouldn't rather talk about his books than anything else. We were still on my most recent published work, the portraits of four of my marine brothers, when Blaine looked at his watch and said I'd better get back to the hotel if I wanted to get a night's sleep before the trip home.

The CIA proved itself just as efficient at JFK as at Marco Polo. I was whisked off the plane and through passport control, where it turned out I didn't need to show my passport. Apparently my two suitcases hadn't traveled in the hold with the rest of the luggage.

They're already in the car, I was told by the large young man in a brown suit who'd been guiding me. I'll need you to identify them all the same. As soon as you've done that, we'll get going.

The plane had been more than half an hour early, and our exit from JFK must have set some sort of speed record: twenty-seven minutes. I'd be home almost two hours earlier than I had predicted. My housekeeper Jeanette was at the apartment. Having allowed myself to disregard in this one case Scott's instructions, I'd called her from the Gritti to give her a heads-up that unexpectedly I'd be coming home tomorrow. She was not, however, to plan on working on that account. I'd manage very well, and she should be sure to take her Saturday.

It was a mistake to tell her I was returning and at what time I expected to be home. Of course, she was at the apartment.

Thank the Lord, Captain Jack, she said, hugging me. I've been waiting for you and waiting.

She had tea and tea sandwiches and cookies ready and insisted that I sit down and eat. I don't know what happened to you in that Torcello, she kept repeating, you're a shadow of yourself, you must have lost twenty pounds! You just don't know how to take care of yourself, Captain Jack!

My damaged pelvis craved a long immersion in hot water. I assured her that I felt well and that we'd have a big talk once I'd taken a bath and changed my clothes. But she shook her head, and said, Captain Jack, you just have to listen to me now. I'm so scared!

Then let's talk right now. I led her into the library and had her sit down on the sofa with me.

Captain Jack, she continued, I haven't been so scared since my Walter was sent to Fallujah in Iraq and I'd watch TV and see all the killing and destruction over there. I'm so scared I'm sick.

Walter was her husband, a master sergeant, whose Humvee was blown sky-high by an IED.

What happened, I asked, taking her hands into mine.

First, Miss Kerry died of an overdose. I didn't think she was doing drugs. What did she need that shit for?

She covered her mouth and said, Excuse me. Such a sweet young lady, so beautiful, and she loved you so much!

Yes, I said, it's horrible. I didn't know about the drugs either.

And now . . . Do you remember, Captain Jack, maybe four months after Mr. Harry died, just about the time you flew to Texas, a man called and said to tell you how you were dead meat?

Of course I remembered. That was a couple of days after I had visited Abner at his Houston office, accused him of killing both Harry and his secretary, and made him listen to the recording on Harry's iPhone of the torture and execution of Harry and Harry's cat by Abner's hit man Slobo.

I was so scared then I couldn't sleep until you came home, she continued. Yesterday and this morning another man called and asked for you. When I told him you're away, he said, Tell him from Jovan: he's a dead piece of shit.

Once again, she covered her mouth.

That's all right, I told her. These are rough people, not like you and me.

Twice the same message, Captain Jack!

What does that guy sound like? I asked. Some kind of accent?

Yes sir, a foreigner.

Stop worrying about it, I told her. He doesn't scare me. He'll probably call again. If he does, just tell him: Captain Dana says he wants to meet you. That's all. Once you've said that, hang up. Don't get drawn into a conversation. And if he calls again after you've told him that, listen carefully to what he says and, after he's finished, thank him, hang up, and write down exactly what he said. Don't argue with the guy; don't get involved. And if there is a number from which he called in the caller ID, write that down too. If there's a message, don't erase it.

There is something else, I continued. After I came back from Texas that time I asked you to be careful about whom you let into the apartment. Remember?

She nodded.

It's the same deal now. Basically don't let repairmen or anyone like that into the apartment unless I'm here. Second, don't let deliverymen into the kitchen unless you recognize them as someone you know who's been making deliveries regularly. If they're new and I'm not at home, tell the elevator man you want the delivery held downstairs until I come back. All right? And now I'm going to take that bath.

Yes sir, she answered. I have a nice cold dinner set out for you on the kitchen counter, and if you want something hot there is some pea soup, just the way you like, ready to be heated up.

I soaked for a long time, fighting the desire to doze off, feeling the soreness recede. When I finally got out and dried myself, I decided I wasn't going to shave or dress. Instead, I put on a sweatsuit and remained barefoot. It felt good to be home. Just as I imagined, Jeanette had unpacked my suitcases, taken the dirty laundry, and put away the rest of my clothes in the closet and chest of drawers far more neatly than I would have managed. She'd found my switchblade and set it down in the precise center of my night table. Seeing it there made me think that, what with Jovan sending those friendly greetings, it wouldn't hurt to have the .45 handy. I took it and a package of twenty rounds out of the safe. I didn't think I'd be dealing with Jovan or his colleagues in my bedroom. A more central location seemed indicated. I put the gun, the ammo, and the knife into the right-hand desk drawer in the library. Then I poured myself a triple shot of bourbon, added a couple of ice cubes, found a tin of cashews, and called Scott and thanked him for making Blaine's travel agency available.

He treated you right? Scott laughed.

Like precious human cargo, I replied. He's great.

That's good. It's wonderful to have you back, old buddy.

You bet, I replied, and asked, What about the finger and the photo, are they any use? Is there any progress on any front?

No progress at all, he replied. Fingerprint and DNA databases are great if you're dealing with someone who has a record. The guy on Torcello hasn't any. There is a one-in-a-million chance that the photo will lead us somewhere. But one never knows. Serendipity is a great operating principle.

And Abner Brown?

Apart from the political front where he's riding high, you mean? No, his companies are defending a dozen or more lawsuits and enforcement actions by various state and federal regulatory authorities, spending tons of money—but what does he care—and they've lost some. Huge fines, loss of licenses, and so forth. But nothing close to what it would take to cripple him or his businesses. There is a federal grand jury that has been impaneled in secret right here in Alexandria, in my own backyard, that's looking into Abner's personal involvement in money laundering and violations of international sanctions. This is very serious stuff, and it does aim right at the jugular. The jury's been at it for some time. The proceedings are secret, but we do our best to follow them for the obvious reason—a possible tie to terrorist organizations—but I'm not aware of anything new happening there. We need to get together all the same, not just because we love you, but because we need to figure out how you should cope with what seems a very serious threat against you, and whether and how that connects with Brown. Will you come to Alexandria tomorrow or the next day? Please stay with us. Susie would love it.

A sickening sense of frustration came over me.

Scott, I said, give me a couple of days. I realize that we know nothing about what had been happening to Kerry. What was going on in her head. The answer to the puzzle— anyway a part of the puzzle—may be right there. I think that before I come to see you I should talk to some people here, especially Moses Cohen. He's my lawyer, I got him through Kerry, and it turns out that he was her lawyer as well and is the executor of her estate. I'd like to know what he knows and thinks. I can't bother him on Saturday—he's Orthodox, for Christ's sake—or on Sunday because he's got small children, but I'll try to get hold of him first thing Monday morning. There is also Simon Lathrop. Kerry was working full-time for the law firm. I'd like to see what information can be gathered there. And I'd like to give this guy Jovan an opportunity to show his face.

Jovan, who's he? Scott asked.

I apologized, because I should have mentioned the messages right away. Here's the deal, I said, and told him about my conversation with Jeanette.

Holy Christ! said Scott. I agree that Abner was probably

behind the Torcello caper, and if that is true he is also behind this new entrant. That shows me an unpleasant level of activity. Yes, you should talk to Moses and Simon, but for Christ's sake be careful when you wander about in the city. I'm not crazy about your giving this Jovan guy, if that's his name, a chance to kill you. It's true, there are patterns in crime, mostly repetitious, but you can't be sure that history will repeat itself in your case. When Abner had your uncle killed, and tried to get you killed, he seemed to think it was important to have the murder look like a suicide or an accident. That will not necessarily be the game now. Jovan may have orders to kill you without fucking around. For instance, as I said about a killer in Venice, he may have been told to shoot you. Anywhere. In the street. As you leave the apartment house. Something really banal, without marine hand-to-hand combat.

I said, I read you, brother.

And I meant it. My brain knew he was right.

Moses Cohen had been a trusts and estates associate at Harry's law firm, Jones & Whetstone, at the same time Kerry was making her mark there as a young litigator. They had also been classmates at Harvard Law School and had both been on the *Law Review*. After four or five years at the firm, Moses decided to strike out on his own, counting in part on J & W clients who might follow him because of the good job he'd been doing, or because his hourly rates would be less than half of what J & W charged, or a combination of both reasons, and also on business that should come to him through his and his family's connections in the Orthodox

Jewish community. Many of those businessmen, he told me, had started small but had become rich, rich enough to realize they needed the kind of estate plan, with a will and a variety of trusts, that they used to think was only for rich WASPs playing golf at clubs they would never be able to join. His calculations proved correct. The office he had in Midtown, on Park Avenue, was a very much smaller and more hip version of the J & W premises. I had taken an immediate liking to Moses, deciding to pay no attention to the suspicion that this strikingly handsome and well-organized lawyer might have been Kerry's boyfriend as well as colleague.

I was in luck; he wasn't in a meeting or out of the office when I called him at nine-thirty on Monday morning.

I thought you'd be coming back; in fact, I thought you might come back sooner, he said. I haven't called you about Kerry because I'm still not over the shock, and I can imagine how you feel. Perhaps that was wrong, perhaps I should have called you right after it happened.

That's all right, I told him. Your call wouldn't have changed anything. But can I see you sometime today?

Sure thing, he said. I have a client meeting between ten and one. Otherwise I'm free. I'll be working on documents and can see you anytime.

Three o'clock then, I replied. Thank you!

Simon Lathrop was the next stop. His secretary recognized my voice—pretty good going for someone who'd heard it perhaps half-a-dozen times—and offered to put me through before I'd asked for him. As I had hoped, he invited me to lunch that very day at the grand club to which Harry had also belonged. He also wanted to ask me to dinner at home, saying that his wife was eager to see me. I explained that I'd scheduled a trip to D.C. to see Scott and asked if we could fix a date after I returned.

That left a couple of hours for work. I finished the part where I described Kerry's and my first night together. So much heartache, I thought, so unnecessary if only she could have been reasonable. And then her awful, unexpected, unimaginable death. I was sure I would have protected her if she had allowed me to stay at her side.

My poor boy, Simon said as we embraced. I'm happy to see you. Not a word about Kerry before we've sat down at table and ordered.

We climbed up the two flights of stairs to the dining room, and I had to congratulate Simon on the spryness of his gait.

Yes, yes, he answered, the new hip is holding up pretty well. I wish all my parts could be replaced. You know, the transmission, the shock absorbers, the brain. That day will come, but it will be too late for me.

He wrote out my lunch order: black-bean soup and cold poached salmon. Good choices, he announced. I'll have exactly the same. And we'll each have a glass of Riesling.

He handed the lunch and bar chits to the waiter and said to me, I'm afraid it's time to talk.

He'd made it a point, he told me, to have conversations about Kerry with all the lawyers—partners and associates—at the firm who'd had substantial work contact with her over the past twelve months. It was easy to identify them: he'd asked accounting to analyze the time sheets. To be on the safe side, since he had only limited faith in bookkeepers, he'd also asked a couple of the senior associates who were her principal assistants to make a list of such persons. That information assembled, he'd had one-on-one talks with all those lawyers, asking for their candid assessments of the quality of Kerry's work; energy levels; moods; relations with clients, opposing counsel, and lawyers at the office; and her deportment in court. She'd had several important appearances and filings during that period in federal and state courts. Finally, he'd asked, though not quite in those words, for an appraisal of her intellectual level and approach to problems. That was the due diligence within the firm. But he'd had as well conversations with her principal clients, Western Industries and a hedge-fund manager she was representing in an SEC investigation. Depending on your point of view, the results were uniformly excellent or depressing (because how and why would someone performing as superbly as she shoot herself up with heroin and Molly and whatever else there was in that cocktail?). There could be no doubt: she had been, until the evening she died, the same admirable Kerry we had known and loved.

And that's not all, he said. According to normal firm practice, her emails would be on their way to be erased. I've arranged to have them saved in an account to which only I and the firm's general counsel (that's a new position at the firm, a partner who is essentially our legal compliance and risk manager) have the password, and I've had her personal correspondence and notes collected and delivered to me. I've got them locked up in my office safe. Everything that wasn't in the ordinary course of business sent by her or at her direction to client files.

Have you analyzed it?

That's a big word. I've read it all, somewhat hastily, on weekends. There isn't anything of real interest there. Stuff relating to her investments. Thank-you notes, appointments she was making, letters to her landlord about repairs, lots of correspondence with the facility where her father had been and with the retirement place where her mother is still living, and nothing, absolutely nothing, that hints at a big problem or depression—or anything connected to Abner Brown.

If only, I thought, if only my uncle Harry's papers had been preserved in this fashion. Instead, those swine, Hobson, then the chairman of J & W, and Minot, his trusts and estates sidekick, at the time already Abner Brown's vassals, had done their best to destroy them. To say it to Simon would have been to rub salt into a wound. I held my tongue. Instead, I said, This is a difficult question—perhaps "indiscreet" is the better word—to put. Did you get the impression that any of the people in the firm you talked to were also drug users, might have done drugs with Kerry?

No, Simon answered, I was on the lookout for telltale signs, slips of the tongue and suchlike. But no, there was nothing. Not that I suppose it means much. Look at Kerry herself. Neither you nor I suspected she was a user.

I accompanied Simon to his office and, after we'd said goodbye, went to see Moses. He was only a few blocks away.

He greeted me at the reception desk and showed the way to his unnaturally neat office.

Who would have imagined what happened when you first came here, he said, and made the will that left almost all your property to Kerry? Who would have thought of her dying this way? By the way, while it's probably not what you had in mind coming here, your will needs to be changed. I don't think that at the time we discussed it either of us was able to think seriously that she'd predecease you.

You're right, I said, but as you said a new will is not my big priority. What I would really like to have is an answer to the question you put just now. Who would have thought of Kerry dying of an overdose? You'd known her very well, and for a very long time. What's your answer? You should know, incidentally, that I've sort of assumed that at some point you and she were together.

Moses blushed, hesitated, and nodded. A long time ago, he said, when she came to J & W after her clerkship. It didn't last very long. Probably I broke it off, because that isn't the sort of thing that people in my community are supposed to do.

A light went on in my head. Of course, Orthodox Jews like Moses were constrained in their relations with women. That was something Kerry had told me, but without hinting at anything that had gone on between her and Moses.

It's all right, I answered. You might as well know that when the idea came into my mind I decided I wouldn't be childish about it.

Thank you!

But what about my question?

It's a long story, Moses replied. I don't suppose you know it, but Kerry had been in treatment ever since college, possibly before, with a series of therapists and shrinks, and she's been on a lot of meds.

No, I didn't know it. Was it anything specific? I asked, immediately feeling stupid and hating myself for it.

If you know anything about this sort of stuff, Moses said, it was the usual. Anxiety, depression, low self-esteem, certain compulsive traits. They're syndromes meds can't cure, but they can make it so that you function.

And hard drugs?

When I knew her, it was an occasional line of cocaine. Nothing much. A lot of people at the firm—and other people I knew outside my community—did that. Do you know that I'm the executor under her will? he asked suddenly.

As a matter of fact, I do, I replied. Simon Lathrop has told me.

Well, strictly on account of that I saw more of her during the last twelve months than during the last ten years. It's hard to tell you this, but she was really fucked up over you. First because of what you did with this guy Slobo—yes, she told me everything—and then because she left you. She couldn't figure how she could have stayed with you, and at the same time she thought that when she left you she made the biggest mistake of her life. So she was quite a mess, of course behind that perfect mask she always wore.

I see, I said stupidly, and added that Simon had told me the father was dead but the mother was still alive. Was that right?

Yes, he replied, the father was very deep into Alzheimer's, but the mother's hanging in there, in that retirement village. Kerry was very concerned about taking care of them. Of course, that isn't as much of a problem as in the past, now that the father's gone.

And is there enough money for the mother?

Yes, Kerry carried a huge amount of term insurance, and there is some money that will come out of the firm.

Moses, I said, have you been through her personal papers,

her personal email, and so on, have you looked for clues to what led to this accident? How it happened that she ended up in that hotel with a syringe in her arm?

You know something about law's delays, Jack. I'm appointed executor, but I haven't qualified yet. I've been through her correspondence that was found at the apartment, checkbooks—all the usual stuff. There was nothing there. I haven't had access to her email.

Can you do something—like what that J & W fellow Minot did—I think he called it a preliminary appointment, so we could get into her email account?

Do you think it's that important? I can tell you right now, without checking the law, that it's a complicated matter.

I do think it's important.

All right, I'll look into it.

One more question: who is H. Krohn? I received an email from someone with that name as part of her address. The rest was "@sbw." She says she is one of Kerry's closest friends and wants to talk to me. Kerry mentioned a couple of times a friend called Heidi something or other. Is this the same person?

Oh sure, Moses answered. Heidi Krohn. She's a partner at Silverstein, Brown & White. Kerry, Heidi, and I were all classmates at the law school, and we were on the *Review* together. Heidi was the president. She's OK, and it's true that she was Kerry's close friend—nobody was closer. Sure, you should talk to her.

I went home directly from Moses's office and found Jeanette so rattled she burst into tears each time she tried to speak.

He called again, she told me, the same guy. I wrote down what he said. Here it is.

She handed me a page from the notepad in the kitchen on which she wrote down messages. It read: Tell fuckhead he's roadkill.

That's practically the same message, I said. Some people have no imagination. Poor Jeanette, some people have no manners either. And did you give him my message?

Yes sir, Captain Jack, I sure did. You told me to hang up after I'd given it, but before I could do that he said, I'll cut his heart out. I'm real scared!

Don't worry about this guy, I said. Lots of people wanted to kill me in Iraq and Afghanistan, and then Slobo, the guy who murdered Uncle Harry. I'll be all right.

Just you be sure to take good care of yourself, she replied. You've got mail and a package.

I looked at the mail. Except for one letter it was all bills and appeals for money. I opened the one that looked personal, addressed to me by hand in solid capital letters. Inside it, neatly folded, was a sheet of stationery taken from the *locanda* in Torcello. On the sheet, written also in solid capital letters was: YOUR DAYS ARE COUNTED SHITHEAD.

I put the sheet back into the envelope and turned to look at the package. It was from Amazon, large enough for something like the Bose radio I'd bought online for my bedroom when I moved into the Fifth Avenue apartment or an object of equivalent bulk. I hadn't ordered anything, but it was possible that someone—who?—had sent me a present. I lifted the package. It was surprisingly light.

Do you want me to open it? Jeanette asked.

I thought quickly. Only Scott and Jeanette knew I was

arriving last Saturday. This package wasn't from Jeanette. Was it from Scott? Why wouldn't he have said that I should expect a present? Simon Lathrop knew I was coming back soon, but I hadn't told him when. He too would have told me that his wife Jennie and he had sent me something.

This could be a mistake, I told Jeanette. Please put it—I hesitated about where, because I wanted the package as far away as possible from Jeanette and me—in the guest room. I'll decide later what to do with it.

It was late enough in the afternoon for a drink. I poured myself a bourbon, took it into the library, and called Scott.

He gave a long whistle after I'd told him about the telephone conversation between Jeanette and the unknown caller, the letter on the *locanda*'s letterhead paper, and the Amazon package.

Someone's putting on pressure, he said. The Cipriani paper is a nice touch.

One that required organization and planning, I observed.

I don't like the package, he continued. It could be nothing, it could be one of Abner's asshole jokes, or it could be a bomb. One that explodes when you open the package—or a time bomb. Is that guest room really far from where you and Jeanette are apt to be?

I said it was as remote as I could make it in the apartment, and I didn't want to have the elevator man put it in the mailroom. It had occurred to me as well that it might be a time bomb.

You're right about not having it moved to the mailroom, Scott told me, just stay away from that guest room and have Jeanette stay away from it too. Leave the package strictly alone. Someone from the Agency will come to collect it this afternoon or this evening. We'd better find out what it's all about. And you had better get over to see me. We've got lots to talk about.

Let's make a plan tomorrow, after your people have examined the package. There is another thing: a friend of Kerry's, one Heidi Krohn, has gotten in touch and would like to talk. I sort of remember Kerry's mentioning her name, but I checked with Moses Cohen anyway. She's genuine, and a good person, and, according to Moses, Kerry's best friend. I want to see her as soon as possible. We know almost nothing about Kerry's life during those months after we split except that Simon has told me that she continued to work hard and effectively. Heidi might fill that gap.

Here is a stupid question, Scott said. Have you done something basic, which is to look at Kerry's Facebook page? You know, her postings and other people's comments and so forth. Probably it all adds up to nothing, but who knows? You might find something meaningful.

I told him I wasn't on Facebook anymore, I'd closed my account while I was in Walter Reed, but that was something I'd certainly talk about to Heidi. In fact it was a point I'd intended to raise with Moses and completely forgot.

IV

This is my cell-phone number, Heidi had written. If I don't answer, leave a message and the time you'll be available. I'll call back. As it happened, she answered on the second ring. I told her I'd just gotten back to the city over the weekend and would like to see her very soon. For dinner, if possible.

Good timing, she said. I'm in a car heading back to the office from the airport. The traffic is terrible. Yes, she continued in a warm no-nonsense voice, she was free for dinner, if dinner could be at nine or later and on the Upper East Side, which was where she lived. That would give her a chance to drop off her bag at home and freshen up before meeting me.

I said there was a restaurant I liked on Madison Avenue between Seventy-Seventh and Seventy-Eighth that served dinner late and, at that hour, would be quiet. We agreed to meet there at nine-thirty.

While I was making the reservation, Jeanette let in the Agency's technicians, two very polite former army infantry noncoms who reminded me of my platoon's explosives specialist in Helmand. That was, in fact, where they had previously honed their skills, taking apart IEDs. Their examination of the Amazon package took no time at all.

It could be anything, sir, said the older of the two, really anything other than a charge of explosives. With your permission, we'll take this baby to the lab. The report will go directly to Langley, possibly even this evening.

I called Scott, told him that Abner seemed to have thought of something less crude than a bomb, that the Agency people, who seemed first-rate, had taken the package to their lab for further examination, and that I was seeing Heidi later that evening.

All right, he said. Call me in the morning. I really want to talk.

Jet lag? Release of nervous tension? Some other reason? A tremendous fatigue overcame me, to the point that I literally couldn't keep my eyes open. When Jeanette asked what time I would like to have dinner, I apologized for not letting her know earlier that I'd be going out—it was a plan I had just made—but first I'd lie down for a nap in the library.

That's a good idea, Captain Jack, she answered. If you don't mind my saying so, you look bad. Pale and haggard.

There was no hiding it. I admitted that I was worn out and looked forward to a good rest under her care.

I had expected to fall asleep at once. Instead, I found myself wide awake, unable to stop thinking about Abner.

If the package had contained an explosive device, obviously the wrapping and the shipping labels would all have to be fake. That was clear even in my befuddled state. Amazon doesn't sell bombs, not yet. But according to the Agency's specialists, there was no explosive in the package, and the package looked one hundred percent genuine. Why had Scott and I both suspected it wasn't? The fact that I hadn't bought anything from Amazon, and couldn't think of anyone who'd send me a present purchased there and timed to arrive just as I returned to the city, a circumstance of which only Scott, Jeanette, and I were aware? If that was the reason, it didn't seem compelling. Especially since making a fake Amazon package would be quite an undertaking. A skilled operator working with a forger would have had to take apart a real package, put in the place of its original contents whatever horse's-ass gizmo Abner had decided would make an impression on me, paste on the outside counterfeit shipping labels, and find an appropriate way to put the reconstituted package in the hands of UPS or FedEx, however my package happened to have been delivered. Was it reasonable to suppose that even someone like Abner, a man of endless means and malice, would devote so much effort to one more practical joke in the campaign of harassment he had unleashed against me? The effort would be justified if the package were going to explode when I opened it. It might still seem justified if it turned out there was ricin in it or some other equally noxious chemical or biological agent. We'd find out soon. If the package was inoffensive, chances were that it was also genuine, whatever it contained and whoever sent it, and that Scott and I had overreacted. Scott was taking his role as a nanny too seriously. As for me, clearly I was on edge. I needed to calm down and think more clearly.

But suddenly I saw the other side of the coin. It wasn't

necessarily true that if the package was inoffensive it was likely to be a genuine Amazon article, and, if it was both inoffensive and fake, there were implications going far beyond any campaign against me or my whimsical notion of a solitary forger employed by Abner in his effort to harass me. They derived from the ubiquity and, for lack of a better expression, all-American respectability of Amazon's packages, and the doors to a whole world of crime that dispatching convincing fakes through seemingly normal Amazon channels would open for Abner and his businesses. One sees an Amazon package, and what does one think is in it? A book, a DVD, a scanner, a toy, mouthwash, power tools—an endless and growing array of products available in normal commerce. But suspend disbelief for a moment and imagine that, instead of the foregoing, this parallel Amazon shipped heroin and cocaine and cash on behalf of drug cartels and money launderers. And explosives, as well as fuses, timing devices, and the whole gamut of other paraphernalia you can look up on jihadist websites for use by terrorists and copycats. I was willing to bet any amount that Amazon's packages weren't tested for explosives and weren't processed through whatever apparatus is used to detect the presence of large amounts of cash in boxes such as Amazon uses, for instance, to ship paper for home printers. Why would they be? Arguments over collecting state sales taxes, working conditions in its warehouses, and the effect of its sales tactics on book publishing and independent bookstores all put aside, one doesn't think of Amazon as a criminal enterprise. Now shift the focus and look at Abner Brown's businesses, such as my uncle Harry's road map revealed them to be. You'd find that each of his myriad legitimate "good" businesses had an evil twin, also owned by Abner, sometimes sucking its good sibling dry and always usurping its identity for criminal purposes. That, in simplest terms, was his business model. I didn't think for a moment that Abner owned "good" Amazon. But given his wealth and power and his "interests"—smuggling, drug manufacture and distribution, evasion of North Korea and Iran sanctions, and money laundering, to mention just a few, it wasn't too much of a stretch to hypothesize his having created a "bad" Amazon, concealed somewhere in the state of Washington or whatever other place worked best for the purposes of camouflage and verisimilitude, creating on an assembly line fake Amazon packages charged with the mission of facilitating, through shipment of proscribed illegal merchandise in the U.S. and internationally, the business of its evil siblings. One could imagine it also as an independent contractor of sorts, distributing heroin and cocaine, and other more modern drugs, on behalf of the Mexican cartels and Italian and Eastern European crime families. If that nightmare vision approached reality, nothing could have been simpler for Abner, if he was in the mood to amuse himself, than to ship to me in that innocuous Amazon package whatever had struck his sick fancy.

These thoughts led back to the basic question that had been nagging at me since the last days in Torcello. Why did Abner choose this time, so soon after having arranged to have Kerry murdered, to show his hand? Since he had apparently decided to have me killed too, why advertise that intention? Why the cat-and-mouse game? When he sent Slobo to kill Harry and Harry's secretary, Barbara Diamond, he gave no advance notice. I couldn't believe that he had told Kerry she was next on his list. She was a smart girl, and she'd seen how dangerous he was. If she'd been told her number was up, she'd have sought help. She would have called Scott. She knew he'd have her back; it didn't matter that she and I were no longer together. She had kept up friendships with former colleagues at the U.S. Attorney's Office and had connections at the New York office of the FBI. At the very least, she would have gotten hold of Martin Sweeney, the retired FBI agent I'd hired to be her bodyguard after I made Brown understand I had the goods on him. What was different about me? Why bother with the letters I received on Torcello and as soon as I returned to New York? And why send that Amazon package? If it was genuine, but its contents were the equivalent of a drop-dead note or one of his habitual billets-doux, I'd still guess he was the sender. What was the point? If on the contrary it was a fake, he was plenty smart enough to know that I would come to the conclusions I had just reached and wouldn't keep them to myself. Why would he decide to reveal this new and terrifying aspect of his empire, the mere existence of which was bound to galvanize law-enforcement agencies?

Sadism would have to be a component of any explanation of his dealings with me—perhaps it was the motor that drove most of his actions—sadism and its corollary, the desire to dominate, to abase. If Abner thought that, rattled by his antics, I would stumble, he underestimated me grossly. On the other hand, nothing I had seen so far had shown him to be a good judge of character. When it came to me, add rage and loathing to sadism. He must really hate my guts. How could it be otherwise? Each time he thought of the countless investigations, enforcement actions, and lawsuits targeting his businesses and possibly threatening him personally, my face must appear before his eyes. It was I who figured out that Harry's suicide was disguised murder, who found the phone on which the murder scene had been recorded, who got Slobo to confess that he had killed Harry and Barbara Diamond, and I who in turn killed Slobo. Worst of all, it was I who found Harry's road map to Abner's criminal enterprises and turned it over to the government.

Perhaps in order to get away from these thoughts, at some point I did doze off and for at least half an hour slept very hard. The telephone awakened me. It was Scott.

You won't believe this, he said. Inside the package, wrapped in all the usual bubble wrap, as though it were a jar of Stilton, is a can of rat poison. "Bonham's Just One Bite. Kills rats and Norway rats." Scotch-taped to it a card with a message typed in solid capital letters: ENJOY!

Scott was laughing his head off.

Holy shit, I said. Can you trace the sender?

Inside, I was cursing. So the package was genuine. My elegant theory about Amazon's evil twin was going up in smoke. Amazon sold rat and every other kind of rodent poison. After Slobo killed Harry's cat, I'd ordered mouse pellets from Amazon for the house in Sag Harbor. It had never been necessary before.

Scott laughed again. We're a step ahead of you; we've already tried. Amazon has no record of such a package. The information on it doesn't correspond to anything in their database. Plus, so far as we've been able to find out, there's no such thing as Bonham's rat poison, and, much more to the point, no such product is sold by Amazon. Put that in your pipe and smoke it! The name, though, is similar to that of a couple of popular products. Somebody's got a great sense of humor.

We do have a lot to talk about, I told Scott. I can't thank you enough. Or the Agency. Can one send the Agency a thank-you note? Or flowers?

You can skip the flowers if you manage to stay alive and get your ass over here. This is a big deal.

No kidding! I replied. I'll call you first thing in the morning.

I suppressed a guilty feeling of self-satisfaction as I hung up. So I was right: Abner ran a counterfeit Amazon! A fact so mind boggling that it suggested an answer to the questions I'd been putting to myself about why he chose to send me stupid messages and now this package. One that perhaps trumped all others. It came down to this: the possession of a fortune estimated on the basis of officially known assets at in excess of sixty billion dollars—and surely far greater if you added the value of the illegal businesses and the billions in cash he probably hid in secret accounts at banks operating in jurisdictions that welcome them—and his ability to impose his extremist views on members of Congress and state legislatures had imbued him with a sense of power and personal invulnerability so limitless that he no longer paid attention to normal concepts of prudence and risk. They were made for little people and had nothing to do with him. Why shouldn't he then play with me like a cat with a mouse? He was going to kill me, but in his own way and in his own time. In the meantime, he was having fun. That's why he hadn't yet told Jovan or one of the Torcello archer's brothers or cousins to kill me with a well-aimed hollow-point bullet.

But wait. Might it not also be true that this game gave me a chance to turn the tables on him, despite all his power? I'd watched plenty of real-life and animated cartoon cats trying to catch mice. I knew the strange moments of vacancy and absentmindedness that punctuate the hunt. The cat has the mouse cornered, but suddenly, instead of pouncing, he has some other idea. Or his mind goes blank. The mouse scurries away. Sometimes the cat regains his concentration quickly enough to corner the mouse again. Sometimes he loses her, and, in real life, if you're there, looks at you with a puzzled air that says: Come on, stupid, help! Where'd that mouse go? All right, Abner Cat: I will wait for that moment when your playfulness will mix with distraction. Because that's when I, Jack Dana, will get you. Just what that meant, I wasn't sure. I hoped it meant I'd kill him, but I wasn't stupid enough to think I'd get to use the switchblade or the Ka-Bar on him, or even to put a bullet between his eyes. He was too well guarded. Unless I got very lucky, I'd have to settle for sending him to a supermax. Which would I prefer? Seeing him put away for life with ample time to contemplate his disgrace and ruin or watching him die? I wasn't sure.

Sometime during that interminable afternoon, I did fifty push-ups, fifty sit-ups, and thirty pull-ups on the bar Harry had installed for me in the bathroom when I first moved in with him after the months spent at Walter Reed, showered, and dressed. I arrived at the restaurant where I was meeting Heidi five minutes early and ordered an extra-dry Gordon's gin martini straight up with a twist. Not waiting till she arrived wasn't very polite, but, given the lateness of the hour, I thought she'd forgive me. Nine-forty. No sight of Heidi. Glad that at least I had my drink, I checked my iPhone. Lots of junk mail but nothing from her. She was good and late, but I had no doubt that she'd show up. How many hours was it since the lunch with Simon? I was feeling seriously hungry and asked the waiter for bread. Both my father and Uncle Harry had been strong believers in not drinking hard liquor on an empty stomach. I shared their belief, but it had become difficult to put it into practice, bars no longer serving nuts or crackers to nibble on. According to a bartender I'd asked about it, the reason is hygiene! It was now considered unsafe—if not disgusting—to have more than one customer stick his unsterilized fingers into a bowl of peanuts. Whatever. I've never heard of a barfly catching typhoid fever from a pretzel, but that doesn't mean it couldn't happen or hasn't happened. For instance in Karachi. If the alternative consists of having Purell wipes dispensers on bar counters or having to slip on latex gloves before fishing out a peanut, I'm willing to give up nibbles.

The issue became moot when the waiter, after what had felt like a long wait, at last brought the bread basket. I wolfed down a piece of focaccia, went on sipping my martini, and daydreamed about the first time with Kerry. It had been the evening of my return from Brazil. I had spent four weeks incommunicado, working on my third novel, on a cattle ranch in the Mato Grosso belonging to a client and friend of Harry's. When the time came to go home, the ranch manager drove me to the Cuiabá airport. The propeller plane I was taking from there to Brasília connected with a flight to New York. There had been no Internet access at the ranch, and cell-phone reception was virtually nonexistent, so that the first time I was able to read my email since I arrived in the Mato Grosso was when I settled down in the Cuiabá departure lounge. Right away, I saw the message from Kerry. Three weeks old, it said that Harry was dead. I called her immediately, and she told me the circumstances, which defied understanding and belief. A suicide by hanging, he'd killed his adored cat before taking his own life, no letter left for me or anyone else! There was no reason, absolutely no reason, I had told myself as I thought about it obsessively, for Harry to have taken his life. Kerry and I had lunch the next day at a Japanese restaurant in the city and agreed to have dinner that evening at her apartment to talk about what had happened in greater detail. Until then I'd been aware of her as Harry's favorite associate, the cynosure of his eyes, whom a year or so earlier he succeeded in having elected to partnership at his law firm. I had seen her no more than twice—at parties given to celebrate the publication of my first and second novels, and at a large dinner after the second party. She was athletically built and almost as tall as I. Her pale face, her eyes more green than blue, and a huge chignon of curly black hair made for a striking appearance. But except for that formidable chignon, she looked and dressed both times I saw her previously, as well as at the Japanese restaurant, like other successful young women partners in top New York law firms or investment banks. That evening, though, when she received me at her own apartment, she'd let her hair down to her shoulders and wore a long blue-and-green sheath of Indian silk and gold lamé ballet slippers that drew attention to her feet, which were extraordinarily large even for such a big girl. It has seemed to me since then that a sure sign of falling in love is the realization that aspects of a woman's appearance she isn't proud of, like those oversize feet of Kerry's—anything that she makes halfhearted efforts to keep out of sight—become the aspect of her body you single out and particularly cherish. That is what happened to me later that evening when we were having drinks seated at the opposite ends of her living room sofa. By habit or design, she stretched her legs so that her naked feet were an inch or two from my left hand. I dared to caress them, as if they needed reassurance. To my astonishment, the feet were not withdrawn. They began, instead, to rub against my hand, a gesture like that of a cat rubbing his back against your leg to show he is pleased or, on the contrary, to remind you that there is something he wants to which you have foolishly forgotten to attend. The acceptance of my caress, her way of reciprocating—both incontrovertible signs of trust—filled me to the brim with tenderness and gratitude. Later that evening, we made love, then resumed our conversation about Harry and the discovery of pervasive criminal behavior in Abner Brown's businesses he had made in the course of acting as Brown's principal lawyer, and before morning made love again twice. A couple of weeks later, I asked Moses Cohen to prepare a new last will and testament for me and left to Kerry almost all my earthly goods, just as though she were my wife. That was how I thought of her, never doubting the solidity of our love. Then came the misunderstanding. The catastrophe. She left me, and the dream shattered.

My conscience was clear. Slobo deserved to die. That did not prevent me from tormenting myself. If I had I known that the consequence of what I did to him would be to lose her, wouldn't I have left him to criminal justice, however much I despised it? Had I done so, the daydream or nightmare continued, she would be alive. I would have shielded her from Abner Brown and his thugs. And I would have stood between her and drugs. I understood that she might not have shaken off her addiction, however much stability and reassurance I gave her, but surely she would not have been mainlining cocaine and whatever she'd mixed with it at that cheap Chelsea hotel. Had she not believed me when I told her over and over that I'd kill Slobo? Did she think I made empty threats? That seemed impossible. Then why hadn't she beaten into my poor dumb head that if I stepped over the line with that bastard she wouldn't forgive me? I knew the only plausible explanation: the revulsion and its strength came to her too as a surprise. A revulsion that was understandable, but one that she should have been able to overcome. Such was my unchanging ultimate answer. Monsters like Slobo cannot be rehabilitated. The concept as applied to them, I would tell myself, is grotesque and absurd. Society has no duty to lodge and feed them for the balance of their natural lives and—why not?—teach them useful skills. Computer programming, a second or third language, cabinetmaking! No, they deserve to die, and I deserved credit for not having tortured him first, the way he had tortured his victims.

But all this going back and forth was no use. My sorrow and regret were so sharp that had I not been in a public place I would have howled.

Ten o'clock. I hesitated between ordering dinner or another martini and decided a martini was the safer bet. Since my purpose wasn't to give Heidi a lesson in good manners but to hear all she had to say, I shouldn't embarrass her by eating my pasta when she arrived. I ordered the drink and once more checked messages on my phone. Still nothing from her. I'd give her ten more minutes. I wasn't put to the test. The martini and she arrived at the same time. Wow! These hardworking girls must spend almost as much time at the gym as at the office. Like Kerry, she was beautiful and really very fit. Apart from that, very different: Heidi was no more than five foot seven, with brown eyes and straight dark blond hair worn in a stylish pageboy. In fact, everything about her was chic: the black leather jacket that she said she'd keep on a little longer, the knee-length dark red wool skirt, the ribbed black tights, the matching dark red pumps enclosing small and pretty feet.

Before she could start on what I feared would be a lengthy apology, I asked what she would like to drink.

She pointed to my martini and said, The same as you, but with an olive.

The apology turned out to be very brief, more like a matter-of-fact explanation than an expression of regret. The traffic was terrible, all the way from the Van Wyck Expressway to the bridge; at the office she found a call from a client she had to take being held by her secretary, and another call she had to return; when she got to her apartment she realized she wanted to take a shower and change out of her jeans; and she walked to the restaurant instead of hailing a taxi. *Et voilà!* From Lexington and Eighty-Eighth, she added.

That seemed to be all for the moment, so I asked whether she wouldn't like to look at the menu.

Don't need to, she told me. I know it, and I always take the same thing. The Neptune salad and linguine *aglio e olio*. That's if the smell of garlic across the table doesn't bother you.

I laughed and said it didn't. The linguine and the seafood salad were exactly what I would have as well. After she confirmed that red wine was all right with her, and that, in general, she preferred it to white, we fell silent again. Wondering how we would get around to talking about Kerry, which after all was the reason she'd given for getting together, I told her that I'd seen Moses Cohen earlier in the day and that he'd said she and Kerry and he had all been on the *Law Review* together. Kerry told me you and she were friends, I added, but she didn't give me the background.

That's just like her, she answered. Moses is a good guy. We've stayed in touch.

He's my lawyer, I soldiered on. Kerry recommended him after my uncle Harry died and I needed help with settling his affairs.

She made no comment.

We'd finished our first course, and I began to think that unless I gave her a real nudge the dinner would be over before she got beyond telling me such items of interest as that she liked the wine I'd chosen and, in general, the wines of Alto Adige and Friuli, as well as Venetian cuisine.

With the need to move on in mind, I put down my fork and knife and said: Moses also told me that you and Kerry were very close friends. He may have said best friends. Kerry had also said you and she were close. Looking back on it, I'm surprised that we didn't meet while she was alive.

You were together such a very short time! she replied. And so very absorbed in each other! But she did speak to me about you. Before and after you broke up, so I feel I know you pretty well, and also what happened between you. That's why I thought I could write to you. I was glad when you suggested having dinner this evening.

That's very true, I said, it was a terribly short time. Four months and a few days. We were very happy, I was happier than I'd ever been, and then suddenly she left me. No, that's not really fair. I had a premonition that something was wrong. As soon as I returned from Sag Harbor and gave her a full account of the final confrontation with Slobo. And things only got worse.

It had occurred to me that a neutral characterization of what happened that night between Slobo and me was called for, and that was the best I could come up with.

I don't know how many times I've been over the story I told her, I continued. It was too graphic. I should have fudged.

She wouldn't have let you get away with it, Heidi answered. Don't forget she was a crackerjack lawyer and a former prosecutor. You might have made it worse. Look, she hated what you'd done—in her eyes, because that guy was no longer a threat to you, it was murder, not justifiable homicide, and she picked up on something like boastfulness in the way you talked about it—but she thought you were too smart not to understand the effect your story would have on her, so at least she had to respect you for telling the truth.

She was wrong, I answered. I was far too dumb. She knew how I hated Slobo for what he'd done to Harry—he didn't just kill him, he beat him first—and for what he'd done to

Plato, the cat I'd given Harry that both of us loved. And for pushing Harry's secretary under a subway train. A nice woman I'd known since I was a boy. Kerry knew I'd sworn to kill him. She knew I didn't want to leave him to the Suffolk County D.A. and a Suffolk County jury. If that was how she felt—that if what I did couldn't qualify as self-defense she wouldn't be able to bear to have me touch her—she should have laid it on the line. Then even someone as thickheaded as I, who'd killed men far less guilty than Slobo, men who'd done me personally no harm, would have gotten it. I can't be sure thinking about it a year later. Probably I would have gone after Slobo the same way. But I might have called the ambulance right away, instead of letting the bastard bleed. I can't tell. She meant everything to me.

I stopped talking and drained a full glass of wine.

Heidi surprised me by putting her hand over mine and saying, It's all right, Jack. Kerry knew you were suffering, and she wished she had handled it differently or could go back to you. She just didn't know how to make herself do it. But I don't believe she stopped loving you—whatever that means—and you shouldn't think she had. It wasn't only stubbornness either. She wasn't stubborn; she was more like a car without a reverse gear. Once she got herself into a situation—you know, a way of feeling—she didn't know how to back out. She told me it was almost as simple as that. That's a lot of what all the shrinks, all the therapy, all the anxiety and depression, and the medications were about.

She never told me about any of that. Or the drugs. She did tell me about her parents. I realized that was hard for her to do.

Yes, it was, but she thought she must tell you that so you'd understand she was the principal source of their support, and she couldn't risk losing her job. The rest of her problems . . . she was ashamed, she believed you wouldn't be able to accept the truth.

I interrupted. She was wrong. Of course I would have accepted it. I would have done whatever was needed to help.

She covered my hand again.

Yes, Jack, but she couldn't be sure. I hate to say it, but I must: you loved each other, you had lots of great sex, but you remained strangers. There wasn't enough time. Kerry needed time.

You seem to know a lot—no, everything!

I blurted that out, without managing to suppress the note of bitterness in my voice.

That's right, Jack, I do, but I'm Kerry's oldest and best friend. We had almost no secrets from each other, not even when telling them hurt the one who told and the one who listened. Anyway, I had no secrets from Kerry. You must understand that Kerry kept things and people in separate boxes. There was a box for Jack, a box for the parents, boxes for different aspects of her work, and on and on. It was her way of maintaining order, of fighting against the worst of anxiety. Yes, and a box for sex different from what you and she had, for sex where there was no question of love, and, I am certain, a box for stuff she'd keep even from me.

She broke off and took her hand away.

Look, she said, I hope I've made it clear that I understand how you felt about Kerry and how you feel now. Talking about it has broken the ice between us, but we are here together for another reason. It's what happened to Kerry. I want to tell you that I'm sure that Kerry didn't overdose in order to commit suicide—she wasn't at all suicidal, hadn't been for years—and I'm not at all sure that the overdose was an accident. I think she may have been murdered.

Me too, I murmured.

Good, she continued. In that case I assume we have the same notion about where the inspiration for the murder would have come from. I have friends at the Manhattan D.A.'s office, and I've read their report on the case. It throws no light on what most likely really happened, and obviously no light on who may have done it or how he or she went about it. So let's put that aside. But I do have an idea about timing—the reason why Kerry might have been murdered at that particular time. She was scheduled to appear the following Friday before the grand jury that's been meeting in secret in Alexandria, Virginia, looking into new money-laundering charges against a string of Brown's companies and this time—it's a first—against Abner himself. Someone may have tipped Abner off about her appearance and about the fact, known only to the U.S. Attorney's Office, that she had come into possession of important new information. There may have been a leak picked up by Abner himself or his lawyers. If Abner or the lawyers thought—and it's not improbable—that the evidence was uniquely in Kerry's possession, someone may have concluded that it would be good for Abner if Kerry was permanently prevented from presenting it.

I see, I said. Do we know what that evidence is?

I think I do, at least in part. There is a file I've put in a safe place. I believe there's more that Kerry hid somewhere. I hope that working together we will be able to find it.

You've got yourself a partner, I said, and held out my hand. She shook it, and let me hold her hand for a moment. Will you tell me about what you have and what we are going to look for?

Of course, she said, but it's late now, and I have a court appearance in the morning. I'll only give you a thumbnail sketch: it's the method used by one of Brown's commodities trading firms working together with his bank—he may have other banks in addition to that one, but only this one is mentioned—to launder really huge amounts of drug and sanction-avoidance money as well as proceeds of really big bribes paid to foreign government officials. The sexy thing is that what she found does show Brown's own involvement. As for the rest of the evidence, while I'm pretty sure it exists, I don't know what it consists of. I do know that Kerry thought it was dynamite.

When will you have time to tell me more and make some plans?

Tomorrow. Would you be able to have a relatively early dinner, for instance at eight?

Yes, I said, realizing that meant I might not make it to Washington to see Scott that day. Would you like to meet here? Would you mind coming to my apartment, which would at that hour be more private than this place or any restaurant I can think of? My housekeeper is a good cook.

She laughed.

I know that too, she said. I'll be glad to come, but having been told about the rapid progress between you and Kerry, I want us to start off on the right foot. You might as well know that I'm not attracted physically to men. It hasn't always been so, and it may not be so forever. But that's the present position. Understood?

Yes, I answered, understood and admired. I'll expect you tomorrow at eight. No wonder you were Kerry's best friend.

Make it seven-thirty, if possible. I'd like to leave time for one or two martinis just like these. By the way, do you think they've got a tail on you?

I don't think so. No, in fact I don't know.

Please try to find out. If there is a tail, I'd like to make sure I don't get onto their shit list unawares. If I know what's up, I can probably take care of myself.

V

As soon as I came home from my run the next morning I called Scott.

You're right as usual, I told him. The threat is different this time. It's so diffuse! When Abner sicced Slobo on me, I managed to goad him into actually saying the bastard's name. Afterward, because of the figure I'd seen on the beach, I felt I could recognize him and was pretty sure I could take him out. For instance with my switchblade. But just now, when I went out running, and slipped the knife into the pocket of my windbreaker, it was more as a nostalgic gesture, a wink at that prick Jovan, than as a weapon I'd get to use. By the way, I was curious when I left the house whether I had a tail, but no one followed me, on foot or on bicycle, and no one odd looking was hanging around the building when I returned. Perhaps my morning schedule isn't of interest. They know I run and that I run in the park, and that's enough. Now I should report about my dinner with Heidi.

Scott gave one of his long whistles when I told him about Kerry's scheduled appearance before the grand jury sitting secretly in his own backyard in Alexandria and the file belonging to Kerry that Heidi had in her possession.

This may be it, he said. Heidi may have put her finger on why Abner decided it was time to move on Kerry. And now he figures he'd better move on you as well. He knows you're sure to try to get whoever murdered Kerry and to pursue any leads she discovered. He'll think of killing you as a pre-emptive measure. I'll check through my contacts at Justice into what this grand jury is up to now. And look: I agree you should have dinner with Heidi and, if necessary, stay in the city another couple of days. But I do need to see you, you old mother. Not just because I love you. We have to talk seriously about making sure you don't get killed. Also there is that Amazon package. I can't just sit on that stuff.

What do you mean? I asked.

I think the FBI has to be brought in, he replied. There is the small matter of a federal criminal statute: misprision of a felony. Not reporting one to the authorities. Sometimes the feds take it very seriously, particularly in cases like this one that involve egregious criminal conduct. I want to discuss with you how we go about reporting.

The implications didn't sink in until sometime after we'd hung up. If he went to the FBI, would I have to file some sort of complaint? If so, how much would I have to say about the background—my past dealings with Abner, the killing of Slobo, my suspicions about Kerry's death, Heidi's discoveries, Torcello and the new threats, and anything else she or I might unearth? Would the FBI take over the "case," cutting me out? That's not what I wanted. Heidi or perhaps even Moses could tell me whether I could dig in my heels and take the view that receiving a stupid-ass package didn't require me to run to the FBI or the NY Police Department. It was advice that Scott's position with the Agency possibly prevented him from giving. Shit! The FBI had been screwing around with Abner for over a year now based on specific information—Harry's road map they'd gotten through me— and what had it accomplished? Zero against Abner and close to zero overall. Both Scott and Simon had mentioned some fines and settlements. What did Abner care about that? And what did I care about them? I wanted whoever had killed Kerry dead by my hand. And Abner? The task seemed almost impossible, but a resolution was hardening inside me: somehow, somehow or other, I would have to try to kill him too.

The immediate priority, though, was to avoid exposing Heidi to danger. I was prepared to believe that if someone had been following me on my run I would have realized it. But that didn't mean that I wouldn't be tailed next time I went out or that the building and anyone identified as coming to visit me weren't under surveillance. How such an identification of my visitors would be made I had no idea, but I was sure there were ways—for instance photographing people who came in or went out and then sorting out who they were. I needed help from someone in the business of surveillance. Fortunately, I was convinced I knew the ideal person. Martin Sweeney, the guy I had retained as a bodyguard for Kerry. He'd worked out well, and he had a partner who should be available to step in if needed. I consulted my iPhone. Sure enough, Martin's telephone number and email address were there. I had no idea how often he checked his email. To save time, I clicked on his number. He answered right away, and, after I'd identified myself, he told me how sorry he was about Kerry.

Such a nice young lady, so brave and, if you don't mind my saying so, very decent. I would have never thought she was a user. A heavy user! Someone who'd overdose!

Perhaps she didn't, Martin, I answered. That's part of a long story I want to go into with you, but I have a more immediate need for your help. Would you, or you and your partner—I think his name is Lee—be able to figure out whether I'm being tailed? We'll discuss what to do if in fact I am.

You've got me coming fresh off a job, Martin told me. When do I start?

How about today? I asked. It's a little after ten. Could you be over around eleven? We'll have a cup of coffee and talk.

The cup of coffee turned into an early lunch.

Such a nice young lady, such a nice young lady, he kept repeating. Then he told me: I've got a daughter, she's twelve, curly black hair like Miss Kerry—some Irish have hair like that—and green eyes, and I used to say to myself, I'd like her to grow up just like that young lady!

Listening to him, measuring the depth of his emotion, and profoundly moved myself, I decided that it made no sense to limit his assignment to checking whether I was being tailed. The task that lay ahead was huge. I would undertake, with Heidi's help, the part that had to do with locating and understanding such additional evidence of Abner's crimes as Kerry might have assembled. Scott would give a hand too, but what he'd said about the Amazon package made me worry about constraints on him. I wanted to kill the bastard who killed Kerry myself, but to find him, I imagined, would require plumbing the world of clubs, dealers, and users, a world I knew only from books like Edward St. Aubyn's and the movies—a world with which I hoped Martin and his partner had some familiarity and that I hoped they could access. If I was wrong about that, they'd find someone with knowledge and the right connections. The thing to do was to get them on board. Going after Abner was another matter. I had no doubt it would be a solo job, for which I was uniquely qualified.

Martin, I said, your daughter couldn't have a better role model. Kerry wasn't about drugs. She was good and loving and generous and very, very bright and hardworking. Drugs were an outside force. Like a drunk who slams head-on into a careful driver. Someone gave her that injection. Against her will. Or she didn't know what was in it. I want you to help me find whoever did it. But you've got to let me start at the beginning. All right?

Yes sir! He nodded. I just can't help myself when I start thinking about her.

I began, as I thought I must, with our breakup over what I called my not taking energetic-enough steps to get Slobo to the hospital on time—it was important for him to understand her even better than he seemed to—and went through everything that happened since my last days on Torcello all the way to Heidi, her impending visit, and her concerns. The only piece of information I withheld was the Amazon package. I'd fill him in, I thought, but only after I'd seen Scott and figured out whether it was really necessary to go to the FBI.

Martin was a former agent. The last thing I wanted was to get into some sort of crossruff between Scott's and Martin's loyalties.

Let's take this one step at a time, I concluded. First, the tail. I'll go out this afternoon for a little walk around the neighborhood. A test run. If there's a tail, we might consider changing my date with Heidi to a restaurant, and I'll try to get rid of whoever it is by jumping into a taxi as I am leaving the building—

Good plan! Martin interrupted. If you do decide to take the young lady to a restaurant and are meeting her there, which is what I'd recommend, I might have Lee wait for you with his car so there's no time for the tail to get organized while your doorman hails the taxi.

Fine, I replied. But for the time being let's assume Heidi and I will have dinner here. And even if there is no tail, I would like you or Lee to follow Heidi home—she lives somewhere near Lexington and Eighty-Eighth Street—and make sure we didn't miss anything.

He nodded.

Then unless something Heidi tells me changes my mind, sometime tomorrow I'll go to see Scott Prentice in Alexandria and spend the night. You and I will get together on my return and decide how we check out the club—perhaps there was more than one—that Kerry used to go to and the people over there she hung out with. Assuming there were such people.

Martin nodded. If you like, he said, we can do some preliminary work beginning tomorrow. We have pretty good contacts at the DEA here in New York and at the narcotics group at the NYPD.

You're on, I said. You can bill weekly or however it suits you best.

I'd been working on my book for about two hours after Martin left when the phone rang. I thought it might be who-ever harassed Jeanette with his threatening calls. But no, it was my agent, Jane Bird, with the news that she'd gotten a miniseries offer for *What We Did Together*, my most recent book, a portrait of four men alongside whom I fought in Iraq.

This is fabulous, fabulous, she was saying, and I could pic-ture her practically levitating in her chair from excitement. Not just because of the price you get up front but even more because of the stream of income once the miniseries takes off. And the uptick in book sales. All your book sales, not just *What We Did*! This calls for a celebratory lunch, and it will be my treat!

I like Jane. Harry had put me in touch with her through the journalist wife of one of his partners. Spending a couple of hours with her over a meal suddenly seemed like exactly the right medicine for my nerves and general sense of disarray.

You almost have a deal, I told her. But it will have to be din-ner. Lunches interfere with making more money for you by writing books. And probably not this week. I may be going to D.C. tomorrow, and if I do I'll spend the night, and I'm likely to go to Sag Harbor for the weekend. Just to see whether the house is still there.

We do have a deal—she laughed—especially since I've bro-ken up with my boyfriend and I'm once again able to make dinner dates. I'll call you on Monday.

The phone call had interrupted the flow of ideas, and I found I couldn't reconnect immediately with the text. This

was as good a time as any for the test walk in the neighborhood I'd mentioned to Martin. I put on my parka and told
Jeanette I'd be back within the hour. The doorman on duty
was a talkative Albanian I liked. I paused on the sidewalk to
talk to him—and to make sure the tail didn't miss my exit—
and headed uptown. Out of the corner of my eye, I spotted
Martin sitting on the steps of the Metropolitan Museum.
When I next checked, he was walking in the same direction
as I, a hundred or so yards back, along the park side of the
avenue. I continued to Ninety-Third Street, where I turned
east and walked into the bookshop on the east side of Madison, one that I liked because it was well stocked and, more
to the point, did a good job selling my books. The owner was
in and made a fuss over my long absence. When would there
be a new Dana novel? I told her I was working on one and, if
nothing interfered, it would most likely appear in about nine
months, perhaps sooner.

That's a long time for your fans to wait, she complained.
You've spoiled us, letting us have your novels more frequently.

It couldn't be helped, I replied. Harry's death set me back.
There was a period after it happened when I couldn't write at
all. So I went abroad and only returned a few days ago.

So that's why we haven't seen you. Your uncle was such a
dear old friend! she exclaimed.

I nodded, kissed the cheek she offered, and promised to
come back to sign books whenever she wanted. Martin was
lounging beside the window of a men's clothing store next
door. When I caught his eye, he shook his head.

Nothing, he told me.

I wonder what that means, I replied. Perhaps they think

they've got it all figured, where and how to waste me, and don't need to bother with my comings and goings. What about this evening? Shall we stick to the plan all the same and have you or Lee be on duty by the time Heidi arrives? And follow her home? I invited her for seven-thirty, and I should think she'd go home not later than ten-thirty.

Absolutely, he said. No change. One of us will check in once she's inside her own building.

Seven-thirty indeed!

I had taken Heidi at her word and asked Jeanette to be ready to have dinner on the table at eight-fifteen. That would give us, I figured, enough time before dinner for those martinis she'd said she wanted and plenty of time before and during dinner to talk about Kerry and Abner. The prospect of putting her revelations to use had revved me up, and finishing my novel so that it would be out of the way suddenly seemed more urgent than ever. I returned to my text, paying no attention to the hour, and stopped only a few minutes before seven. Holy God! I changed my clothes without taking a shower and rushed to put gin, vermouth, ice, and the cocktail shaker on the bar table in the library. It being a cool evening, I lit a fire and stood with my back to the fireplace, luxuriating in the heat. The pelvis Walter Reed put back together had been sending unpleasant reminders of its existence ever since my morning run. I'd been running five miles in Torcello, could it be that my six-and-a-half-mile run was too much? Should I have worked up to it gradually? The thought was unwelcome. The bastard who'd shot me had put an end to my active service. That was bad enough. Hampering harmless civilian activities was intolerable. I was sinking into a foul mood. It wasn't lightened by the knowledge that most likely I wouldn't have stayed in the Corps beyond the two remaining years of my engagement—not the way the war in Afghanistan was going—or that the injury was in its own way responsible for getting me to write novels and find my new life's work.

Jeanette came in and asked whether she should bring in her tray of canapés. Smoked salmon, she told me, and egg salad. I looked at my watch. Seven thirty-seven.

Please do, I said. I'll try to leave one or two for the young lady.

Enjoy! I can make some more.

There was no reason not to have a drink to go with the canapés. I made one carefully, following Harry's recipe. Five-sixths gin straight out of the freezer, one-sixth vermouth freshly extracted from the fridge, and an almost transparent lemon peel. Pour frigid liquor into crystal wineglass to chill it. Place ice cubes in shaker, add the gin and vermouth, shake vigorously, pour liquid back into wineglass, twist lemon peel, and introduce into liquid. The recipe was foolproof. Raising the glass to my lips should have made Heidi appear like a genie out of a bottle. No dice. I eased myself into an armchair near the fire, pressed the on button of the CD-player remote—I remembered having inserted a recording of *Dido and Aeneas*—and bit into a second egg-salad canapé. She'd show up all right; the only question was when, and the answer wasn't all that important. Jeanette had made a chicken sauté that could be kept waiting. So could I. Except for the four hours spent at my desk revising the draft of my novel, it had been and would continue to be a hell of a day: the futile exercise I'd gone through with that nice Martin Sweeney on the lookout for a nonexistent tail; the prospect of the time Scott and I would spend planning, to borrow a locution or two from my least-favorite secretary of defense, for unpleasant and dangerous knowns and for known and unknown unknowns, including the implications of the faux Amazon package; and now the need to face disclosures Heidi had up the sleeve of whatever elegant jacket she had donned. On the CD, Dido was crying her heart out:

> *When I am laid, am laid in earth,*
> *May my wrongs create*
> *No trouble, no trouble in thy breast;*
> *Remember me, remember me, but ah! forget my fate.*
> *Remember me, but ah! forget my fate.*

I found tears were rolling down my cheeks for her and the self-absorbed and heartless Aeneas and for every stupid slob who breaks the heart of someone he loves. In the suicide letter Slobo had forced him to write, Harry planted a clue that he'd hoped would bring down the House of Abner: he enjoined me to search the family Bible. I had been slow on the uptake, but finally the import of the clue—Matthew 7:7, "seek, and ye shall find"—penetrated my thick skull. When I took my great-grandfather's Bible off the shelf and opened it to that chapter and verse, there it was, staring me in the face: the sheets containing the road map to Abner's criminal empire. Harry hadn't been wrong to count on me to remember that much of the Gospels. We're not much good at forgetting, in our family.

So it wouldn't have surprised Harry, it might even have

struck him as singularly fitting, that I also recall Matthew 8:22, and what Jesus said to the disciple who asked, after the command to depart had been given, for leave to bury first his father: "Follow me; and let the dead bury their dead." If that wasn't the most brutal affirmation ever uttered that life must go on, I'd like to know one that beat it. There was no doubt that when Jovan—or whatever his real name was—came after me, I'd kill him, and I'd do whatever it took to make him talk before he died and give me the man who killed Kerry. But was I obliged to go looking for Jovan? And, by the way, how was I to go about it? Or the guy who murdered Kerry? Two needles in a haystack, unless there was only one needle, and Jovan had killed her. The FBI, the Treasury, and I'd forgotten what other agencies of our brilliant government had been trying for over a year to nail Abner based on the information I'd handed them on a silver platter. According to Scott and Simon, they hadn't gotten very far. Was it my destiny to be their truffle hound? To sniff out and feed evidence to them, regardless of the cost to me? Fuck that. Just between you, gentle reader, and me, I'd done more than enough for my country in a war I loathed but fought because it was my country's war and because in my ironic hypereducated family my great-grandfather, the abolitionist, my grandfather, my father, and I have stood with Stephen Decatur and never failed to raise our glasses to our country or spill our blood for her, right or wrong. Uncle Harry didn't lack for patriotism either—he just wasn't cut out to be a warrior. My family! That was a sick joke too. Only I was left. Wasn't it about time I packed it in? For instance: why not take my beautiful and apparently very available agent Jane out to dinner or—better yet—invite her to Sag Harbor for the weekend and screw the daylights out of her, instead of getting sloshed waiting for Kerry's lesbian pal? The pal who, I was beginning to suspect I would discover, if I kept on peeling the rotten onion, had been sleeping with her.

I tossed back what was left of the martini and started fixing a refill. Great gods of gin, I genuflect to you! While I was shaking the martini shaker as furiously as I would Jovan if I had him by the scruff of the neck, the answer issued forth from my subconscious like thunder: "Avenge not yourselves!" What? I could have died laughing. Thanks a lot, Saint Paul! If that's what you believed, what you wanted to write to the Romans, that was a nice formulation. But don't dish that bullshit to me. It doesn't cut it. I, blasphemous Jack Dana, proclaim to the four winds that vengeance is mine and not the Lord's, and it is I, Jack Dana, who will repay.

I heard the doorbell dimly through the pleasant gin-induced haze. Had I dozed off? It wasn't impossible. My wristwatch read eight thirty-seven. Nice work, Miss Heidi Krohn! Screwing up Jeanette's plan to get away early and see her sister. I scrambled to my feet and headed for the front door. Jeanette had gotten there first and was taking Heidi's coat, a black form-hugging velvet number, and propelling her in my direction. Jeanette held a bunch of yellow roses.

They're for you, Jack, Heidi said to me, but they need water, so I'm entrusting them to Mrs. Truman. Kerry told me Mrs. Truman's name. Will Mrs. Truman, will you, Jack, forgive me for being so late? I couldn't resist walking home from the office, and then walking here. I'd been preparing for a deposition and badly needed to clear my head.

This was, I realized, coming from Heidi, a fulsome apology, one I should accept with good grace. I also realized that she had brought the same flowers, yellow roses, that I had given to Kerry when I returned from the Mato Grosso, the first time I went to dinner at her apartment. A weird coincidence or a fiendish signal that she really knew and remembered everything about Kerry and me, down to the smallest details?

We were missing you, I said, but now that you're here, everything is Zen. Come, you have a lot of catching up to do in the martini department.

She sat down in an armchair facing mine, on the other side of the fireplace, stretched out her legs, and examined the surroundings with great interest.

This is a beautiful room, she said. Exactly as Kerry described it. She talked about your uncle's fine book bindings. Do you mind if I take a closer look? I have a bibliophile grandfather. Books and bindings mean a lot to me.

After I had given her the drink and we had both sat down again, Jeanette brought in the roses and put the vase on the library desk. I found it impossible to play dumb.

It was very kind of you to bring flowers, I told her. Neither Jeanette nor I have gotten used to my being back in the city, so these must be the only flowers we have right now in the apartment. Yellow roses. They're among my favorites, and I can't help wondering whether this is a confluence of our tastes, a charming coincidence, or a sign that you know that I brought just such a bouquet to Kerry the first time she invited me to dinner. Her apartment, by the way, was full of tulips! The first tulips of the season, it seemed to me.

She laughed. The last hypothesis is the right one. I knew. Shall we say that I'm still establishing my credentials?

If that's the purpose, I answered, you may rest your case, and I'll make a confession. It makes me just a little uneasy—not enough to upset me—to have you know all about Kerry and me, everything that Kerry had learned about me included, and to know so very little about you.

She laughed again. Give it time, Captain. Getting to know people takes time, more time than is needed for a quick recon job. Reconnaissance is your specialty, isn't it? Force reconnaissance at that! But I have to stop this. I find I am flirting with you, and that is not a part of my battle plan. Do you think I might have another one—she pointed to the shaker—they're delicious.

Yes, you may, I said, if you will allow me a personal remark. Your velvet coat is stunning. Just like everything you wear. Have you a grandfather couturier to balance the bibliophile?

She had on what my mother would have called a little black dress if only it had been black. As it happened, it was made of burgundy silk.

How did you guess? She laughed again. Not quite a couturier but big on Seventh Avenue. That's how the Krohns have made their money. My great-grandfather started out sewing shirts on the Lower East Side. Next thing you know he had a sweatshop on West Thirty-First Street where people working for him sewed and sweated. My late grandfather moved the operation to Seventh Avenue, and that's where it is today, making fancier and fancier ready-to-wear women's clothes that you'll find under the Krohn label at Bergdorf Goodman, Neiman Marcus, and Saks, if you want to see what we still make in the U.S. Most of what Father now sells to department stores and online under labels that don't include the magic word "Krohn" is manufactured for them in China or Vietnam. There you have it, the key to my independence and my chic: money on my father's side of the family. My mother's family is all certified lefty intellectuals. City College in the old days, and Harvard and Yale now that they let in people called Rappaport and Schwartz. The bibliophile is a Rappaport.

She laughed once more—I was beginning to like the sound of her laughter—and added, I guess we both know the story of Kerry's visit to Abner when he said he expected her to give him a blowjob like a good Jewish girl from New Jersey. A charming literary fellow! If Kerry's name was Black it must have been originally Schwartz, and if she's from New Jersey she must be into giving head. Another Philip Roth creation straight out of *Goodbye, Columbus*! Just think, suppose instead of Kerry he'd seen a Krohn. He'd have raped me!

I had decided to let Heidi babble on through what had turned into a longer cocktail hour than I had envisaged and waited until we were at table, eating Jeanette's sauté, to remind her of the business purpose of our dinner. What more could she tell me about the file she'd recovered? Had she by any chance brought it with her?

No, no, the file is in the safe. It wasn't so much a matter of recovering it, she said, as of following instructions. I can give you the exact date: Tuesday, the first of October. The poor thing must have felt threatened, though she never let on. Anyway, she clearly wanted to get the file out of her possession and into some other hands. That Tuesday morning, then, I received a hand delivery in a Jones & Whetstone envelope showing her as the sender. Inside was another envelope, also addressed to me and scotch-taped in every direction, and a handwritten note asking me to keep the envelope for her in a secure place and open it only on her instructions or if something happened to her. Of course, I called her immediately wanting to know what was going on. She revealed nothing, literally nothing. She'd been going through her mother's personal papers and had come across a journal her mother had kept that was fascinating, and very important for her, but otherwise not a file she'd want anyone else to see. I thought that was pretty weird and asked why she didn't simply burn it. Oh no, she said, I couldn't possibly. One day I may want to write a novel or a family memoir, and these pages are essential material. I went on thinking this was weird, but naturally I told her I'd do what she wanted and would put the envelope in my firm's office safe, under my personal file number. Oh well, she said, I guess that'll do, but I'd rather you put it in your personal safe-deposit box. And do it today, please. I was very busy; otherwise I would have asked to see her and would have tried to get to the bottom of this. As it was, I just told her that I had no personal safe-deposit box—which is the truth—and that no one except me would have access to a file I put in the office safe marked as belonging to me rather than to the firm. She said she guessed in that case it was all right, and hung up.

If only you'd seen her, I murmured.

I know, she said, I know. I can't get it out of my head. But it was one of those things that's nobody's fault. I went to D.C. that evening and didn't come back until late in the afternoon the next day. I called her once I got home. She was out and didn't get back to me until around noon the following day— that was Thursday—just as I was leaving for lunch with a client, and we made a date to get together on Saturday. Dinner was better than lunch, she said, she'd want to sleep in. Why didn't I suggest doing something together Friday night? Very simple. First, I didn't think there was any urgency. Second, I was going to the opera with my parents. It was all so stupid and so crazy.

She stopped to choke back a sob.

I don't think that you've done anything wrong, I told her. Have you been able to find out since what scared her?

Heidi shook her head. The police actually got through to her voice mail at home. All messages had been erased. I don't know what they did about voice messages at the law firm. Simon Lathrop should be able to tell you.

He didn't mention it, I said. I'll ask him. So what was the next step with the envelope? I suppose once you came out of shock you got it out of the office safe and opened it . . .

Yes, it's a file, consisting of many sheets, reporting on due diligence that Jones & Whetstone did on the Brown Enterprises holding company, the one that owns all the legitimate businesses other than Abner's residences and ranches and perhaps a part of his oil and gas investments, when it was being prepared for a public offering. I know that Kerry told you that your uncle Harry discovered the existence of Abner's parallel crime empire through that work. I can't tell whether what this file consists of is transcripts of notes taken by J & W associates or Harry's summary and analysis of their notes. Unfortunately, if it's the work of many associates—which is what I believe—their names aren't given, and there are no file numbers or other usual means of identifying the authors. Anyway, whoever prepared these notes found a disconnect between the shipping documents—bills of lading and the like—that First National Brown Family Bank, which is a legitimate, real banking organization created under the laws of Texas and owned by Abner, and anything those shipping documents purported to cover, and the underlying transactions. For instance, there are shipping documents relating to huge volumes of rare earths being bought from Congo for hundreds of millions of dollars. Very nice, except that if you go to the trouble of tracing those documents to their source, you find that there was no such purchase, that nothing was loaded on the ships, et cetera, et cetera. Why? Because the criminal First National Brown Family Bank, organized under the laws of Malta unlike its legitimate twin, used the funds realized on the sale to buy arms from non-U.S. manufacturers for resale to countries under sanctions, or potentially nuclear-proliferating materials from North Korea or Pakistan, that were then shipped to Iran or—much more troubling—consignees who could well be al-Qaeda or Hezbollah, or the al-Qaeda affiliate operating in Yemen. The rare earths are a fiction. The list is extensive, and it doesn't pretend to be exhaustive. It illustrates what was going on and how the feasibility of what went on hinged on the existence of the Brown Family Bank, with its huge and rock-solid capitalization and access to the Federal Reserve discount window. That access was the indispensable open sesame—it made it possible to use extremely cheap funds available without any practical limit to earn huge margins on the phony money-laundering transactions or usurious interest on loans, some of which were real and some imaginary, some repaid and some written off because the loss could be washed against some kooky illegal transaction. And here is the zinger: it would seem that transactions above a certain amount, I can't tell you what it is, had to be authorized by Abner personally. So that you have his signature—or sometimes just initials—on the American side of these deals. Deals that are really transparent to any banker understanding finance. He couldn't possibly get away with claiming he didn't know what he was doing.

God Almighty! I exclaimed. Why did she just sit on this? What was wrong with her? Why didn't she take it to the guy she and I saw together when she and I turned Harry's materials over to him, the U.S. attorney, whatever his name was. Why did she lie to you about what was in the envelope?

Heidi was sobbing. I offered her my handkerchief, which she accepted, and refilled her wineglass.

This is very good wine, she said, and delicious chicken. I'm sorry I haven't got my nerves under better control. Why did she act the way she did? I can only speculate. First hypothesis: she came quite properly to the conclusion that these new materials, which she identified in her own handwriting as having been found by her in J & W's files, were the firm's property and were covered by the attorney-client privilege. Don't forget, Abner and his businesses were Harry's clients and major, very major, clients of the firm. I am pretty sure that Kerry explained to you how privilege works.

I nodded. I haven't forgotten, and I haven't forgotten the exceptions to the privilege that should have let this stuff be given to the authorities.

Good, she replied. She had probably in the end come to that conclusion. Don't forget either that we don't know exactly when she came upon this stuff. How much time did it take her to study it? How much time elapsed between when she finished and the first of October, when she sent it to me? Perhaps only days. And she was working her way first through the file and then through the privilege problem alone—I am certain she couldn't have asked my advice, because there is no exception for disclosure to a friend.

Second hypothesis: she had in fact already told Ed Flanagan—that's the U.S. attorney—in outline or perhaps in some detail what she had, although she hadn't yet turned over the file. I'm sure you remember I told you she was scheduled to appear before the grand jury looking into money laundering by Abner and his businesses exactly one week after she was killed. I believe she gave that information to Flanagan or someone at Justice, which is why they wanted her to testify. I also believe that somehow Abner found out about it and decided there was no way she'd give that testimony. It's probable that the description she gave to the FBI or Flanagan was too general for it to be much use without her to verify and explain. Otherwise, an FBI agent or assistant U.S. attorney could have testified to what she had told him or her. Hearsay rules don't apply in grand jury proceedings, so her presence wouldn't have been indispensable if the story she had given was adequate. But I think as a matter of preparing to get Abner, the U.S. attorney leading the charge on the laundering case would have wanted her live testimony and, above all, would have wanted the file.

Third hypothesis: This one explains why she got so scared. Abner himself or someone who makes those fucking calls for him telephoned her and said something like Listen carefully, you little slut. Give back the file you've stolen or else—and previewed a list of things that she might expect to happen to her, from gang rape through torture to ultimate execution. You can fill in the blanks. So the first thing she thought she must do was to get the file into safe hands, in a safe place. That's what she did. The question I can't answer, which may undercut this hypothesis, is why Abner's boys haven't been turning over every stone looking for the file. For instance, there was absolutely no indication of a break-in at her apartment either before or after she died. You'd think they might have wanted to go through her papers. And I haven't heard of a break-in at Jones & Whetstone, which would be the other logical place to look for a file she'd squirreled away.

Simon didn't mention any such thing either, I interjected.

Well, that doesn't surprise me, but it may not mean much. Remember that the guy who forced Harry to retire and was later booted out from the firm himself and took the Brown business with him to the Houston law firm surely has moles at J & W. Possibly they've looked. They may still be looking. So a burglary at J & W may not have seemed necessary.

Another answer to the question, she continued, may be that Abner thinks the file is in your hands, that somehow Kerry, even though you and she had broken up, something he probably knows, would send the file to you when faced with danger and the possibility that the file might be taken from her.

It took me a moment to think through Heidi's hypotheses.

All you say, I finally told her, makes sense in an insane sort of way. I'm groping my way toward a few questions that you might help me with. But let's first have dessert.

Jeanette had cleared the main course and was preparing to serve the apple tart she'd baked.

I'll take care of the tart, I said, and the coffee. And don't bother throwing these dishes into the washer. Tonight, it's my job. You go on and tell your sister I'm sorry we kept you late. I'll see you the day after tomorrow, unless I am visiting Scott Prentice, in which case I'll see you when I come back. I'll call you tomorrow at your sister's and tell you whether I'm going or staying.

Jeanette's sister lives in White Plains, I explained once Jeanette had finished thanking me and left the dining room. She'll take the number four train to One Hundred Twenty-Fifth Street and catch the Metro-North there. Her sister will meet her at the White Plains station.

Look, I said, here is where I stumble. Abner's fortune—his known fortune as calculated by *Forbes* or Bloomberg—is way up there in the Warren Buffett sphere. How much money can this guy make on the money-laundering business? Isn't it peanuts—in spite of the scale of the operation—in comparison with the legitimate businesses? I do know he's Polluter Number One, Climate Change Denier Number One, and all that; Kerry talked about that, perhaps even Harry did. That I sort of understand. You make more money if you don't adhere to environmental-protection standards. But nothing like what you've just described. Why does he bother?

I think there are several comments I can make, she answered. First, we've been talking about money laundering because that's where we seem to have the goods on him. But as you know from what Kerry told you, and from Harry's road map, all his legitimate—your word—businesses have criminal twins. We can't even begin to guess how much the criminal twins as a group contribute and where their profits ultimately are stashed away. In Singapore? In Malta? In

Kuala Lumpur? Brought back to the U.S. without incurring tax? We don't know. Very likely it isn't peanuts. Second, the guy is evil. He likes doing evil. I imagine it's the spice of his existence. Do you want to take Lucifer as an example? The angel who shone brighter than all others and yet was hell-bent on rebelling? Excuse me, I didn't mean to make a pun. It just popped out. Or to take a mere mortal, Saint Augustine and his pears, how when he was a boy he just had to steal pears from the neighbor's orchard, not because they were better pears than the ones in his own orchard but because doing evil, stealing, made the fruit taste better. Hitler and his men? Stalin? Mao at his worst? Pol Pot? Did it profit them to kill countless millions, or did they do it out of total contempt for life and love of doing evil, a passion for malice? What about the jihadi, blowing up people, including children, decapitating, amputating limbs, stoning sinners, and on and on? They say they do it in the service of Allah, but don't you think that the real reason is that they like to maim and kill?

She fell silent.

All right, I said. What's our next step, what are the other materials you hope to find?

I am convinced, she replied, although I have no proof, that there is more. We have to get to her personal email accounts and her iCloud. They may be tucked in there, or we might find clues to their existence—or nonexistence—elsewhere.

Thank you! If all goes according to plan, I told her, I'll go to visit Scott tomorrow. Back in a couple of days. I'll be in touch when I return, and we'll get down to business. You're really something. By the way, what was your major in college?

You mean my smarty-pants allusions? I was a Harvard College English major, and when I get carried away I let it show.

We had coffee and, having refused her offer to do the dishes, I helped her into that fabulous velvet coat and put her in the elevator. The kitchen in fact was spic and span. I went into the library, put a log on the fire, and waited for Martin Sweeney to call. The phone rang a few minutes later.

The lady's a fast walker, he told me. No tail, no problem.

That's great, I said, just where are you?

At Eighty-Fifth and Fifth, he answered, I want to check out your building once again.

Come up after you've done that, I urged him on the spur of the moment. We'll have a nightcap and talk about plans.

He was up in no time. I poured him a Jameson with soda and a neat single-malt scotch for myself. We were clinking glasses when the telephone rang. The caller identified himself as Detective Rod Walker. Immediately, I put him on speakerphone.

Does a Mrs. Jeanette Truman work for you and live at your apartment? he asked.

Yes, she does, I answered, feeling weak, as weak as when Simon told me over the phone in Torcello that Kerry was dead.

She was attacked on Eighty-Fourth Street, between Park and Lexington Avenues, and badly beaten. The ambulance took her to the Lenox Hill Hospital. If you can get over there, you'll be able to find out more about her condition. I could wait for you and get your statement there. Please go directly to the emergency room and ask for me, Detective Walker.

I'm on my way, I said, and hung up.

As it turned out, I wasn't quite on my way. The phone rang again. UNIDENTIFIED WIRELESS CALLER was displayed in the caller-ID window. I pressed the talk and speakerphone buttons.

Greetings from Jovan, you fuckhead, said the familiar voice. Tonight I beat. Maybe next time I kill.

VI

We'll go on foot, I said, it'll be faster than a taxi.

Why had they done it to Jeanette? Why beat up an old black lady who'd never thought a bad thought or done a bad thing in her whole blameless life? The answer never changed, however many times I asked the question. Maximum evil, that's what he's after. Hurting the innocent. Heidi has the prick pegged. No more doubts or hesitation. Whatever it takes, I'll make him pay.

We got to the hospital in record time, but without Martin I'd have wasted the minutes we'd saved while I tried to find my bearings. Out of breath and sweating, Martin found the emergency room like a homing pigeon and spotted Detective Walker without having to ask for him. It occurred to me that this was not the first time they had met.

It's ugly, Walker said, but I don't believe she's in danger. Mr. Dana? There is some information I'd like to get from you. If you don't mind, I'll record what you say. You should be able to see Mrs. Truman right after we finish.

My mind was wandering, but with Martin's prompting we

went quickly through the basic stuff about Jeanette. Widow, husband an army master sergeant killed on deployment in Iraq. Two daughters, with children, I believe married, living in Oakland, California. One sister, a divorced retired librarian, living in White Plains. Yes, Mrs. Truman has been working for me as a live-in housekeeper since my uncle's death last year and had been working for him in that capacity for more than thirty years; live-in since the death of her husband.

This is an unusual mugging, said Walker. For one thing, these days muggings rarely occur in your neighborhood. This would be the first one this year. Quite a change from not so many years ago. Mrs. Truman wore her pocketbook bandolier-style. It was still on her shoulder, unopened. She had her MetroCard clutched in her hand and didn't let go of it during the attack. The assailant beat her on the face, most likely hard slaps. Her nose is broken; the lips are split; eyes are swollen shut. I don't know whether the jaw is broken. She's got broken ribs. Obviously a concussion. I don't know about internal injuries. This brings me to my question: do you know of anyone—a personal enemy, hers or her late husband's— who would have stalked and attacked her? It doesn't look to me like a random assault. Would you agree, Martin?

Martin shook his head. Nah, he said, not the way you describe it.

What do you think, Mr. Dana?

I hoped the question would go away. It didn't. Walker continued to stare at me.

A personal enemy? I said. It's out of the question. I don't believe Mrs. Truman has a single enemy. Since she was widowed, her whole life has been looking after my uncle and, now that he's dead, after me. That and, of course, her church in White Plains. As for her husband—I wouldn't know, but he died nine or ten years ago. It seems out of the question.

And you?

I'll give you an answer, but it's not simple. Since I returned from Italy a week ago—I'd been away almost a year—there have been threatening calls made to the apartment, to my telephone. The threats are directed at me, but a couple of times Mrs. Truman was the one who answered the telephone. My advice has been to tell the caller, in case she answered again, that I would be glad to talk to him or to meet him, and having done so, to hang up. I'm sure she has followed my instructions. By the way, the caller appears to identify himself sometimes as Jovan.

I spelled for him J-O-V-A-N. Probably he is the same man who called this evening, a minute or two after you called, and spoke to me. I think I can quote him exactly: "Greetings from Jovan. Tonight I beat. Maybe next time I kill." It so happened that Mr. Sweeney was there and heard him. He can confirm my version.

Is that about right? I asked, turning to Martin.

Yeah. He nodded. Exactly as Captain Dana said minus an expletive.

Walker checked his recording device.

I see, he said. This is very interesting. Have you any idea who Jovan is, or why these calls are made? By the way, have you reported this harassment to the police?

No, I don't know who he is, and no, I haven't reported the calls, I replied. And I don't really know why these calls are made—except, as you put it, to harass me.

I'm surprised, said Walker. Why haven't you turned to us?

In the first place, I haven't felt personally intimidated. Second, I didn't believe I had anything useful to tell the police department. Obviously, if making a report could have in any way prevented this attack, or gotten protection for Mrs. Truman, I was horribly wrong. I must say, though, that her being singled out as the target of violence is something that never crossed my mind.

And how about you? Have you enemies you're aware of?

Clearly, yes. My uncle Harry Dana was murdered last year, in the first days of January, at his house in Sag Harbor, down in eastern Long Island. The murder was made to look like a suicide. The next day, his long-term secretary was pushed under a subway train. Then in May of last year—on May fourth, to be precise—an attempt was made on my life at that very house in Sag Harbor, which I had inherited from my uncle, just like the apartment on Fifth Avenue where I live. I killed the intruder. The intruder was a hit man by the name of Slobodan Milić. He was the man who killed my uncle and his secretary. I recorded his confession before he died and turned it over to Mr. Flanagan, the U.S. attorney for the Southern District, shortly after the events I've described. It occurs to me that the person making the threatening calls and whoever attacked Mrs. Truman may be in some way connected with the hit man I killed and that desire for revenge may play a role in all this.

I kept an eye on Martin Sweeney as I spoke, hoping that if I was too close to the line in editing the information he would alert me by his facial expression or body language. To my relief, he remained entirely impassive.

A couple more questions. You're unmarried, right?

Yes.

Isn't it rather strange for an unmarried young man—you're a little over thirty, I'd guess—to have a live-in housekeeper and to occupy a large apartment on Fifth Avenue? I believe that all the apartments in your building are large.

The guy was getting on my nerves, and I was about to tell him so when Martin broke in.

Easy there, Rod, he said. The captain here is a war hero, a decorated Marine Corps Infantry officer, and a bestselling novelist. You heard of the film *Returning*? Maybe you've seen it. It's based on his book. If he wants to live in a Fifth Avenue apartment with a full-time housekeeper that's his business. He can afford it!

Thanks, Martin, I said. I don't mind the detective's questions. But I believe I've said all I have to say. Unless there is something specific you need to know, Detective Walker, I'll leave you now and find Mrs. Truman and her doctor. I also need to call the sister. I assume she'll get in touch with the daughters.

No problem, Walker said. I have your telephone number and address. I'll need you to sign a statement after I've typed up this interview. Will you be available?

I'll be going to Alexandria, Virginia, for a couple of days, I replied, as soon as the doctor tells me that Mrs. Truman's condition is stable, and probably I'll be spending some weekends in Sag Harbor. I'm in the telephone directory over there. Otherwise I'll be around.

Without a word having been exchanged between us, Martin followed me as I set off to find the attending physician.

When my poor father had the big stroke that put him into a vegetative state, I was a senior at Yale. I got the call in the middle of the night from our next-door neighbor, who'd been alerted by my father's cook, jumped into my car, and headed for Cambridge determined to get to the hospital while Father was still alive. Massachusetts state troopers stopped me doing ninety and ribbed me about being a good son when I told them I was hurrying to my father's bedside. In the end, they let me go, after taking all my cash. By the time I got to the hospital he had already been installed in a bed in the ward. In the course of previous visits, for the little strokes, he'd trained the hospital to understand that paying the difference not covered by insurance between the cost of a private room where he'd have privacy and that of the ward or a semiprivate room was unthinkable. That last time, he had nothing to say. Harry and I took over and made sure that his remaining days as a vegetable were passed in comfort, that he was beautifully bathed, powdered, and diapered, and that no bedsore broke his skin. So this visit was my first to a civilian emergency room, which revealed itself as yet another circle of hell, a brilliantly lit cavern in which patients slumped over in chairs or stretched out on gurneys moaned or mumbled or screamed nonsense while shapes recognizable as relatives or friends crisscrossed the space, pursuing nurses and doctors, bent on securing their benevolence. Other shapes besieged the white Formica-enclosed islets of privilege, where nurses and young interns cracked jokes and interrogated computer screens.

Fatal and perfidious dinner, I thought, what had I done? If only I'd asked Heidi out to a restaurant instead of wanting like an asshole to show off Jeanette and the apartment, if only Heidi had been on time, if only Jeanette had gotten away earlier. If only . . . Nonsense, they would have gotten her whatever time she left. Somebody told them: Beat her. There was no way they weren't going to do it.

Martin was tugging at my sleeve. Snap out of it, Captain, you're losing it. I'll find the doctor. You stay right here.

The Pakistani doctor, a friendly man with a little mustache, said the beating had been bad; she looked really bad but was lucky. There was a concussion—presumably from the impact of her head hitting the sidewalk, but he didn't think there were other significant internal injuries—CAT scans had been ordered to confirm that and determine the extent of intracranial bleeding. Neurological tests would be necessary. Her jaw had not been broken. The plastic surgeon would set her nose in the morning and possibly sew up her lip. She had many broken ribs; he wasn't sure how many. Slaps to the face and kicks. There was nothing to be done about the ribs, except to leave them to nature. We used to tape broken ribs, he continued, but now we understand that entails risks.

I would like to see her, I told him.

He nodded and led us to a gurney at the end of a corridor.

Can't we get her into a room? I asked.

He shook his head. We have to keep her here so she can have her CAT scans and neurological work done first thing tomorrow morning.

Jeanette's face, normally very pale—more lait than café, according to Harry—was a shiny black and swollen like the face of a corpse fallen in battle and left unburied for days. I half expected the usual fetor and flies. Her eyes were closed. But she was alive.

No use trying to speak to her, said the doctor, she's in very deep sleep. I'll still be on duty when the tests are done. If you wish I'll call you, but don't expect a call before eight, eight-thirty. By the way, I'm a big fan of your novels.

I seized his hand and thanked him.

Martin, who thought of everything, gave him my telephone numbers as well as his own.

Stay here another minute, he said.

When he returned, it was to report that a private room was available and that he'd told the admissions person I'd want it for Jeanette. Round-the-clock nursing was available too, but I would have to stop by the nursing office when it opened to make the arrangements.

By the time I'd taken care of the room and called the sister, who said she'd been calling my apartment and was sick with worry—and reassured her as best I could—it was past midnight.

Martin, I said, putting an arm around his shoulder, I'd be lost without you, but it's really late. You should hop into a taxi and go home.

Not a chance, Captain, he answered, not if you can spare some more of that Jameson. I've already texted Lee. He'll take over tomorrow morning while I get my beauty rest.

I had better leave you for a moment, I said to Martin after I had served him his drink and poured an Oban for myself, and send Scott an email telling him I'll have to stay in the city until Jeanette is out of the woods.

He nodded. Good idea. Let's talk about Miss Krohn after you've done that.

Look, Captain, he said when I returned to the library, we've got some serious problems to discuss.

Only if you knock off the "captain" shit. My name is Jack.

Thanks, Jack! I'm honored to do that. Look, Jack: you may not be thinking of that now, but you're in real personal danger. What they did to Jeanette wasn't some sort of happy-anniversary card they sent you. It was bold, brutal, and well aimed. I've no idea what they'll try next, but they'll sure try something. The question is whether there'll be some intermediate fun and games before they close in for the kill. It depends on whether there is something they want while you're still alive.

There is a document, I said. Heidi has it. Based on what she's told me, it's dynamite. They may think I have it and they can get it from me. It's a good idea to keep them thinking that if it keeps her off their screen. That means to me that we have to make sure they don't establish a connection between her and me. Unless there is some indication that they think she's the problem, I doubt that providing her with security, something like what we did for Kerry, is a good idea.

Is the document in a safe place?

I think so, I told him.

Can I have another? Martin asked, and held out his glass.

A good idea.

My bartender duty performed, we drank in silence until he spoke again.

Do you have by any chance a list of the people working in this building? Martin asked suddenly.

I do, I said, as of last Christmas. It's in my computer, marked to show the checks I sent them. Ordinarily, I'd give cash, but I was away. Let me print it for you.

When I returned and gave him the sheet, I said, I can't be absolutely sure whether they're all still here or whether there is somebody new. I've been back such a short time!

Thanks, said Martin. I want to check out these people. One-half seem to be some sort of Serbs or Croats or maybe Montenegrins. The rest are Irish and Polacks. Interesting mixture. I bet they're clean, but that doesn't mean they don't talk. You know, such as Mr. Dana said he's going away for the weekend, or He said he's staying in town, or There is a young lady who comes to visit all the time, or Yeah, the housekeeper has her evening off on such day. Who they talk to I have no idea, but it could be anybody. A cousin visiting from the old country. Someone they go bowling with. You get the picture.

I do. Checking them out is a smart idea, and I'll find out whether there are any new hires.

Good deal, he replied. By the way, your firearm is registered, and the registration is in order?

Yes, of course, I said.

And New York City validated?

Yes, I said, and I have a license to carry it concealed. Not that I lug my Colt 1911 with me.

Good deal, Martin said again. I wouldn't want a character like Walker to grab the chance to run you in and perhaps get you into a lot of trouble.

What's this all about?

You saw the little pin he had in his necktie, a gold Christmas tree? I was surprised he wore it so openly. It's the Tannenbaum Society. Open to policemen. I'm sorry to say some of my former colleagues belong too. It's mostly secret, something like the old John Birch Society only weirder. It doesn't stop him from being a good cop, but I don't like and don't trust those guys. They've got strange agendas and strange friends.

Interesting, I said. More and more interesting. Now I'll tell you another reason why I want Abner to believe I have the document he wants. It will make him move against me. And that will be my chance to kill his thugs. I wish he'd come after me himself so I could cut his heart out. I know. It won't happen. And now, why don't you go and get your beauty sleep? Call me tomorrow—anytime. We'll get together and figure out what else we should do.

I must have slept five hours straight and woke up feeling rested and alert. It was a dry morning. A run would do me good. I set my landline phone to forward calls to my iPhone—I didn't want to take a chance on missing the doctor's call—got into my running shoes, stuck the switchblade into my windbreaker pocket, and headed for the park. My building's door was locked at that hour, and Emil, the night man, opened it for me. We exchanged the usual comments about the weather, but I felt a tinge of unease. Was it by any chance he who reported my comings and goings? Who else could it be? If there were such informers, did they coordinate passing on the information, or was it all very casual?

I ran fast, thinking that the one temporary concession I'd make to my pelvis was to limit the distance to about four and a half miles, and was glad to see that no one was overtaking me. A quick look around the building as I was leaving had revealed nothing unusual, and no one had followed me from Fifth Avenue into the park. That, I realized, didn't prove anything because if Jovan & Co. had me scheduled for an early morning run, whoever was to tail or attack me could be waiting inside the park rather than outside my building, especially if they had also figured out that I was in the habit of entering the park at Seventy-Ninth Street. I took a look at the figures running behind me, and headed north: women, who I assumed were not a problem, men of various ages and body builds who didn't look anything like Slobo or the thug in Torcello, and one guy who had real potential. Big and fast, with a stupid face. What was I to do about him? The obvious test was to change my pace. He followed my lead, but that could mean only that we were both good runners and he liked regulating his speed according to mine. I could simply leave the park and see what he'd do. The problem was that he and his handlers might think he'd scared me. Rapidly, I decided to keep going another mile and cut toward the Ravine, which I was pretty sure would be deserted. A great place for him to do his thing and for me to do mine. In a beautiful setting! The waterfall is at its best in the autumn, I told myself. Let's see if my new buddy enjoys it as much as I.

He followed me like a cocker spaniel. For all I knew he was wagging his tail. I put on some speed, clambered up and down a rock or two, and got us to the chosen spot. Behind me was a big slab of granite, perfect for the sacrifice of Isaac. As I expected, we were alone. The waterfall was also as expected—gorgeous. I admired it, keeping an eye on my pal, wondering what he'd do. Surprise, surprise! He did absolutely nothing—no, that's not quite right. Standing about fifteen feet from me, he started running in place and doing fancy stretches. He looked like an idiot, but his approach presented a dilemma. I didn't think I could attack him without further provocation. After all, as my mother liked saying, it's a free country, and his following me on my morning run wasn't per se a reason for knifing him. There was also the little legal problem: I killed the fellow in Torcello in self-defense, and a pretty good argument could be made that I killed Slobo in self-defense as well. Justifiable homicide was my ticket! If this was Jovan or Jovan's little brother I certainly wanted to kill him too, but I didn't want to go to jail. Or even take a serious risk of going to jail.

Hey you, I called out. Come over here and explain why you're following me. If you've got some kind of problem, let's deal with it.

No way, the guy answered, no way. No talk.

I couldn't tell whether the voice was the one I'd heard on the telephone, but I had no doubt about the accent. What I should do next was a puzzle, from which I was distracted by the ringing of my phone. I pressed the answer button and this time heard the voice that I knew, the voice that had spoken to me about Jeanette.

You get it, shithead? We know where you are. Twenty-four/ seven. Now we only fuck with you. We kill when we want.

He hung up. The guy who'd followed me stopped dancing around and took off full speed toward the West Side. Without hesitation I followed. Out of the Ravine, past the Loch, through the loveliest part of the park, across the West Drive. We left the park at One Hundred Third Street and headed west. He was a good runner, but I was better, staying right on his ass, the switchblade ready in my pocket, waiting for him to turn and fight. He did no such thing. We zoomed past Manhattan Avenue, Amsterdam, and Columbus and were reaching Broadway when suddenly I understood. He wouldn't duck into some tenement building or ethnic luncheonette; he wasn't going to introduce me to his friends. He was taking the subway—uptown! I looked back. There was no one behind me and no one ahead on my side of the street except him, and when he started down the subway stairs I was right there behind him. I grabbed the handrails on both sides, raised myself, and kicked him with both feet in the small of the back. I put all my strength into it. He flew forward, facedown, landing with a thud and a long yell of pain. I climbed the stairs. Still no one there except me. As I could see, the shops on Broadway were closed. Only a Starbucks was open. A guy was standing in the door. Hanging out? Leaving? I resisted the desire to run downstairs and stomp on my buddy. Instead, I took a taxi to the corner of Madison and Seventy-Ninth Street. At a diner down the block I had fresh-squeezed orange juice, scrambled eggs, and coffee. I knew that Jeanette had left everything I needed for my breakfast in the fridge, but I didn't have the heart to deal with it.

There was a good chance I had hurt the guy real good, I reflected as I ate, and caused lasting damage. The big question was whether I'd tell Martin Sweeney or Scott about it. That my Nanny Sweeney and my Nanny Prentice would disapprove—for openers because of what might have happened if I'd been caught by the cops—was a certainty. But the point was that I hadn't been caught. Nobody was going to trace this job to me. They beat Jeanette's face into a pulp and broke her nose and ribs. I hoped I'd at least cracked this guy's skull.

VII

By the time I got to the hospital later that morning, Jeanette had been moved to a private room and opened her eyes when I spoke to her. I felt sure she recognized me. I even thought I saw the beginnings of a smile. The Pakistani doctor who'd asked me to call him Sonny told me that was possible.

A dim sort of recognition, he said. She's had a heavy dose of painkillers, and now that the first neurological tests have been done we've sedated her a little. By the way, there is intracranial bleeding. Fortunately it's not extensive and not in the really crucial areas of the brain. We may hope that there won't be permanent neurological damage, but we won't know that for several days. It depends in part on whether the bleeding continues and how much additional bleeding there will be. I'm glad to tell you that there don't seem to be any other internal injuries. When you come to see her tomorrow morning, she should be more responsive.

I thanked him again and told him how happy I was to know she was under his care.

He shook his head and said, Since she's no longer an emergency-room patient, a hospitalist will be looking after her. I'll find out his name and if possible introduce you.

I confessed that hospitalists were a specialty I'd never heard of before.

He smiled and said, Most people haven't. They're full-time hospital employees who in the new system take responsibility for patients. It's different from the old days when a patient's regular doctor would be in charge.

There's one other thing, he added, you should have Mrs. Truman's regular doctor get in touch with the hospitalist. Do you know her doctor?

I told him I didn't. Probably he's someone in White Plains, where her sister lives.

You should find out, he said. She'll need to be under his care after she's been released from here or from rehab.

He saw me raise my eyebrows, and added, Yes, I'm afraid that a stay at a rehabilitation facility will be desirable. By the way, you should understand that I've taken particular interest in her not only because of her connection with you but also because in my country I've treated people who'd been beaten by the police. I know what those injuries mean, that kind of a beating. Stay right here; I'll be back.

The hospitalist wasn't available, but Sonny gave me his name and telephone number. He also gave me his own cell-phone number. If you need help with the system, he said, get in touch. I'll do what I can.

The private nurse I had hired arrived just then. She worked an eight-hour shift, she said; if I stopped by after five, I'd be able to meet the evening nurse, and if I couldn't, she'd fill the evening nurse in and make sure she wrote down my telephone numbers. I found I liked this sturdy lady who, for all her matter-of-fact air, caressed Jeanette's cheek and spoke to her, calling her sweetheart, as indeed I had gotten to like Sonny, and paradoxically felt uplifted by my contacts with them, as though something good had happened to me. There were good people in this world as well as monsters, gentle, unassuming people who were ready to help. Perhaps they outnumbered evil shits like Abner and his acolytes. Of course, Sonny and the nurses were paid to care for their patients, but somehow it didn't matter that money changed hands. Their merit was just as intact as Martin's or his partner Lee's. Martin especially, whom I'd gotten to know well enough to be sure of my judgment, was a genuinely good guy. The sort of brother I would have wanted for my team of marines.

It was hard to go back to the apartment. I'd spent the night there and stopped by to take a shower and get out of my running clothes and knew that nothing would have changed since then. That was the problem. I had never known the apartment without Jeanette. She had been inseparable from my uncle Harry. I'd never thought about it, but presumably she went on vacation at the same time he did and came back when he returned. However that worked, she was always there, and I couldn't think of the place without her, without her voice greeting me. Yes, everything was exactly as I had left it. The radio was still on, and WQXR's usual programming—something by Dvořák—rolled on while I made my bed and neatened the bathroom. Then I carried my laptop to the kitchen, made a pot of tea, and sat down to check my email. Scott, Heidi, Martin, and Moses Cohen. Scott asked me to call his private cell phone, which I did at once.

His first question was naturally about Jeanette. When I explained that she was likely to be unable to speak until tomorrow—if then—and probably no decisions could be made about her treatment and convalescence before a couple of days had passed, he said in that case it was unrealistic to think I could get to Alexandria before the weekend. It made more sense for him to come to New York on Friday afternoon and combine a visit to his mother with seeing me. His mother now tired quickly in the evening. He'd have tea with her and dinner with me, if I was free, and go back to Alexandria Saturday morning, after breakfast with his mother.

That's perfect, I said. Depending on just about everything, I might go to Sag Harbor on Saturday.

I've got some special news for you. It's a secret from everyone else, but both Susie and I wanted you to know right away. She's pregnant. If it's a boy, his name will be Jack.

I choked back tears. Good things could happen.

I wish you were here, you old mother, I told him, so I could give you a big hug. Your life is turning out so well, exactly as it should. What a relief! This is something we'll celebrate on Friday. But look, on another front, there are some developments. Perhaps I should hold them until we're together. What do you think?

Really interesting?

Yes.

Let's hold them. Call me or send me an email about Jeanette.

Understood. Do you recommend holding off calling others?

Not a bad idea.

We hung up.

He'd asked me to call his private cell phone. . . . Clearly he thought it, as well as his office cell phone and landline, was being tapped and perhaps actually monitored instead of just being recorded for future reference. Telling me that it wasn't a bad idea to stay off the phone with others could only mean that I too might be under surveillance. In my case, there was a way out—one that I would assume worked until Scott told me it didn't. I'd buy a burner, carry two phones, and use the burner when I had to say over the phone something I'd rather keep private. Then I realized that he was in fact repeating a warning he'd given to me once before, a year and a half ago, when my hunt for Slobo intensified.

I called Martin next, figuring this was a call that would take no time. I was right. He said he could be over in half an hour, forty-five minutes.

On the same theory, I called Moses before calling Heidi. What an amazing lawyer! He was in a meeting, but if I stayed on the line he would duck out so we could speak.

I'll be very brief, he said. Kerry's Facebook page is no problem. I was her Facebook friend, so I have access. There's absolutely nothing of interest there; I've been through it carefully. You may want to ask Heidi to look carefully too. She might pick up something I wasn't sensitive to. She should also let you log on as her and review it yourself. As for getting Kerry's password from Facebook, so one could log on as Kerry, forget it. At present, the best we could do is to get Facebook to close her account once I'm appointed executor. Email accounts are different. There's a bill languishing in Albany that, if and when it's passed, will give the executor access to them. As for applying to Google itself—the only email accounts I've known Kerry to have in, I'd say, the last ten years have been Google accounts—the situation isn't desperate long term, because Google will give access to the personal representative, which is me once I'm appointed, but it's a drawn-out process. It can take months. Months you have to add to the time it will take me to go through the Surrogate's Court stuff. I'm pretty sure you can get to the email account with a search warrant, but that's a whole other story. The practical result is that you and Heidi might try self-help. Try to think up what passwords Kerry might have used and see if you can get in. But if you bomb out too often, Google will decide that the password has to be reset. It'll send the reset link to some backup account, probably Kerry's now-nonexistent office email, and if that happens, it's like—forget it!

This isn't great news, I said. I'll talk to Heidi, and we'll try to cope. By the way, you were right. She's first-rate.

Isn't she? replied Moses. Too bad she plays on the wrong team.

What sexual team she played on was mattering to me less and less, I realized, so long as she was my teammate in the grim tasks that lay ahead. I said goodbye to Moses and called her.

That was a great dinner, she said. I'm already suffering from chicken sauté withdrawal.

Look, I said, various things have happened, one of them serious, that we should discuss. Face-to-face would be best. I really don't want to impose on you, or take too much of your time, but could we do that over a meal at a restaurant? Probably dinner, so you'll be less rushed. When might you be free?

You're going to think I sit by the phone waiting for you to call. How about tonight?

Perfect, I said. Would you like to meet at the same place as the last time? Any hour that's good for you.

I'd like that a lot, she answered. Nine o'clock because I have a brief to finish. But I promise to be on time.

One person you could count on not to be late was Martin Sweeney. I went to the bathroom after talking to Heidi and was drying my hands when the doorbell rang. Force of old habit: I expected Jeanette to open it and rushed to the door only at the second impatient ring.

Sorry, Martin, I said, I was at the other end of the apartment. Would you like coffee or tea? I'll have tea, but I can easily make coffee for you.

Tea was all right with him. We drank it in the kitchen. As I was telling Martin about Jeanette and my conversation with Sonny I remembered that I should get in touch with the hospitalist.

Go ahead and call him, Martin said.

Miracle of miracles, Dr. Stein not only answered but actually knew Jeanette's name and was aware of her condition. He couldn't exclude the possibility of permanent neurological impairment, time would tell, but he echoed Sonny's opinion that I should be able to see some improvement the next morning.

All things weighed, that was less upbeat than Sonny's assessment. I pushed aside my growing anxiety and faced the question of whether to tell Martin about my run in the park, the telephone call that came at the Ravine as I challenged Jovan's little brother, and in particular—the part of the story I would have liked to hold back—kicking him down the subway stairs. My hesitation, which I hoped to disguise by turning on the electric kettle, waiting for the water to boil, and adding some water to the teapot, didn't last long. If Martin and I were going to continue to work together, this was something he had to know. So would Scott, however much I hated the thought.

Jesus, Martin exclaimed. Holy Jesus! You're out of your mind. Did anybody see you?

I told him that I'd looked behind me and ahead of me, and there was no one. The shops were closed. All except the Starbucks on the southwest corner of Broadway. The guy and I were at the subway station on the northeast corner. There was no way anyone at Starbucks could see into the stairs going down to the platform.

Martin nodded. I'll grant you that, but someone there could see the guy disappearing down those stairs and you following, and a minute or so later see you reappear and hail a cab on Broadway. Right?

I guess so.

And then, assuming whoever that someone was, if he or she happened to be there when the police cruisers and the ambulance got there—I think soon after the uptown local arrived at the station and discharged passengers who found this guy—as I say, if he or she was still there, they might put two and two together and say, Hey there was that man in a sweatsuit or whatever you wear when you run . . .

A spandex running suit, I interrupted mechanically.

Even better, it makes for a better description, a tall strong-looking blond man—you can add whatever you like, depending on the witness's power of observation and memory.

It's all perfectly possible, I said, if whoever it was who saw the scene remained until the police and the ambulance arrived. That would seem very odd, though. At that hour, six-thirty or so, people don't hang out at Starbucks doing their email or surfing the web. They get their coffee and muffin and head for work.

How do you know? The story gets even better if whoever it was whipped out his smartphone and snapped your picture!

All right, Martin, I said, feeling that my face was flushed, what am I to make of all this, and what do you suggest I do about it?

What you should make of it is that potentially you're in deep trouble. We don't know if this guy is alive or how badly injured. If he's alive, he may choose to talk just enough to help identify you. Would he talk? Depends on what he opens himself up to. Let's say he's alive, and you're identified. Anything from various types of assault to attempted homicide. If he's dead . . . or if he dies in the hospital, you fill in the blanks. What should you do? Keep your mouth shut. Don't tell Scott. Don't tell Heidi. You'll put them in a very difficult position. You've told me. OK, I work for you and I'll keep my mouth shut. But, Jack, please don't forget that you're up against experienced and vicious criminals. Don't underestimate them or what they're capable of.

I'd recovered my composure—or so it seemed to me—and said, All that has been duly noted. But we have to move on, and we have several subjects to discuss. First, telephone conversations. I've gotten the impression talking to Scott that he thinks my line may be tapped. By his people? By the Bureau? By Abner? He gave no indication. I assume if the landline is tapped they—whoever they are—will be listening to my cell phone as well.

Martin nodded.

I hope you'll join me for lunch. I'll buy a burner on the way back and use it exclusively for conversations I'd like to keep private. It means I'll have to carry two cell phones, but that's not the end of the world.

Good idea, said Martin. Let's not get ahead of ourselves, but you will want to consider replacing the burner when it's out of minutes instead of buying more time online.

Noted, I answered. Now about Heidi. Look, I've told you she's got this file of documents in her office safe—she says only she can have access to them, and I trust her, she's a very smart lady—that would seem to have enough in them not only to get Abner indicted but probably to send him to the big house. Why hasn't she taken it to Ed Flanagan yet? Quite frankly, I don't know, in the onrush of information she's given me and everything that's been going on I haven't asked her. But I will tonight. It might be that she wants us to find first another file she thinks Kerry squirreled away somewhere. The immediate problem is that, as you have observed, these bastards are very dangerous. First, I'm worried about her safety. Second, I'd like your advice on how she and I should go about meeting. So far, there doesn't seem to be a regular tail on me. But can we be sure? Besides, if there isn't one today, I can grow one tomorrow. In any case, I think it's clear that for the time being she shouldn't come again to this apartment. Do you agree?

That's easy. She shouldn't.

For instance, I continued, I'm having dinner with her tonight. At a restaurant in the neighborhood. Madison and Seventy-Seventh. I can go there in a taxi, which should thwart any tail that you haven't spotted. What other precautions should I take? Should we get her a bodyguard?

These guys are so fucking vicious and devious that at this point it would probably be a good idea. Lee and I have our hands full with you. Should we see if any of the good people we know are available?

Let me speak to her first. But how do you think I should manage our meetings?

What you've planned for this evening is just right, he said. Let's play the rest by ear. You should use the burner when you call her.

All right. That's what we'll do. Shall we go to lunch now?

Yeah, that would be good, but can we first speak for a moment about something different that's on my mind? It'll just take a minute.

Of course, I said.

Jack, my wife and I have talked. Jeanette won't be able to come back to work anytime soon. Even if she recovers sufficiently, she may be too scared to come back ever if you tell her what really happened. The wife and I don't see how you can live in this huge place by yourself without any help, and I'd be worried about your hiring someone new from an agency or however you'd normally go about it. You can check references all you want, but with these pricks—excuse my language—you can't be careful enough. So we're worried about you. Even Nora, that's my daughter, is worried.

My good friend Martin, I said, let's go and eat. We'll walk and talk. The restaurant is practically around the corner, on Third, between Seventy-Ninth and Eightieth. The food's OK, it's quiet enough there to hear yourself talk, and the tables aren't crowded together. Not a place for eavesdropping. Now about Jeanette and the apartment. I agree that there's no telling when or whether she'll come back to work. We first have to see about her convalescence. I'll certainly offer her a nice pension, and, if it can be done without hurting her feelings, I'll encourage her to retire. We'll see. But you and your family shouldn't think I'm someone who can't cope or isn't willing to cope without a full-time live-in housekeeper. I kept Jeanette after Harry died because she's been at the apartment ever since I used to visit my uncle as a boy. He was really attached to her, and I'm not ashamed to say that I kind of love her. She's the one remaining link to my past. And about that huge apartment. I don't need an apartment like that and I know it. But it was my uncle's apartment, it's his furniture, some of it actually family stuff, and the paintings and objects he collected. I've hardly changed anything. He was like a father to me, perhaps more of a father than the real one. That's why I feel at home in the apartment, just as perhaps I will someday again feel good about the house in Sag Harbor. As you pointed out to that creep Walker, I can afford it. Very easily. So relax! I'm not some sort of hopeless case even if I don't really like the idea of doing my laundry or carrying it to the laundromat and picking it up. Someday I'll replace Jeanette, but there's no hurry. By the way, I've told you all this so you'd understand me better. That's all. I'm very grateful to you and your wife for your concern. And, of course, to Nora!

Thank you! For your information, poking around I learned that there is an expensive and probably OK laundry that picks up at your building and delivers. So that's not a problem. But I still think you need someone in that apartment, and I have someone exactly right for you that you can trust. A Hong Kong Chinese. He's legal, he can clean, do laundry like nothing you've ever seen, and he's a great cook if you like Chinese. He can also take very good care of himself. No one's going to beat him up. You might even find you're glad he has your back. I don't mind telling you on the QT that he has on occasion worked for us. That's how I know he can really be trusted. His name is Feng.

Martin, if you vouch for this guy I'll be glad to try him out. I'm curious though: why is this paragon available?

It's a sad story, he answered. The old gentleman he worked for finally died of cancer. He was someone we knew very well, and we wanted to be sure he was in good hands.

Then please ask Feng to come to see me. Preferably at a time when you can be there as well.

The restaurant was two-thirds empty. We took a table in the corner and, after we'd ordered our pasta, I decided to get back to business.

One of the reasons I don't mind not giving Kerry's file to the U.S. attorney just yet, I said, is that it may be easier to find the guy who murdered Kerry before Abner is indicted and goes on the defense.

You're going to try to get Abner to sic the guy on you, the

way you did with Slobo? Martin asked. The same trick may not work twice.

I nodded and said, That's right. It might not. Though I don't detect much originality in Abner's method of operations. How are we going to do it otherwise?

Police work, police work, and more police work, Martin replied. Lee's going to hit Le Raton. That's the name of the club where Kerry was that Friday night when she died. He's figuring out how to get in. It seems that for men it's strictly by invitation. Like a private party.

I'd like to get down there soon myself, I said. Scott will be here on Friday, and I'm going to have dinner with him. Perhaps if I don't go to Sag Harbor on Saturday morning—I somehow doubt I will unless Jeanette is kept in the hospital over the weekend or is well enough for us to make some other arrangement—I could get down there Saturday night. Whatever you and Lee think is best.

Good deal, he replied. I'll alert Lee. That club, by the way, isn't open every night. Friday and Saturday nights for sure. Other nights are announced to clients. Speaking of Lee, if you don't mind I'll ask Lee to keep an eye on your building and on the restaurant this evening. Let's see if these guys have figured out where you're likely to go to dinner.

We finished lunch and went down the block to an AT&T store. As I was paying for the burner, my iPhone rang. It was Detective Walker.

Mr. Dana, he said, I've got the statement typed up and I'd like to stop by your apartment and have you sign it. I also have some questions I'd like you to answer. Will you be at your apartment anytime soon?

In twenty minutes, I said.

Good. I'll be over in half an hour.

I glanced at Martin. He had the facial expression of someone using his tongue to detach from a molar a piece of caramel candy he's decided he doesn't like. Do you mind, he asked, if I sit in on your visit with Rod Walker?

On the contrary, I told him, I'd like that.

At a quarter of three sharp, the doorman telephoned to say there was a detective downstairs asking to see me. Please send him up, I said, and opened the front door.

The statement Walker had typed up was an almost verbatim transcription of the interview at the hospital. I showed it to Martin. He read it over and nodded.

All right, Detective, I said, I'll be happy to sign.

The response from Walker wasn't immediate. He had gone, without my invitation or leave, through the open double doors from the library to the living room and could be seen examining the art on the walls and Harry's collection of Viennese bronzes on the sideboard that came from my paternal grandparents' house on Pinckney Street in Boston.

Quite a place you've got here, he told me when, some minutes later, he returned to the library. I see Mr. Sweeney is here. May I ask in what capacity?

I consult for the captain on security issues, Martin answered for me. You got a problem with that? Just in case you're curious, I'm also an attorney, admitted to the bar in this state.

All right, Mr. Dana, is it the case that you live here all by yourself?

Yes.

I suppose with your Marine Corps background you make sure you stay in shape. There is no gym in this building?

I shook my head.

Have you installed gym equipment in the apartment? You know, a stationary bicycle, weights, or a rowing machine?

No, I haven't, I answered. I go to a gym on Third Avenue.

Yes, which gym is that?

I said the name, which he wrote down initially in a cardboard-covered notebook.

Stupid of me, he said, and took out a recording device from an inside coat pocket. Having had me repeat the name of the gym, he played it back. It works, he announced.

I shrugged.

Do you do anything else to keep in shape? For instance, do you run?

So that's where he was going. It was a good thing that Martin had warned me. But how the hell did he get to me so fast?

Yes, I do.

Most mornings?

Yes.

In Central Park.

I nodded.

Including this morning?

Yes.

And did anything unusual happen?

Yes and no. I became aware of another runner who seemed to be following me. When I slowed down, he slowed down; when I ran faster, he did too. I thought at first he'd picked out someone running at a speed he liked and decided he'd let me pace him. Then I realized there was more to it. He'd follow me if I left the road and so forth.

And what happened next?

I decided I'd cut across the North Woods—I don't know whether you're familiar with that part of the park—

I am, Walker interrupted.

And run to the West Side, I continued. This other runner followed.

What did he look like?

Tall. Perhaps not as tall as I. Heavier. Dirty blond. Wearing a gray running suit.

And what happened then?

Martin, at whom I sneaked a glance, was expressionless. Did this mean I was doing well? No way to tell. I'd better keep on trucking.

You mean after he followed me? We got to a spot called the Ravine. There I stopped. He stopped too. Started doing what you might call usual runner stuff—stretches and running in place—but gave no indication of planning to move on.

Can you describe the other runner's face? Walker asked.

I really don't think I can, I replied. Sort of ordinary.

Maybe I can help you. I'm going to show you a photo.

He took out his smartphone and after fiddling with it showed me an image.

Is this the young man?

It's possible. I can't be sure.

Really?

Yes, really.

All right, Walker said, but do you remember what happened after this young man had finished doing his stretches?

I called out to him: Have you got some problem with me? If you do, let's talk about it. The guy answered, No way, no talk. Then he ran off toward the West Side.

Slow down, Mr. Dana. Didn't you pull a knife on him before he ran off?

What an absurd idea! I exclaimed. Of course I never pulled a knife on him.

Not even after the telephone call?

What telephone call?

I was genuinely surprised.

Walker spoke slowly: You heard me, Mr. Dana. I said, Not even after you got the telephone call?

Whoa, hold your horses, Roddy boy! Martin spoke up suddenly. Suppose you answer the captain's question. What telephone call are you talking about? Some telephone call to Captain Dana that you know about that he received there at the Ravine? Do you also know perchance from whom? And what was said?

Walker was visibly flustered. Strike that question, he said, we'll move on. What happened after that young man, as you say, ran off? Did you follow?

Whoa boy! Martin said again. Nobody's striking any questions, and don't bother deleting anything from what you've recorded. I've got it all down right here—he patted his pocket—it will make good listening. Do you want to discuss why it will make such good listening for the Internal Affairs Bureau?

Walker's jaw was set, but I thought he was going to speak. Instead, he shook his head. It occurred to me that he didn't want Martin to record him. If that was the case, he thought better of it.

That will be all for now, Mr. Dana, he said once again very slowly, we will be in touch if we have more questions.

Bullshit, said Martin, rising from his armchair. There won't be any other questions and you won't be in touch. Get the fuck out, Roddy boy, and don't bother the captain again. This is good advice. It can save you a shitload of trouble. Get going! I'll show you to the door.

Holy Moses! What do you make of that, I asked Martin when he returned, and added, Thank you! Thanks a lot! You kept me out of some really hot water.

That's right, he said, I did. Now let me make a call. There's a piece of useful information we might be able to get.

He'd memorized the number he was calling or had it on speed dial. Yeah, it's me, he said. The fellow who fell down the subway stairs at One Hundred Third Street, what's the story on him? Only broken wrists and elbows and a bad concussion? Really bad? I see. At St. Luke's under observation? What's known about him? Couldn't talk because of the concussion but his fingerprints talked for him? No kidding? A Serb called Goran Petrović! Spell the last name—thanks! Wanted by Interpol and the police in Italy, drug dealing and human trafficking? Child sex trafficking too? And that's all! So you think he'll be held on the Interpol warrant without bail until the extradition hearing. Mazel tov! Couldn't happen to a nicer guy.

Martin ended the call and turned to me. You dodged a bullet, Jack. I don't think Walker will be back or that the NYPD is going to spend time looking for the idiot who pushed that prick down the subway stairs. Can you imagine Mr. Petrović filing a complaint? Or giving testimony? The scumbag that just left either didn't know the background or thought he could pull a fast one. Interesting who sent him and filled him in on that phone call. Your pal Jovan? Whoever Jovan works for? Sleeping with the enemy, I'd say, and for once they weren't very smart.

But you're really something, Sweeney, I said. Why do you know so much, and how do you get to make a telephone call like that?

Twenty-five years in the Bureau, Jack! The last ten years in the Balkan organized-crime unit, which is how Scott Prentice and I got to know each other real well, and six years before that in major white-collar crime, concentrating on money laundering. You get to meet a lot of really upstanding people! Lee was with me in organized crime.

And you decided to retire?

You bet. Full pension and freedom to earn money working for rich guys like you. Little Nora isn't so little anymore, and she's a straight A student. I'm looking at paying for college and graduate school.

Let's get this job done. If we do, nothing will give me more pleasure than to contribute to Nora's scholarship fund.

We'll be grateful for that, he replied, the wife, Nora, and I. When are you going to see Mrs. Truman?

Around six, I told him. Her sister, Marjorie, is coming too. Then I'll meet Heidi at nine. And between now and the hospital and the hospital and the restaurant, I'll try to work.

Sounds good. Lee will take over when you go to the hospital, and he'll stay on the job until the young lady is safely home. You've got his cell-phone number? Call him if there's a change in the program.

VIII

I told Martin I'd get some work done before leaving for the hospital, and that had been my firm intention. At that point work should have consisted of going on with my story of Harry's murder. But having written about two-thirds of the book by my reckoning—I was not many pages away from the confrontation that ended with my killing Slobo—I gave in to the urge to share my manuscript with a friendly but supercritical reader and showed it to my editor. She said she loved my draft—and then stabbed me in the back! She sent it for vetting to the in-house legal department! As always, the lawyers "had issues," and my editor and I agreed I had better take care of them before going into the home stretch. This was the time to make such adjustments as might be needed to save the publisher and me from lawsuits and liability, before the text was complete and revised, and I felt ready to ask my agent to submit it officially to the publisher. Whom, if anyone, was I libeling? the lawyers wanted to know. Had I invaded anyone's privacy? So instead of pushing forward I squirmed at my desk composing an epistle to the lawyers, trying to respond to their litany of worries, some of them so stupid I wondered whether those jurists know how to read. Because if they'd read my manuscript, and had understood what they were reading, they would have seen what I'd made clear as a bell on the first pages: the story was true; nothing had been invented; I'd told no lies and pulled no punches; I'd spared no one, least of all myself. Yes, the names of certain persons had been changed, I warned the reader, to protect the innocent. And, although I didn't say so, I invented the name I gave the monster Texas billionaire who'd commissioned Harry's murder. I also invented the names of his lackeys, the lawyers I called in my book Will Hobson and Fred Minot, who sold Harry for thirty pieces of silver. If the shoe fits, let them wear it! If the book is published and they read my pages, they'll know who they are. In the meantime, I chuckle whenever I think how my lovely agent Jane and my editor haven't realized that Abner Brown is also the name of a fictional villain as evil and ruthless as my real-life Texas monster, whose schemes are ignominiously thwarted by a young boy, the brave hero of a children's book that my beautiful mother adored and insisted on reading to me long past the age at which I became able to read it by myself. If they missed the allusion, how many book reviewers and readers would get it? I planned to have fun keeping count.

Getting steamed up about Abner and his crimes was no problem, but composing that dignified and irrefutable reply to each of the lawyers' objections was another matter. My eyes were closing while I typed. The alternative to a nap that I didn't have time to take was to goof off and hope the urge to sleep would pass. The *New York Times* lay conveniently on my worktable. I'd barely glanced at the first page in the morning before leaving for the hospital. Except for a brisk game of online tic-tac-toe, I knew no better way to goof off than to read "All the News That's Fit to Print." Anyway not since I discovered that it was possible to whiz through the daily *NYT* in less than thirty minutes. The Sunday paper takes longer, mainly because I read the marriage announcements in the Styles section, congratulating myself on the men and women I haven't married. The secret of my speed? I skip everything concerning Afghanistan and Iraq—been there, done it—Israel because there's nothing there but bad news and problems without solutions, Africa because it's one more big heartbreak I don't need, and India, Pakistan, and Bangladesh because I've paid my dues reading *A Passage to India*. Thank God the *Times* doesn't jump on stories about Latin America, Australia, or Canada. Those they do run can be disposed of in a flash. That leaves Europe, Russia and China, and our poor benighted country. I read selectively. For instance, the government shutdown, now in its third week. The *Times* prognosticated that it would end tomorrow. Why tomorrow? An article captioned "Boehner's Last Stand" laid it out: the distinguished Speaker of the House had decided to let the government reopen because the president agreed to eliminate health insurance subsidies for members of Congress, some members of the executive, and their staffs. No shit! "It's all about not walking away empty-handed, about Mr. Boehner persuading his Republican members that they forced President Obama to give something up in exchange for not wreaking havoc on the economy," the *Times* explained to dumbfounded yokels like me. I'd chosen the right reading material. Furious and wide awake, I got down to work, corrected the typos and punctuation in the letter I'd written, and, hoping it would stop the lawyers' guns, emailed it to my editor.

On the dot of six, I was at Jeanette's bedside. Her sister, a smaller and thin version of Jeanette in a gray wool coat with a black velvet collar, was already there. Not having met her before, I introduced myself.

The nurse has gone to look for the doctor, she told me. Is she like that all the time, lying there, eyes shut, just breathing?

She began to cry.

That's how it's been so far, I said, but she'll get better. You'll see, that's what the doctor says. Why don't you try to talk to her, Mrs. Bidwell? Maybe caress her. She might respond to your voice better than to anyone else's.

The sister wiped her eyes and nose and spoke, very distinctly, holding Jeanette's hand. The response was like a rumble at the end of which Jeanette's features moved, composing themselves into something that we thought might have been a smile. Or it could have been a grimace of pain.

This is better than anything I've seen until now, I told her.

But it's so bad, Captain Dana, the sister said. Bad. Her face . . .

The hospitalist arrived with the nurse, checked the chart and the vital-signs monitor, did his best to calm the sister, and asked whether she and I had time to discuss Mrs. Truman's case. We both nodded.

All right then, he said, sitting down. Look, this is still early, but here is the picture, roughly speaking, so that you can get prepared for what will need to be done. I stress: this is all preliminary. As you see, her nose is taped. That's because the plastic surgeon has set it. Apart from the cranial bleeding, there are no internal injuries, her heart is good, her blood pressure is about where you would expect, so all that part is positive. We're treating the broken ribs with analgesics. They hurt, but we try to avoid stronger painkillers. The situation is less positive with regard to cranial bleeding. There are lesions. It's likely that they will affect her motion. In all probability not very seriously, not after physical therapy, but the neurologist thinks there will be some effect, whether in terms of strength of limbs or mobility or both. Time will tell. We don't yet know whether there will be any cognitive impairment—you know, speech, memory, reasoning. The neurologist is optimistic, but I stress that this is preliminary. He will be doing rounds tomorrow at eleven if either of you wants to meet him. However, he's asked me to tell you that probably he won't have more definitive advice until next week. Midweek. Any questions so far?

I'll see him here tomorrow, I answered. Mrs. Bidwell, would you like to spend the night at my apartment and join me?

I can't, Captain Dana, I've left my two kitties alone at home with no one to feed them or give the old one her pills. Doctor, will Jeanette be all right?

She will be all right, Mrs. Bidwell, subject to the concerns I've mentioned. Please don't forget that human brains are amazing. They recover in ways that surprise everybody. So please be patient, be hopeful. Can we talk about some practical issues?

I nodded.

We need to keep Mrs. Truman here probably through next week. I understand that she isn't on Medicare or Medicaid and that you, Mr. Dana, have guaranteed the costs. Will this be a problem?

No, it won't. She should stay as long as needed and get all the care she needs. I'll be glad to pay.

The Lord bless you, Captain Dana! the sister broke in, sobbing.

Please, Mrs. Bidwell, I said. Don't worry about it. It's what my uncle Harry would have wanted me to do, and it's what I want to do.

At the same time, I must confess, I wondered what had possessed Harry, why he hadn't made sure she was on Medicare or had some other sort of health insurance. How could such a thing have slipped through the fine mesh of that old fox's mind?

That's very helpful, Dr. Stein continued. You will want to consider also the following issues, which are not immediate. Assuming that Mrs. Truman goes from here to a rehab facility, where should we look for it? In Manhattan? In Westchester, where I understand you live, Mrs. Bidwell? We'll give you a menu of choices. After that, the next issue to face will be getting Mrs. Truman nursing help for some period of time, whether she goes back to live with you, Mr. Dana, or with you, Mrs. Bidwell, or with her daughters.

The girls live in California! the sister cried out. I'll want her with me! That's what she'd want.

That's very understandable. You and Mr. Dana will want to discuss the details. I should warn you that it is unlikely that

Mrs. Truman will be able to resume work—anyway not in the foreseeable future.

Look, Mrs. Bidwell, I said after we'd taken leave of the doctor and the nurse, would you like to come to a diner just a few blocks from here that's quite good? You could have an early supper. I won't join you in that, because I have a dinner date at nine, but I'll have a drink that I badly need. Perhaps you'll have one too! Then I'll get a car service to take you back to White Plains. It will be late by then, and I don't want you wandering around alone in the dark.

Where were my brains, I was asking myself while I waited for her answer, why didn't I send Jeanette out there in a livery car? There was no good answer to that question. All I could do was console myself again with the thought that they would have gotten her soon anyway, at some other place—that's all.

The sister agreed. We walked in silence to the diner on Madison Avenue where I'd had breakfast the day before. She allowed me to order a substantial meal for her but, in the end, refused a drink. Another time she'd accept one, she told me. Not having entire confidence in the Greek waitress's skill with a gin martini, I asked for a double bourbon, took a healthy slug, and began the conversation that couldn't be ducked.

We know so little about each other, I said, so I have to ask you some personal questions. You said you'd like Jeanette to come to be with you after rehab. Do you have an extra bedroom? Will that work out?

Oh yes, Captain Dana, she cried out, there is a nice second bedroom, just as nice as mine. That's where Jeanette always sleeps. It's an apartment we own together. Your uncle, God bless his soul, helped us buy it, and we've always planned that Jeanette would come there to live with me when she retired.

That's great, I said, good for Uncle Harry. Another question: it's possible that at least for some time Jeanette will be using a walker or something like it. Will that be a problem?

No sir, it won't. Your uncle made sure we bought the apartment in a building with handicapped access, including the elevator and bathrooms.

What a huge relief! I said. I look forward to visiting once we've gotten Jeanette there. There is another subject. As the doctor said, Jeanette may not be able to go on working. Anyway, I've thought for some time that it's sort of silly for you to be alone in White Plains and for her to be looking after a bachelor like me who doesn't entertain, is away a good deal, and is nothing but trouble when he's here. I'm sure Jeanette has told you about some of that. There will be no money problem if she retires, which is what I think she should do. I will guarantee a pension for her that should be more than adequate once she's well—I was thinking of simply continuing what I pay her now—and, of course, I'll pay for all the medical and nursing expenses until she gets well. I'll make sure that the pension gets paid no matter what happens to me and gets adjusted if inflation gets out of hand. Last thing, we'll get her on Medicare with all the bells and whistles. I can't imagine how it happened that it wasn't taken care of.

It's her fault, Captain Dana; she didn't want it. She said she never got sick. And that's the honest truth.

Yup, I said, and then you get something like this, that no one could foresee. Does the rest seem all right to you?

It did. She ate her dinner with a beatific look of relief on her face. I called the car service and ordered another bourbon for myself. No, Mrs. Bidwell didn't take coffee. Just like Jeanette. Before we parted, I assured her that as soon as Jeanette's condition was sufficiently improved, I'd make arrangements to bring the girls from California on a visit.

Feng, I said to myself, for better or worse, your hour has come. I'll call Martin and get him to bring you over. I'll be damned if I want to start washing my own underpants. I've got enough other troubles.

I'd gone to the hospital in jeans. By the time Mrs. Bidwell was in the car, I had just enough time to go home and clean up and change. Lee, I noticed, was sitting on a bench on the other side of the avenue. He saw me, and I returned a sign of recognition that I hoped was discreet enough not to be recognized as such by any sentry—if there was one—sent by Abner or, for that matter, my own doorman. The Montenegrin elevator man was on duty, a man with a deep interest in meteorology. I couldn't help wondering as we reviewed the likelihood of rain over the weekend whether he was trying to ascertain my plans. Was there anyone working in the building I was still willing to trust? The Irish guys, on the theory that they were unlikely to go bowling or drinking with Jovan's friends and associates? It was a slur to think so. The building's manager, a solid County Cork man, had a Mexican wife and three small Irish Mexican children. Perhaps the whole crew, Mr. Duffy included, tippled slivovitz in joyous congress with Jovan, dissecting my comings and goings. Mistrust and body armor: the keys to survival in Iraq and Afghanistan. Is that how I was going to live in Abner Land?

Out of habit, I picked up the telephone to check on messages. Sure enough, there was one, recorded at 7:08 p.m., which must be when I left the hospital. Jovan's voice. The fellow who'd told me Jeanette had been attacked. Like what you saw, roadkill? he said this time. We're not finished.

I was at the point of erasing the message and stopped myself. Perhaps the thing to do was to forward it to Scott or a number Scott would give me. I couldn't believe the voice could help identify this prick, but perhaps storing it would be useful if we ever took him alive. That was tomorrow's work, I decided. Right then, I couldn't bear the thought of calling Scott and telling him about Jeanette and this call. Two more days and I would see him in New York. I got dressed and slipped the Colt in the waistband of my trousers. The party had gotten too rough to rely on my switchblade alone. Feeling stupid—but this was what Martin and I had agreed on—I buzzed for the doorman to hail a taxi and had myself driven six city blocks to the restaurant. I've a sprained ankle, I told the driver. Not allowed to walk more than a few steps. The five-dollar tip may have lifted his mood, but gratification did not express itself through speech. Where had the Jewish and Italian taxi drivers gone, those guys who actually talked to you? The table I'd reserved was ready. I positioned myself once again where I would see Heidi as soon as she walked in, and ordered a martini. It doesn't take much to jog a bartender's memory. Gordon's gin and a twist of lemon peel, he crowed. The question now was how late Heidi would be.

She surprised me, arriving before the waitress brought the drink. I pushed the martini in front of her and ordered another one just like it for myself.

You're a miracle of good manners, Captain, she said, but your memory is shoddy. I take them with an olive!

Ouch, I said, intercepted the waitress, and specified the olive. Actually, it's your fault, I told Heidi. You rattled me by not being late.

That's just one of the many tricks I use to keep you off-balance, she replied. Stay alert! I'm starved. Let's order dinner and talk.

There seemed to be no reason to choose other dishes or another wine. We stuck to the now-established menu but asked the waitress to give us time to finish the drinks we already had and another round to come before bringing the food.

I've got a lot to tell you, I said, not much of it being good.

She nodded, and I went on to relate in sufficient detail for the import to sink in the events that had transpired since she left my apartment after the previous evening's dinner. The telephone call from Jovan or one of his colleagues boasting about the attack on Jeanette, her injuries, the visit to the hospital I'd just made, the same voice calling the moment I'd left Jeanette's bedside, the tentative decision—for such I realized it had to be—that Jeanette would retire and would be living with her sister.

That sweet, gentle lady! Heidi exclaimed. Whoever decided to do this is really sick.

Yes, I answered, it's unforgivable, and I'm convinced that the psychopath behind it also orchestrated Kerry's overdose.

Could I have my second martini now? On an accelerated schedule?

Heidi remained silent until the waitress brought it, and for a moment I wondered whether she was going to down it in one swallow and ask for a refill. Apparently, she thought better of it. I think you're right, she said finally. So that's the end of Jeanette's culinary reign. Let's face it, I'm glad I got to eat at least one meal she cooked.

Don't despair on account of the cuisine, I told her. Provided you like Chinese food, there is a possible successor waiting in the wings.

Then I decided that I would disregard Martin's advice and told her about kicking my running mate down the flight of subway stairs and about the bizarre interview with Detective Walker.

This isn't good, she said. Walker belongs to the Tannenbaums! They're bad news. I'm aware of them from my days as an assistant U.S. attorney. You're lucky this Goran is bad news too—otherwise, Captain, I fear they'd think with some justification they had you by the balls. Guess what, I wouldn't be totally surprised if there were some sort of Abner Brown connection here. Strictly political connection. Much as I hate fascist cops, I don't think they work hand in hand with the bosses of the likes of Jovan or Goran, although like all other cops they may use hit men like that as informers. Doing favors for like-minded troglodytes is another matter. By the way, your former special agent Martin Sweeney seems to be first-rate.

He is, I replied. That brings me to a related subject. I've got him working for me to make sure I don't have a tail who might lead them to you. On some other matters too. So far neither he nor his partner has seen anybody tailing me, but I'm shaken by Jovan's most recent call. He is too well informed. The related subject is whether I shouldn't engage

Martin or one of his colleagues to look after you. I may be radioactive. I don't want you to be hurt.

For the third time since I met her she put her hand over mine, and said, Thank you! That's what you did for Kerry. She could have used protection even after she broke with you and you left the country. Of course, she wouldn't have accepted it. It would have been a waste of time to propose it. I'm a not-so-nice Jewish girl, so I might accept if I didn't have another solution. But I do. The Krohn businesses have a security organization. You know, we have problems going from espionage—competitors trying to steal our designs— all the way to pretty crude attempted burglaries when our goods are in the warehouse or the showroom or are being transported. I think I'll explain the situation to Father without giving details, maybe I'll lead him to think it's something to do with my past activities as a prosecutor, and ask him to assign however many guys it takes to look after me. There's an advantage: it won't cost you! If for any reason Father can't or won't do it, we'll talk. All right?

She'd withdrawn her hand. I risked taking it back and giving it a brief squeeze. I like doing business with you, I said.

That's just as well, because we'll be in business together— partners. OK? Until this gets done, she said, giving my hand a slightly longer squeeze and promptly taking her hand away, so let's talk about other partnership matters. Might as well make this meal fully tax deductible. Can Moses get at Kerry's email?

I told her what I'd learned.

That's too bad. I'll think of passwords and you try to think too. We should coordinate so that we don't get her account—I think she only had one—shut down by both of us typing in the wrong password. What about looking for the guy who killed Kerry?

That's sort of in the works.

I explained what Martin's partner had begun to do and said I hoped to get down to that club very soon. Perhaps next week.

I may want to go with you, she mused. Let's think about that. Depends on how you decide to play it. There is something I can throw into the mix. I know the name of Kerry's pusher. A guy who testified at trial when she was prosecuting the kingpin who was perhaps the biggest heroin dealer in the New York area. She'd flipped him to Team America, and after he finished cooperating helped him get off with a very light sentence and no probation. Then she became a client. For cocaine, which is not what he's really into. Your Martin or his partner might be able to find him. They might even know him. Pierrot the Cat is his street name. The real name—I was able to find it—is Pierre-Jean Lecat. I don't have his cell number. Anyway those guys change them all the time.

We'll get them started, I said. By the way, I've a question for you that Martin raised. Why didn't you go to the U.S. attorney with Kerry's file instead of waiting for me to return?

Good question, she said. Here is the not-so-good answer. I'll probably go down in Martin's estimation, perhaps yours as well. I had no doubt you'd be coming back and that you and I could work together. I wanted to wait for that. I didn't want to throw down my gauntlet to Abner Brown while I was all alone. Witness protection and suchlike are no substitute for having a partner.

You've got one now, I said. My friend Scott Prentice is

coming here on Friday. I'm having dinner with him. I'd like to ask you to join us, but he has a very personal reason to celebrate, and I think I'd better see him alone. Did you notice, by the way, that I assumed you'd be free? What cheek!

Tsk, tsk, she answered, you get to go back to zero. I'm going to the opera with Mother and Father. An unfortunate Friday habit, because that's their subscription night. But with prior notice I can sometimes arrange to be free. They invite someone else or give my ticket back to the Met as a contribution.

Duly noted, I said. And then, unless Jeanette's situation takes a worrisome turn for the worse, I'd like to go to Sag Harbor on Saturday morning. I could, of course, go down to that club—Le Raton, the Cat, what a world!—on Saturday, but frankly I think I need a couple of days off. There's another reason. Abner last tried to get me killed in Sag Harbor. I don't necessarily think he's bound to pull the same stunt this time, but there is something obsessive about him, so perhaps he would. I'd like to give him a chance and give myself a chance to nail whomever he sends to do it.

And you'd like to invite me to come with you as your bodyguard? she asked, grinning.

The thought hadn't occurred to me, and I didn't jump in with an answer.

In case you do, and you promise to remember that for the time being I'm the not-so-nice Jewish girl who doesn't like sleeping with men, I'll accept. You see, Jack, we're in this together.

Let's have a grappa, I said. Departure on Saturday from your house at ten-thirty?

Senz'altro! You've got a deal.

I'll walk home, she said, after all you came in a taxi so it's not as though you would have been followed.

That's right. But please be very cautious and let Martin's partner Lee, who is waiting outside, shadow you.

That was all right with her. We hugged on the sidewalk, and she headed uptown at a pace that might have been set by a marine drill sergeant. Having seen us embrace, Lee understood she was the lady he should follow and fell in a short distance behind her. I went back into the restaurant, ordered another grappa at the bar, found I didn't want to finish it, and went home. There was again a message waiting, left less than a half hour earlier, this time from Martin instead of Jovan.

Do you mind if I come up? he asked when I called back.

For Pete's sake, Martin, don't you ever rest? That's what you were supposed to do.

I will when this is over. Jack, may I come up?

Sure, I said, I'll break out the Jameson.

He appeared so quickly one might have thought he'd been standing all the while behind the door.

I poured him a whiskey, and in his excitement he blurted out what he had to say before touching the drink.

Listen to this, Jack, it's good news or bad news, depending on how you read it. This guy Goran is dead. Cardiac arrest. A few hours ago—get this—just before he was supposed to be moved from intensive care to a regular ward. The doctors thought he was out of the woods. What do you think of that? It's not in the news yet, not even online; I got it from the guy I called about Walker.

Unbelievable.

You're right. I'll bet whatever you like, I'll give you odds, these bastards killed him. They thought he might start singing while he was held pending an extradition hearing. Who knows what sorts of songs he had and how much he could have bargained for.

Any reason other than your Sherlock Holmes instinct to think so?

Yeah, the convenient timing of this cardiac arrest. Mind you, this was professionally done. No obvious traces were left. If I were to bet, potassium chloride injected into the intravenous feed.

So why is this good news or bad news? Sounds to me like very nice good news. One more bad guy gone. No chance of his identifying me, though I must say I don't see what harm that would have done. I readily admitted we had an unfriendly meeting at the Ravine. He certainly couldn't have identified me as the man who kicked him down the stairs. He didn't see me. Couldn't have seen me!

Very true, very true. The bad news comes if they have some other way of tying you to that One Hundred Third Street caper. Some witness we don't know about. If there is such a witness, and if no one figures out that our boy Goran was killed at the hospital and didn't die of injuries, you'll be looking at a much bigger potential criminal liability. Two big ifs. I don't deny that.

Is there anything we can do about it?

Only one thing I can think of. I'll whisper into my NYPD friend's ear that they should have a thorough autopsy and really study the cause of this guy's death. Could he have been injected with this or that? I'll mention potassium chloride.

These sons of bitches had to know what they were doing. You inject a guy with the wrong thing, or instill the wrong stuff into the intravenous feed, and *boing*, all the monitors go ape. They had to know what would work and wouldn't set off alarms.

Have another drink, old pal. We'll stand down tomorrow. Let me tell you my story.

First I related Heidi's explanation for not having gone to the U.S. attorney.

Some lady, he exclaimed. They don't make them better.

You're right, I said, and told him about Jeanette.

He proposed to bring Feng over the next day, to which I agreed. Then I played Jovan's most recent message and explained its astonishing timing. The son of a bitch knew I'd gone to the hospital and knew when I left, I concluded.

I don't like this, said Martin. I don't like this at all.

IX

For a change I ran south the next morning, thinking that if I had company I would lead whoever it turned out to be into the Ramble, no worse a place to settle private accounts than the Ravine. The .45 remained in my right-hand desk drawer. My sense of the ridiculous, joined with the conviction that only Secret Service men run with their artillery holstered somewhere out of sight, had won out over caution, but the switchblade was in its place, in the pocket of my windbreaker. Lee wasn't on his accustomed bench across the avenue. I couldn't remember what arrangement Martin and I had made, whether he'd said Lee would be on duty at that hour, but I was glad not to see him there. Granted I was paying both of them handsomely for their services, the notion that one or the other of these fine family men—I'd learned that Lee and his wife had three children of preschool age—should be out in the street at five-thirty in the morning just so that Captain Jack Dana could get his exercise at an hour that happened to suit him was the sort of thing that had gotten the French Revolution going. I hit the park's East Drive, looked around, and, seeing nothing suspicious, picked up speed. None of the few runners going in my direction broke their pace or changed their behavior when, still on the southbound leg of my run, I'd stop and turn to check who was behind me. A banal itinerary suited me fine. I took the Sixty-Fifth Street Transverse going west and zoomed up the park's West Drive. As I was nearing Eighty-Sixth Street a question occurred to me: was it possible that I did have a tail after all, a runner who hung back far enough not to be fooled by my stop-and-go antics? I came to a halt and waited by the side of a drive, letting runners pass. And there he was, another one of those beefy very fast men who closed in on me and likewise came to a halt, perhaps thirty feet away. Was his face scarred like Slobo's and impossible to forget once you had seen it, or was he merely cautious? Whatever the reason, he wore a red ski mask matching his fancy Lycra suit and red running shoes. What was I to do? I took a leaf from Slobo's book and gave him the finger. He reciprocated by spitting a huge glob of phlegm, the kind of skill I admired among my tobacco-chewing marines. What were we going to do next? Some sort of replay of the confrontation with Goran in the Ravine? Nothing, it occurred to me suddenly, was to be gained by it. I'd simply continue my run, letting him follow as long and as far as he liked, and respond to whatever action he took. That left up for decision the balance of my route. Would I turn east at Ninety-Sixth Street and head home once I'd reached the East Drive or take my new friend to the North Woods and pick up the East Drive above the Ravine? The more extensive itinerary appealed to me, if only because I was feeling pretty good, my pelvis pretending it had never been to Walter Reed. I waved to my running partner and got going. Who am I to plumb the cesspool of criminal minds? Perhaps having this fellow accompany me had a purpose. Such as what? Making sure I knew they were on my case? I'd have had to be pretty dumb to doubt it. Whatever! We ran very fast down the East Drive until we reached Ninety-Sixth Street, where I decided it was time to cool down. We left the park companionably at Seventy-Ninth Street and jogged up Fifth Avenue to my building, my pal a little more than half a block behind me. Should I invite him to come up—out of the question, we hadn't been introduced—but he rated another friendly wave of my hand. To my chagrin, he left it unacknowledged. In the meantime, the day doorman had come on duty. I greeted him cheerfully, wondering whether he'd be getting on his cell phone to notify his Serbian colleagues of my return. There was no way to know. But if I was still alive at Christmas, I'd think long and hard before distributing tips. Sure enough, there was a message on my telephone, and it wasn't Heidi or Martin or Scott. You guessed it: the voice I heard was Jovan's. Fuckhead, he said, now we play. Kill later.

Bad manners! He didn't leave a callback number.

Show yourself and I'll have your ass in a casket, I replied, addressing my empty kitchen. And just in case you're curious, right now I'm going out to breakfast.

I didn't bother to add that I was going to shower first.

I don't get it, Martin said later that morning, after I'd described to him the morning's run. Lee was there, in his car, parked on the other side of the avenue. You didn't see him, but he saw you. He certainly didn't spot any sort of tail. A guy in a red Lycra suit and red running shoes would have been hard to miss. What's going on?

I'm pretty sure I understand, I told him. These guys know I enter the park at Seventy-Ninth Street. The tail—the late Goran and now this guy—doesn't wait near the building. He's at the entrance to the park. If I show up, he follows. If I don't, he calls his handler and does whatever it is they do in their spare time. Anyway, if your suspicion about leaks from the building is right, the tail may get a heads-up on his cell phone as soon as I leave.

Possible, very possible, Martin muttered.

You want to hear Jovan's voice again? I saved the message. Same voice as yesterday evening. The message was waiting when I came back from the run.

So what's the plan, Captain Jack? I'm stumped.

We move ahead, one step at a time. Why don't you ask Feng to bring the coffee here. I'll tell him he's hired, and he can move in today or tomorrow—whatever suits him best. He'll have to take Jeanette's belongings out of his room and put them in the guest room, which is anyway where she'll be if it turns out that for some reason she comes here from rehab instead of going to her sister's. While you're doing that, I'll forward Jovan's messages to Scott.

I had taken an immediate liking to Feng. He was big and looked tough enough to be in a kung-fu movie, was dressed in a black Mao suit, spoke intelligibly, could write down messages, and was polite but not to excess. Martin was right. I wouldn't have to worry about Jovan & Co. messing with him.

Martin, I said after Feng and I had shaken hands on the deal and agreed that he should bring his stuff over right away,

I've got to go to the hospital to see the neurologist on his rounds. If you're free, let's have a quick lunch together. I should be back in a little over an hour.

I am free and I'd like to, he told me.

Good! Heidi wants to ask her father to get his company's security people to provide protection for her. If they're good enough, that's clearly a fine idea. Can you check into it? His name is something or other Krohn. I think you'll find him on the web. You're welcome to wait for me here. Use my laptop, do your telephoning, work on my book, whatever strikes your fancy!

It's not good for Jeanette, I told Martin when we settled down in the restaurant. The neurologist thinks there is a significant possibility of cognitive impairment—he doesn't know yet what kind or the extent—in addition to problems she may have with locomotion. She should stay at the hospital at least until the end of next week. As for rehab, he mentioned Burke. That's where my friend Simon Lathrop went after his hip replacement. A great big plus is that the inpatient facility is in White Plains. It will be easy for the sister to visit. Do you suppose it was the telephone caller—Jovan?— who did it, or this guy Goran? If it's Goran, I'm gladder than ever I kicked him down those stairs. If it's Jovan or another one of those guys, this case won't be closed until he's dead.

Prison should be enough, said Martin.

I'm not sure that's how my mind works. How about an answer to my question?

I don't know. We might never know. Most likely won't know until we've caught Jovan.

What about security for Heidi?

Krohn and Son Enterprises. It's quite an operation. Real estate as well as textile manufacturing and fashion. Miss Heidi is a very rich girl—or anyway someday will be. I ran a check on their security department. It's first class. Former policemen, special agents, and Shin Bet operatives. It's run by a retired Mossad officer. They'll take good care of her.

Good. Next point. I've got a name for you, Pierrot the Cat or Pierre Lecat. According to Heidi, he's a pusher Kerry flipped while she was prosecuting a major dealer. One way or another, he later became her supplier. Heidi doesn't know how he can be reached, but she thinks you'll be able to find him.

Very likely.

Would you try to? Let's see whether there is anything useful he could tell us. I sort of doubt it, because I think there is no logical connection between who Kerry bought drugs from and whoever it was that administered the overdose, but who knows? Perhaps he does know something.

Lee and I will get on it. We'll have something for you tomorrow at the latest.

Good. I think I told you Scott will be here tomorrow. We're having dinner. Then on Saturday morning, inshallah, I'm going to Sag Harbor. Back on Sunday. By the way, Heidi's coming with me. It still seems like a good idea not to have her show her face around here, so I'll pick her up at her place. I'll make it easy for Jovan so he won't have to tail me. I'll tell the elevator man and the doorman I'm picking up my car at the garage and heading for Sag Harbor.

Congratulations! If you don't mind my saying so, that's fast work.

Now, now, Martin! It's not like that. Business oriented and strictly platonic.

That's too bad, if I may say so. If I may be serious, though, and try to do my job, please listen. Do you think going to Sag Harbor is a good idea? These guys are really out to get you. You're more exposed there than in the city. *Entre nous,* I like having Feng in your apartment. Less chance of monkey business in a place where you'd least expect it.

I do think it's a good idea. I have to take a look at the house. Getting reports from Mary Murphy—she's my combination housekeeper and house watcher—isn't the same thing, and *entre nous,* as you put it, I want to give Jovan, assuming it's him, a chance to get close to me. Again *entre nous,* I'll cut his heart out.

Unless he shoots you first. Firearms have been invented, remember? It will be easier to get a clear shot at you out there. Or blow you up with a hand grenade. Would you at least take Feng with you? That way you'd have the house covered.

Is this guy in your profession, by any chance?

Was. Hong Kong Police Force Special Duty Unit—the nickname's Flying Tigers—and later very successful private detective. Saving your reverence, I don't know that Marine Corps infantry has much to teach those guys. Had to leave the territory in a hurry after he came upon a situation the mainland people wanted kept under a cover and did his job all the same. That's the kind of guy he is. No way he can go back, not anytime soon. On account of various things we've done together, the Bureau helped get him an immigrant visa so he can stay here and work, but being hired by the Bureau or one of the police departments would be harder than hard.

Probably impossible, especially at his age. Even once he's got his citizenship.

Let me think about taking him to Sag. Probably not this time. I want to give these guys the chance they're looking for.

And expose Heidi to danger? Just think what they could do to her if they kill you or put you out of action and she's there.

I am thinking about it. The answer is that she wants to do it and I'll take care of her, but I really will think some more about taking her and about taking Feng. Let's you and I talk tomorrow morning, after my run, unless one of us has something special to report.

All right.

By the way, I don't think there is any need to continue watching my building. We know that one way or another they're keeping tabs on where I go. So good luck with the Rat and the Cat!

We'll be on the case, but Lee won't hit the Rat tonight. He plans on spending time down there tomorrow.

I needed to be alone, away from my nannies, once and all, and especially Nanny Sweeney. True, starting in the afternoon, I'd have live-in Nanny Feng to contend with at home, but that was all right. He'd keep his distance—at least for a while. All that the nannies understand is caution, while the simple truth is that the Corps didn't train me to dig in and sit in a foxhole watching shit land all around. Shit! I was once the leader of a U.S. Marine Force Recon platoon, the guys who go where no one else wants to go, track down the enemy, and do whatever it takes to kill. In my heart, that's where I'd remained. I wasn't going to hunker down and wait—wait for what?—not while Kerry's killer and the thug who crippled Jeanette were on the loose, scratching their balls when they weren't looking to murder me. The time had come to move out. For instance, Abner and I—we needed a heart-to-heart talk, and it might as well be right now, while my adrenaline was way up. Le Raton would come next. Let Lee prepare his report and deliver it when he was good and ready, but I might have news for him. I wasn't going to wait; I was going to check it out myself. There was also my book, a living, breathing presence in my office, impatient and waiting for me to write. The way I felt, I could do it all.

One-thirty. Twelve-thirty in Houston. There was no reason that Abner would have changed his private telephone number. Did I give a fuck whether he or anybody else recorded our chat? I didn't. I called him on my landline phone. The saccharine southern good-girl voice I knew came on, and, when I said, This is Jack Dana calling Mr. Brown, cooed sweetly, And this is his assistant Eileen, how nice to hear from you, Captain Dana, after all this time, hold please while I check whether Abner is available.

He was!

Why aren't you dead, asshole? he said pleasantly. What's on your fucking mind?

Ask the goon you sent to kill me on Torcello why I'm not dead, the idiot with a bow and arrow. He'll tell you! Oh no, excuse me, he'll never talk or bother anyone again. And you want to know what's on my mind? Then listen up! I'm tired of you, Abner. Of you, your hit man who killed Kerry Black, your thug who crippled my housekeeper, and the rest of your murderous clowns. I want you and your goons dead.

You're tired of me? So what's that to me, asshole? I've been tired of you ever since you barged in on me in Houston last year. How do I make you go away and stay away?

It's simple: give me the goons who killed Kerry and beat my housekeeper.

You a stand-up comic or something?

Sure! Just keep laughing. How about it? Will you give me those goons? Because I swear that you won't have a quiet moment until I've killed them or they've killed me. And if you don't send them soon, like in the next few days, I've got some tricks up my sleeve I know you won't like. Think it over!

You're a real asshole, came back the reply. I don't know what goons you're talking about. Even if I did, and even if I could give them to you, why would I? What's in it for me? You think I give a fuck about your bullshit threats? Wise up! Your pansy uncle threatened me, and look what happened to him. The fucking queer had brains but no luck. Ditto the Jewish slut: brains but no luck. You've got no brains and no luck, asshole, and you've taken more of my time than you deserve.

Click.

That was that. A bracing exchange. I'd miss that guy once I'd killed him or put him in supermax. I was right to resist the temptation to mention Kerry's file. He knew what I meant by tricks he wouldn't like. We didn't need to get into a what-happens-if-I-give-you-these-guys conversation. There was no point. He'd want me to say that if he gave me the goons I'd make him a present of Kerry's file, and that wasn't going to happen.

Another telephone call and once more I was in luck. My trainer, Wolf, at the Third Avenue gym came to the phone right after that nice chat with Abner. Hey, great to have you back! We made a date for a big session of Krav Maga starting at six. I thought I'd better fine-tune my skills.

Feng had moved into the apartment and was busy waxing the furniture in the library. What would Captain Dana like for dinner?

Since I'd already given him a credit card to shop for food and whatever else was needed for the house, might as well put it to use and try him out. Here is the deal, I said: Captain Dana would like dinner at nine. Chicken with red peppers, a green salad, Macoun apples, and Stilton. And a red 2009 Côtes du Rhône to be found in the wine closet. And espresso—if you've figured out how to use the machine.

I know the machine, sir. Very nice choice of menu, if I may say so.

That was good to hear. Since he'd put me in a good mood, I decided I owed him an explanation. Dinner had to be later than my usual eight-thirty in order to flow into a late appointment I had made downtown.

The workouts at the gym in Dorsoduro had been worth the fortune they'd cost in euros. Wolf told me that, far from losing ground, I'd made progress. From now on we'd concentrate on speed. I also made progress that afternoon on my book. Not only had I written the one thousand three hundred words or so I tried to put down each day I worked— yup, here's the loophole, I can't honestly say I work every day—but I did revisions. No wonder that at nine, having showered and put on newly washed blue jeans and a Thomas Pink shirt, I felt entitled to a martini. Feng offered to make it as dry as I wished. In the spirit of adventure I accepted. The drink was beyond reproach, as was the meal. I found myself wishing Heidi were there. Not yet ten. Using my burner, I called her office number. She too answered at once, chipper and seemingly delighted to talk. If the equipment they had to carry could be made lighter and still retain its quality, these young women lawyers would make first-rate Marine Corps Infantry officer material. They had the right stuff. I would write to the commandant and tell him so.

Don't you ever stop working, Superwoman? I asked.

Only to have dinner with you.

Too bad. I've just had my dinner, courtesy of Feng, the pearl of Hong Kong. Also martinis. Wished more than once you were there.

You should have whistled. I'd have run over.

Look, on a serious note. I've had a telephone chat with my best friend in Texas. It might get very hot in the kitchen cooking the Tex-Mex stuff he and I like. I hate to say it, but I know it would be a mistake for you to come out with me on Saturday. Let's have dinner on Sunday night instead, in the city. OK?

No, it's not OK, partner. I'm coming. If you don't call before ten Saturday morning to say you're picking me up, I'll drive out in my own car. You'll get a chance to make up for your bad manners, though, by taking me to a late lunch at the American Hotel.

Click.

Some girl! I wished that taking her along to Le Raton were not so obviously a rotten idea. I was going down there to look and listen, and not to banter with this incorrigible lesbian flirt. What should I wear to a shithole like that? A leather jacket? I didn't own one. I settled on a double-breasted navy-blue blazer I'd acquired during my scholarship year at Balliol. By now it was bit tight around the shoulders, but otherwise a fine example of shabby chic. I stuck a red silk square in the breast pocket. Perhaps with this touch I could pass for a clueless Brit who thinks his blond looks and posh accent will get him past any door.

Jesus Holy God! Captain Dana, sir! What are you doing here, sir?

Even if I hadn't known the street number of the Rat Hole, as I had mentally renamed Le Raton, I'd have deduced that I'd come to the right place as soon as I saw the queue of superannuated and mostly tanked-up Wall Street and similar types that had formed at the glistening red door of an otherwise unmarked establishment. It was guarded by a bouncer big and solid enough to impose order without raising his voice. It seemed wise to observe the proceedings for a moment before addressing him. But my reserve turned out to be superfluous.

The bouncer advanced in my direction, crying out again, Captain Dana, sir! Don't you remember me? Corporal Eric King, sir, Weapons Platoon, Charlie Company, sir! One of your own men!

It was my turn to swear.

Holy shit, Eric, I exclaimed, you saved my fucking life! You nailed the guy who shot me. Last time I saw you the docs had me strapped to the stretcher and you were waiting on the chopper. You held my hand!

That I did. You were bleeding so fast we thought we'd lost you.

Well, thanks to you, I got patched up almost as good as

new. But not good enough to return to active duty. What about you, Eric?

I got out a year after you were hit. Figured my luck was running out. Also my career in the Corps. You'll remember that little detail. For now, welcome to the Rat, sir! Would you like to go in?

Yes, eventually, but right now I'd really like to catch up with you. This is so unexpected! What time do you go off duty?

Late, sir, not until the last customer leaves. But we can talk in a back room. I'll get one of the guys to cover.

He spoke into a walkie-talkie. The red door opened, and another giant appeared, this one black.

Sir, this is Sam, said Eric. Sam, this is Captain Dana, the meanest platoon commander a marine ever had. Sam's an infantryman, sir. Three deployments to Iraq. Hold the fort, Sam, while the captain and I have a drink in the back.

I shook Sam's hand and followed Eric into a large space lit by overhead strobes and filled by a crowd consisting mostly of men, drinks in hand, groping a much smaller number of young or youngish women in various stages of undress or wearing dresses or caftans that permitted easy access for exploring hands. A few couples made up of a man and a woman or two women were writhing on a small circular floor.

This way, sir!

The back room was furnished with a sofa, opposite which hung a huge mirror, and two chairs. After I'd sat down on one of the chairs, Eric asked what I'd like to drink. Bourbon on the rocks, I told him. He excused himself; a moment later he returned with a bottle of Wild Turkey, a small bucket of ice cubes, and two glasses, and poured our drinks.

Cheers! We clinked, and he sat down on the sofa facing me.

This is really so unexpected, I repeated. I thought your hometown was in North Carolina, somewhere near the Appalachian Trail. And yet, here you are!

Damn right, sir, Linville Falls, sir. In the Blue Ridge Mountains. That's where I learned to track and to shoot.

You sure learned well. Well enough to be the best shot in Company Charlie, perhaps in the battalion. And what brought you here, to the city and to the Rat?

Long and sad story, sir. First, you had me up for company punishment before Colonel White. Broke me from sergeant to corporal and ordered forfeiture of pay. With that in my record and other stuff I was fucked. I knew I'd never make sergeant again. Jesus! And I thought I had it made, E-8 for sure, maybe even E-9 before I retired. That was a sweet dream.

Eric, I interjected as mildly as I could, for Pete's sake you know what you did. You went fucking mad. I couldn't let it go, but I made it as easy for you as I could. I saved your ass from the worst, just like you saved my life!

The cover-up—there was no other word for it—was as clear in my memory as though it had happened yesterday. With the help of a round sum of cash, my own, I got the village elders and the husband to stop talking rape and mutilation. That it had been that and far worse I didn't doubt for a moment. I managed to turn an indescribably brutal rape and beating of the husband, whose ear Eric had sliced off, into disorderly conduct.

You did what you thought you had to do, sir. It broke my life, and it's over and done with. Funny, don't you agree? I didn't think of it when I killed the fucker who shot you. So I put in for discharge and guess what! My wife dumped me just as I was leaving the Corps. Didn't want to live with a fucking dead-end corporal. Cleaned out our savings and investment accounts, slapped a mortgage on the house, grabbed the money and the kid, and hightailed it with some guy to Texas. Shit, sir, I thought I'd track the bitch down and shoot her and then shoot myself. I'd have done it, too, if I wasn't drinking too much to get myself going right away. It's a miracle I didn't. The chaplain at camp straightened me out. Then a couple of years ago a buddy from Linville called and told me about this kind of work. I decided I'd try it. The pay is just a notch up from crappy, but the tips are good. He and I live together, down in Chinatown. This country has turned into shit. I didn't know it back then, but I know it now. Through my roommate I've met people who have the right ideas on how to clean out this shithouse. And do it good, so it stays clean. Anyway, I need money, and I've been working here over a year now. And you, sir, what brings you here? Some of the pussy's OK, but you, sir . . . You can do as well or better without paying.

I didn't come for that, Eric, and please stop calling me sir every other word. We're civilians now. Try calling me Jack. Do you remember a girl called Kerry Black? I've been told she came here a lot. She's the girl who died of an overdose at a hotel somewhere down the street after an evening she spent here.

Sure, Captain, I remember her. She was known here as just Kerry. We only found out her last name from the newspapers.

She was my girl. We broke up more than a year ago, but I never stopped loving her. I love her now. The story that was put out about the overdose—it just doesn't add up. I never heard her speak of this place or of going to clubs, and she didn't do drugs while we were together. I can't figure it out. I left the U.S. soon after we broke up and got back only a couple of weeks ago. The main reason I returned is to find out what really happened.

Jesus, Captain, do you know what kind of place this is? What goes on here?

I know almost nothing, Eric. I've been told it's a club, an after-hours club, I guess, where there's some drug use and stuff. I'm not sure I know what I mean by any of it. I haven't been in an after-hours club since college.

That's what I figured. Look, Captain, let me lay it out for you. Johnnie, that's the owner, has a pretty good thing going. He thinks it's strictly legal, and the fact is we've had no trouble with the police, not since I was hired. The idea is that the Rat is just a place where private parties happen. You come by invitation only—unless not enough regulars show up, and Sam or I look you over and decide to let you in. The regulars are rich guys on Johnnie's list. I don't know how many names he's got. A thousand? Maybe fewer. He sends an email or a text saying there's a party tonight or tomorrow night or whatever. They can RSVP, but that's not required. When they turn up, we know them or they flash the email or the message on their phone and we let them in. The other schmucks wait. That's the assholes standing out in the street now. As I said, maybe they get in. All the guys who go in, the regulars and the schmucks, pay a party fee—three hundred dollars cash or by credit card. The charge shows up as "Bistro Paradise." That way they can tell their wife or accountant it's a restaurant. They also pay for drinks—nothing wrong with that at a private party with an open cash bar—for themselves and a girl if they want to treat her, and a fee for the use of a private room. Rooms like this one. Five hundred for twenty minutes. See?

I guess I do, so far.

All right. Now the girls. That's what this place is about. Most are high-class hookers on Johnnie's girl list. He emails or texts to let them know the party's on and sends a follow-up if more girls are needed. The others are just girls. All kinds—secretaries, waitresses, college students, actresses, whatever. Amateurs. Any woman shows up alone we let in unless she's a dog. They come for the money and kicks. All the girls, hookers and amateurs, pay an entrance fee too, fifty dollars. But a girl gets twenty percent of the room fee if the guy takes her into a room, and she keeps what he gives her for whatever they do once they're there. This is key. That way Johnnie stays out of legal trouble—he's not pimping. No one's forced to do anything, but I can tell you the girls do plenty. I hear the stories from both sides. Even some stuff I'd never heard of before. The amateurs, if they work out, I mean if guys buy them drinks and take them into a room, can ask Johnnie to put them on his girl list. I hate to tell you this, Captain: Kerry was a star. She was here like most Fridays, ever since I started here. Sometimes during the week too. A really good-looking kid!

All the air had gone out of my lungs. I swallowed the bourbon at the bottom of my glass and let Eric refill it. I had the unpleasant feeling he enjoyed telling me the story.

You say she'd go into those rooms.

Yes, Captain. Sir, begging your pardon, you got to understand that's the point of coming here. And she was some dancer! Almost always danced alone. Dressed beautifully, slinky black or red jumpsuits that zipped down the front, and high heels. It wasn't like those half-naked floozies. Real class.

Did she have people here she'd go into a room with most of the time she came?

I couldn't tell you that, Captain. I'm mostly outside, and when I come in it's often because Johnnie needs me to straighten some guy out. The guy who'd know is Pablo, the head bartender. Short guy, almost bald. Or Miguel, the other bartender. They watch what's going on. Or perhaps Johnnie. Only it's no use talking to him. He won't talk about his customers or his business.

Eric, I said, I think you can imagine how I feel. Did she leave the club with guys? You know what I mean, take them home, or go somewhere with them?

That I do know. No, Captain, she'd arrive in one of those black car-service sedans, and there would be another sedan or maybe the same one when she went home. Always alone, always in one of those cars. Except the night she overdosed. She came out the door, gave me a twenty as usual, and kissed me—we'd gotten to be friendly but not that way—and walked down the block in the direction of that hotel. Forgive me, Captain, but she was none too steady on her feet.

Eric, is there any way I could talk to the bartenders, Pablo or Miguel?

One minute. I'll find out.

When he came back he said, You're in luck. Pablo's going to take a fifteen-minute break and join us here. I told Johnnie this is a Marine Corps reunion, and he said we're welcome to stay in the room. He'd be honored to meet you before we leave.

I held out my glass mutely. Eric nodded and poured me a shot.

It's all right, he said, I know how you feel, like when I found out about my wife.

Thanks, I replied. It's rough.

The truth is that a loud voice inside me was saying, Stop talking to this fucking sadist, you fool, banish Kerry from your mind, send her file to the fucking U.S. attorney, ask Moses Cohen to look after Jeanette, and get out of the country. Don't leave a forwarding address. But I knew I couldn't do it. A wave of pity and regret stronger than the disgust I felt was overwhelming me. She was a sick, broken, suffering girl, going through a hell I couldn't begin to imagine. If only she had let me remain at her side . . .

Yes sir, Captain Dana, said Pablo. Eric told me about you. He says you're a war hero. Please let me be of service.

The roly-poly man's volubility was disconcerting, but he had a nice smile.

That's very kind. I'm trying to understand what happened the night Kerry died, and I think it would help if I knew whether she had steady contacts here—customers, I guess is what I mean.

A gorgeous girl, Captain, gorgeous girl. Men would line up to take her into a room. Sometimes she'd do three, even four, in an evening. Some guys would stay with her for an hour or longer. Do you realize how much that cost? There were clients who looked for her each time she came, but if you mean something like a boyfriend, no sir! There wasn't anything like it. You know, she danced alone. She wasn't looking for company.

She got paid for what she did?

You bet, Captain! Sometimes as much as a thousand, sometimes more. I know because she'd tell me. Like boasting. And then she'd give me a big tip.

Pablo, I said, this is a tough question, maybe there's no way you can answer. Why do you think Kerry did this? You know she didn't need the money.

I know what she told me, Captain. She said she was a big-time real estate broker, making a lot. The real-estate-broker part she invented—I know that now because of the newspapers—but she must have made a lot as a lawyer. When she told me she didn't need money, I asked, Why do you go with those guys? You know, fat guys, old guys, guys who've had too much to drink, who smell bad? You know what she said? I like it. I'm horny. I like it when they're ugly. I like it when they're old and can't get it up. I like it when they stink. I like it when they're dirty. So, Captain, you figure it.

I can't, I replied. Most likely I never will. Anyway, it won't surprise you that I feel sick. But there are a couple more things I'd like to know if possible. Do drug dealers hang out here? Can you buy stuff?

No sir! Johnnie doesn't allow pushers or drug dealing. Strictly bring your own. Drug busts are the last thing he needs.

Eric nodded. Exactly right.

This overdose, I said. Was Kerry on drugs? Do you know?

Pablo and Eric both laughed.

Eric spoke first. Captain, sir, sorry to say this, but you've got to be kidding.

Kerry used to say, Pablo broke in, I'm rich so I buy the best shit. High-class snow and E. And that was the truth. She'd give me a line or two.

I see, I see. And what about pimps? Are there pimps here?

Not right this minute, sir, said Pablo. I haven't seen any at the bar.

Yeah, said Eric, they drop in to check how their girls are doing. But there's very little of that. Almost all the hookers here are freelancers, but occasionally a hooker with a pimp brings him over. They get a free pass. Professional courtesy!

I see, I see, I said again stupidly. What about the evening Kerry died, Pablo, do you remember any pimps hanging out here?

Gee, Captain, he answered, those guys are a dime a dozen. They're shit. I don't pay attention to them.

Then he scratched the top of his bald head and said, Well, maybe I do recall a guy who could've been a pimp because he wasn't like the regular customers, a big good-looking black-haired guy dressed real sharp, in leather. Kerry danced with him a lot that evening—something she didn't do. As I said, she'd dance alone. When the guy got hot on the dance floor, he took off the leather jacket, hung it on the back of the barstool, and danced in his black silk shirt. He had powerful hairy arms. I remember when they sat together between sets she'd stroke his arm. Like this.

Did he take her into a room? I asked, overcoming an onset of nausea.

Nah, he didn't. She didn't go in with anyone that evening. I remember, because I asked her what was going on, and she said, It's my period and I don't feel like giving blowjobs. Not tonight.

Do you know that guy's name? Have you seen him again?

No to both questions, Captain. I'm sorry.

It's I who am sorry. Do you remember by any chance whether they left the club together, this guy and Kerry?

No sir, I can tell you definitely they didn't. Here is what I remember. Kerry left early that evening—early for her—and before she left she made a telephone call. She was leaning on the bar and speaking loud over the music, so I could hear what she said. She told the car service to cancel her car, she wouldn't need it. I asked her why, and she said she needed to clear her head; she'd walk to the subway. And she gave me fifty dollars. Just like that! So I know exactly when she left, and I remember seeing the guy at the other end of the bar talking to some broad.

Did you hear him speak?

Sure, spoke English like a Russki.

The three of us left the room. I think I may have staggered, because of the two conversations, not the bourbon. On the way out we were intercepted by Johnnie, who expressed his eagerness to meet a war hero who was also a celebrated author. He'd Googled me as soon as he heard my name. Would I join him in a drink?

I said I'd be delighted, as soon as I'd said goodbye to Eric and Pablo and thanked them.

When I returned, Johnnie invited me to his office, a room slightly larger than the one in which I had talked to the others. He insisted on pouring me a small producer bourbon that indeed turned out to be very good and said how sorry he was about Kerry. An unusual girl, so beautiful, so intelligent, and so mixed up. Hard to understand.

Impossible, I said.

And yet, he replied, many of the girls who come here don't come for money. Or money isn't the main reason. Sex is mysterious. What disgusts you and me will turn someone else on.

I nodded.

My philosophy, he continued, is to give everybody here what they want. Exactly what they want without any obligation. No one forces the girls. They only do what they like. If they do this or that, a guy may give them this much or that much. Or nothing. It's a free country!

I understand, I told him. So this is not a club where you'd run into pimps.

You might meet one if one of the girls invites him, but they don't operate here. Strictly hands off! Johnnie told me portentously. Here we party.

I do understand, I said. I hear there was a man here the night that Kerry died, a big black-haired man dressed in leather whom Pablo didn't know and who didn't seem to be like the usual customers. Kerry danced with him several times. I'm told she normally danced alone. Do you know by any chance who that was, do you know his name?

I know how he got in. A girl brought him. She said his name was Boris. But that's all.

And the girl?

Lena. I don't know her last name. Semiprofessional hooker, I don't mind telling you that. Big boobs. Not that good looking. I don't see her since that night. When I text her, the message bounces. You want her number?

He consulted his phone and dictated the number.

I looked at him carefully. Nice black velvet suit. Ivory-colored silk shirt opened at the collar to the third button. A gold chain with a gold Virgin suspended from it. Nice black curly hair, nice face, nice smile. He must have fun with some of the girls. Kerry? Did that make any difference?

Johnnie, I said, I think you know women very well. Why would a brilliant, highly educated, very successful girl like Kerry go for a guy like that Boris? Can you explain it? I assume they'd never met before. Couldn't be for his conversation!

Why did she come here and do what she did? he asked. You know, Captain, you get a sexy girl, and, even if she's scared, a pimp is like catnip. Those guys have something you can't bottle, you can't duplicate, and it's very strong. And, forgive me, a girl like Kerry . . .

I thanked him. I'm glad to say I thanked him sincerely.

As we parted, he expressed the hope that when we met again I would sign one of my books for him.

X

Scott said he'd like to go down to Le Raton after dinner, to speak to Johnnie, but in the end he agreed it didn't make sense. It was past eleven by the time we had gone over everything that had happened during the week and were ready to leave the restaurant, and he had an early shuttle to catch the next morning. What's more, I really doubted that on a Friday night Johnnie would make time for us, even if he wasn't spooked by Scott's being along. My own immediate goal as far as the Rat was concerned, I told him, was to find Lena, perhaps through the telephone number Johnnie gave me. Talking some more to Pablo and Miguel and getting leads on any girls she seemed to hang out with was another possibility. Once we had her, I was convinced that we'd be able to zero in on Boris. These were tasks for which Martin and Lee were uniquely suited, and I'd already asked Martin to undertake them, after telling him first thing in the morning about my visit to the Rat.

Bringing Scott up-to-date and answering his questions hadn't been easy. I held nothing back—not even, once again

contrary to Martin's advice, what I did to Goran, or what I
had learned about Kerry from my new friends at the Rat,
although to do so filled me with burning shame. Those were
details I omitted in briefing Martin. How could I do otherwise when I spoke to Scott? He was my best friend, the
brother for whom I'd take a bullet anytime, just as I knew
he'd take one for me. But no, what I've just written is not
entirely true. I didn't tell Scott that during the night, after
coming home from the Rat Hole and lying in bed for hours
motionless, unable to sleep and too wretched to get up, I
found the answer to a searing puzzle, which was why Kerry
didn't go into a private room with any of the regulars that
night or, much more astonishing, with Boris. She told Pablo
it was because she had her period, but that had to be a lie.
The police report Simon Lathrop relayed to me and Heidi
made no mention of menstrual flow, and yet this was a detail
too striking and important to have been simply overlooked.
On the other hand, the report stated distinctly that, although
no semen had been found, the condition of the organs was
consistent with sex—vigorous though not necessarily violent
sex. A puzzle? A paradox? I had the solution. Catnip, Johnnie
had called it, those special charms of a pimp. Don't go with
anyone! Boris would have told her, in those Russki dulcet or
perhaps rough tones, don't go with anyone, and I fuck you
later on bed like you've never been fucked. And my solution
explained also why she went to that hotel. Don't go with no
one, he said, later we go hotel! Once there, of course, he wore
a condom. Didn't want to leave his business card. Or perhaps
he never used a condom and never came. Didn't need to. One
of those sex athletes who can go for hours and hold it. At

some point he said, Give arm and don't move, here is syringe, you hold it and I help you shoot up with shit that's better than any shit you ever tried. . . . Or perhaps he killed her first and fucked her afterward. While she was still nice and warm. Yes, I held that back from Scott. I couldn't bring myself to rob Kerry of the last vestige of her dignity. Or was it my own dignity I was sparing? It made little difference.

For his part, Scott told me he'd sounded out the Agency lawyer with whom he worked most often and no longer believed that I—or for that matter he—was at legal risk for not having reported what we thought was Abner's Amazon caper to the FBI or the NYPD.

Our position has to be that we don't know for a fact that a felony has been committed, Scott said. As simple as that. If we did know, it would be a different ballgame. The other side of the coin is that his—or anyone's—being able to send those fake Amazon packages is fraught with such implications that we'd be very wrong to sit on this much longer.

I couldn't disagree. Especially since a second Amazon package arrived that morning while I was out running. Feng, who had ESP or had been warned by Martin, or perhaps both, told me he'd handled the package very carefully, wearing gloves, and had placed it in the far guest bedroom.

Was I right to do that, sir?

Exactly right, I told him and called Scott. He was still at the office, not being due to leave for the airport for another couple of hours.

Shit, he said, here we go again. I'll send the guys over.

The same pair of explosives experts who'd visited just a few days earlier arrived with the same breakneck speed. It seemed that in small things the Agency couldn't be counted on to fuck up.

Clean, Captain, the older one reported after they'd done their thing. No trace of explosives. Do we send it to Langley?

If you're sure it's clean, I'll open it here.

This time, the package was considerably bigger. Same perfect ersatz Amazon outside complete with bar codes and Amazon birthday gift wrapping. The guys were wearing gloves. I asked them to extract the gift card from its envelope. A pithy message: Your time has come. Use it on yourself, asshole! No signature.

Do we keep going, sir? asked the senior operative.

You bet.

Same precautions. The present was ten feet of two-thirds-inch hemp rope with a hangman's noose tied at one end.

What the fuck! The younger operative started apologizing as the words left his mouth.

At ease, I told him. A fucking maniac's at work. Now that we know what this is, would you gentlemen send the package to Langley, the rope included? I won't be using it, not just now, and they'll want to look into the sender and the rest of this stuff. And now, how about some coffee and first-rate coffee cake? Homemade, and I believe fresh from the oven.

Feng shepherded them to the kitchen.

Scott laughed when I described his specialists' visit. He didn't laugh at much else.

I wish this were a bad dream, he said, but it isn't. I don't like the stuff with this Goran fellow. A needless complication and it didn't do a thing for Jeanette. By the way, I'll see what we have on your pal Detective Walker and the Tannenbaum

Society. An extreme-right secret society that's not so secret, with police force and maybe Bureau members! God help us! Martin played his cards just right there.

He's great! I interrupted.

I know, Scott continued. The salient fact is that you're in Abner's crosshairs. He's convinced you have this goddamn file. If you think you fooled him by not mentioning it, you're wrong. He'll try to have you killed soon, before you give the file to the feds and before you make some sort of arrangement for someone else to hand it over in case you're dead or unable to function. If he's right, he wins the jackpot; if he's wrong, he doesn't lose much. What's one more murder? As for your intentions, in case you think you're going to get to kill Abner in some situation that can be described as self-defense, you're out of your mind. And I hope you realize that if you do somehow assassinate him you'll be up most likely for first-degree murder in a Texas court—because where else but in Texas would you do it—and it just so happens that Texas has the death penalty. And hands it out! Who knows what a Texas jury would do to a guy who killed its leading wing-nut billionaire? Would the twelve Texan jurors give a shit even if everything in Kerry's file has come out? Or what a Texas judge would do? How would you adjust to life in a Texas penitentiary? My advice to you, which I am one hundred percent sure is the advice poor Kerry would give you, is as follows: Get the fucking file to the U.S. attorney now. Make a real effort to find the rest of Kerry's stuff, and if you don't find it, let the feds look for it. Turn over to the district attorney in Manhattan what you find out about this guy Boris. Martin Sweeney will know how to go about that. Don't try to kill the guy. And while all this is going on, don't let Jovan or another one of those goons kill you. My son doesn't need a dead godfather. One other thing, brother: if you really want to go to Sag Harbor tomorrow so it will be easier for Jovan to shoot you or blow you up, don't take Heidi. She doesn't need to get hurt. Take your .45 and, if you're as smart as you used to be, take Feng and let him have your back. I know a lot about him.

Had Scott and I drunk one old Armagnac too many? I got up later than usual, and all the same went running in the park. The thought that it might be nicer to run on the beach apparently didn't cross my mind. Feng prepared an English-style breakfast, which I ate with gusto, speed-reading the *Times*. Breakfast finished, I threw a couple of sweaters, my running shoes, .45-caliber ammo, and the Ka-Bar into the duffel. The Colt I stuck into my waistband. Next I called the garage and asked for my car to be out at ten. As part of the exorcism process I'd embarked on, I had traded in Harry's Audi for a Volvo station wagon. Since the curse on the Sag Harbor house, alas, wouldn't lift, I had driven the Volvo there only once or twice before leaving for Italy, and never since I returned. The guys at the garage, though, had been running the engine every few weeks to keep the battery in shape, and Ricardo, the boss man, reported proudly on the phone that it was waiting for me ready to go, just a little dusty.

No, Feng, I'm not taking you with me this time, I told him the second time. Really. This time no, next time yes. It's a deal. Back on Sunday evening, unless I stay until Monday, in which case I'll call.

My Sag Harbor housekeeper, Mary Murphy, was expecting me around twelve-thirty. I'd called my painter neighbor and Harry's friend, Sasha Evans, and invited her to dinner. I called again to confirm and said, Sure, I'd be delighted to come to her house instead.

Anbar Province and Helmand had fried my brains. It was ten, and I hadn't called Heidi to say, as I had told Scott I would, that I wouldn't take her with me and we'd have dinner instead, anyplace she liked, Sunday or Monday. A message came on: Hi, this is Heidi! I'm away for the weekend. If you wish to leave a message, please do so.

Heidi, I cried out, dismayed, I wish you hadn't done this, really. . . .

Naturally, there was no answer.

I opened the email on my iPhone. She'd sent a message: What's happened to your manners, Captain Dana? Instead of driving me out to Sag Harbor and entertaining me by your conversation, you've obliged me to get my old Mini out of the garage and make the drive by myself! You might try to redeem yourself by taking me to lunch at the American Hotel and giving me the best guest bedroom, but I'm not sure it will work. Your disappointed partner, H.

What was I to do? I cursed some more, rushed to the garage, Feng two steps behind me—just to make sure, sir, we don't have company—got into the car, drove back with Feng to my building to pick up my bag, said goodbye to Feng, told John the Serb on duty, resisting the urge to remind him to be sure to so inform Jovan, that I was off to Sag Harbor for the weekend, and stepped on the gas. I'd be damned if I'd let that stupid girl get to the house before me.

Good try, Captain Dana! At least I didn't get a speeding ticket. A cute green-and-black Mini was parked smack outside the house. Without Heidi. Where the hell was she? In the house, idiot, where else? Following Harry's custom, I put my car into the garage, dropped the door shut, and went into the pantry and then the kitchen directly from the garage. There was Heidi at the table, decked out in russet tweeds, having a companionable cup of tea with Mary. She offered me her cheek to peck and shook her head pityingly while I embraced Mary, exclaimed over the pregnancy that was just showing, asked after her husband at the pet shop, and announced that based on her emails I assumed the house was very much in order.

It's in better shape, Jack, than it's ever been, she told me. I wish poor Harry, God rest his soul, could see it. Everything is just the way he wanted it. José Rodriguez has been working really hard—repainting, changing window frames where needed, fixing the cupboards. He's covered your and Harry's entire list. Would you like to check it out now or later, after you and Heidi have had lunch?

I nodded. Later would be better, I said. Heidi and I have a lunch date.

And would you like a cup of tea right now?

You bet, I said. And for you, a gin and tonic?

Wouldn't I love that? But doctor's orders!

She patted her tummy.

Right! How about Miss Heidi? To help her forgive me?

To my relief, she laughed!

Your partner will have a martini while you wash your hands et cetera, she said, provided you haven't forgotten how to make one. You're so full of surprises. Who'd have thought that on top of everything else you're a slow driver!

I've put Heidi into the big guest room, Mary broke in.

Let's make a change, I said. Let's move her into the master bedroom, perhaps it'll improve her disposition. I'll take the guest room.

It was Heidi who went upstairs to do her et cetera. While I was making the drink, Mary cocked her ear to make sure she could speak without being overheard and said, She's very pretty and very nice. I'm glad for you, Jack.

She is all that and more, I replied, but it's not like that and it's not going to be like that. She's Kerry's best friend. You heard her: we're partners. We want to figure out what happened. We don't believe Kerry overdosed any more than Harry committed suicide. It's the same goons. They killed her because she and Harry were like two fingers. She knew too much.

I've been praying for her soul, Mary said. She was such a good person. Harry really loved her!

So did I, Mary, so did I. It broke my heart when she left me. And now you run along home and give my congratulations to Brian. Is the pet shop open tomorrow? Yes? Then I'll try to drop in.

And I'll see you here tomorrow, she said, not too early so Heidi can sleep in.

I knew there was nothing to be gained by arguing with her. If she decided she needed to come in on Sunday, she would, no matter what I told her. So I kept quiet and, instead, gave her a hug.

You've got a talent for finding the sort of housekeepers my

mother would kill for, said Heidi when she reappeared in the kitchen and had taken a sip of her martini. And your martini's up to par. There may be some hope left for your case. Do you want to start telling me why you decided to dump me in the city?

I can, in four words: I want you alive. The party has gotten rough, and something tells me it will get rougher. Unless you're not hungry, perhaps I should hold the longer version for lunch.

Good thinking, Captain! I'm always hungry.

The American Hotel had been my uncle Harry's canteen, where he was fussed over as a beloved habitué. He took me there at least once every time I visited, and I continued to drop in for a meal and sometimes a drink after he was murdered. The headwaiter's chatty amiability was consequently pleasant, but not surprising. Although I hadn't reserved, assuming that Heidi would stay in the city, he led us immediately to a corner table in the back room with no neighbors on either side.

Your uncle's favorite table, Captain, he assured me, as he did every time he placed me there, no noise and no one who can listen to what you and the young lady say to each other. I hope we will be seeing her here often.

We ordered. Another martini for Heidi and one for me.

What's happened to your hollow leg, I asked, when she said, seeing me look for a bottle of red wine that wouldn't break the bank in the wine list as long as the Manhattan telephone directory in the old days, that just a glass of red wine would be enough for her.

Screwed on firmly, she replied, but if I'm not too sleepy

after lunch I'll scoot over to East Hampton to say hello to the parents. My mom got all excited when she heard I was in Sag Harbor—staying with you. Right away, she wanted me to bring you over, but I said that was impossible, even if it's a command performance. In the afternoon, I told her, the great novelist writes! That didn't stop her; she said, Then bring him to dinner, but I was like Easy, Mom, easy, I think he's accepted an invitation from his next-door neighbor. Or do you want to go to dinner there? I could tell her I was wrong.

No, you were one hundred percent right. We're indeed going to dinner at Sasha Evans's, a great old lady and Harry's best friend.

Good. To tell you the truth—I read my mom like an open book—my spending the weekend at your house immediately gave her the Big Idea. You see, she knows what you look like; she's seen your photo on your book jackets. She thinks her deviant daughter may be at last on the straight and narrow!

Would that were so! A path leading straight to me!

Not this weekend, partner! But apropos of nothing, Dad has arranged the security. Starting tomorrow evening, when we get back to the city. He wanted his squad—that's what he calls it—to get over to Sag Harbor, but I said until tomorrow evening you'll look after my security!

She actually put her hand over mine and patted it! But retracted it immediately as the waiter brought two salads and two glasses of Pinot Noir, and said, So talk! Talk already!

I did, after pausing for a moment to organize my thoughts. The increased attention to me—if that's what you want to call it—was one aspect; my weird telephone conversation with Abner was another; and the visit to the Rat and what I learned there about Kerry, and the identity of the man I believed strongly had murdered her, were the third. Perhaps because she was a woman, perhaps because Kerry had been so utterly open with her about everything, including sex, I didn't censor the account. I gave up on Kerry's dignity and mine. Was that a mistake? By the time I finished, Heidi was crying. This time I put my hand over hers and squeezed, repeating, the way my mother used to, Now now there, now now . . .

It's all right, Heidi said finally, after she'd blown her nose into a little embroidered handkerchief she found at the bottom of her bag. I had to know. I think you really did figure out what happened that night, why she went with Boris, what they did. I saw that police report. Simon never told you, perhaps they didn't tell him, perhaps, poor guy, he didn't get it. She and that son of a bitch did anal too. Vigorous! More like assault and battery. We've got to find him. Lena—that's often a Russian name—she'll lead us to him.

I've got Martin Sweeney on it. And his partner, Lee. I think that's the best—unless you think you can get the district attorney or whoever to reopen the case and really look. You and I wouldn't know where to look.

Let's stick with your guys. We'll see how they make out. But you, Captain, I think you're in serious danger.

I laughed. That seems to be the unanimous opinion. The thing is, I'm used to bad people trying hard to kill me. Brings out the best in me.

Very funny.

It isn't, but it is a fact. I've been hoping that one of those bastards—Jovan or whoever—will strike this weekend. With you here, it's more complicated. If you're going to East Hampton, don't you think you could just stay there through Sunday? Rendezvous in the city? I love your company, you know that; I'm talking about getting the job done and avoiding damage to civilians. You know how they've drummed that into us.

Ha-ha-ha! No, Jack. I want to be with you. I'm not a civilian, I'm your partner, and I'm not chicken. You do Krav Maga? I've done karate since elementary school. I'm a serious black belt. I'm a crackerjack shot too!

Sweetie, I said, no, sorry, Heidi, these guys—Slobo, probably Boris, surely Jovan—are professional killers and torturers. Karadžić's men or worse. Jovan won't put on a white karate suit and circle around looking for an opening. He'll use a knife or a gun. With a little luck, I can pull this off. You can't.

We won't argue anymore, and I won't stay away.

All right. We won't argue. Dessert?

Since it's Sabbath, this bad little Jewish girl says yes. Chocolate cake and then a double espresso.

I told the waiter the chocolate cake was for one. I'd have another Pinot Noir. And we'd have two double espressos.

Then I said, Heidi, explain it to me. Why did Kerry, beautiful, brilliant, good-hearted Kerry, turn herself into a doormat for those men? Forgive me, much worse, a urinal? How could that be? No matter how hard I try, I can't fathom it. You know all about the sex between her and me, so you know there was never, not for a second, anything sadistic in it. Nothing remotely kinky. It was tender, classical—I don't know what other word to use—and yet I believe, I'm certain of it, that she liked it. She'd come in a way you can't fake. More than once she came before I did. What was going on then? Or rather, what happened to change all that after she decided to leave me?

I can't explain, and honestly I think nothing happened. Or maybe everything. Here's the best I can come up with. I told you the first time we met that she'd been in and out of therapy forever. Depression. Anxiety. Mood swings. All the demons, all the meds. On top of that—I think it started at Jones & Whetstone, but I could be wrong—coke. Because it was in style. Because she'd go to parties, real parties, not like anything at the Rat Hole, run into some lawyer at her firm or another and get laid, and coke made it more fun. Or was supposed to. I don't know much about her and E or Molly or whatever this other shit was. I'm sure—no, how can I be sure of anything?—she didn't do heroin. I've told you Kerry had her life divided up in compartments. How much did she hold back even from me? To what extent had she resented my family's wealth, my self-assurance? There must have been such resentments, and defenses that went with them. You want to know what happened to turn her into a Rat Hole slut? You like psychobabble? No? I don't either. I think it all boils down to low self-esteem. So low it was nonexistent. Nothing could be bad enough for her. Why just then? It may have been some crazy idea that she'd kicked you in the balls and you didn't deserve it. But look, Jack, don't pay any attention to me. I'm brokenhearted, just like you.

Yup, I said, let's go home. I should have paid closer attention. Especially when she went overboard with her apology for not standing up to that bastard Hobson when he spread the lie about Harry's dementia being the reason he forced him out of the firm. She needed her income from the firm to provide for her truly demented father and her mother. There was nothing culpable about her behavior. But how analytic was I supposed to be? I loved her more than I had ever loved any woman.

I took her home the long way, meaning we went entirely out of our way, to the very end of the Long Wharf, and stood there awhile, looking out over the water. Seagulls were going crazy. A boat must have dumped some garbage. I wasn't going to tell her about the Mashomack Preserve at the near shore of Shelter Island, or how I had hiked there with my mother and Harry, or how I had hoped one day to hike there with Kerry. A tune from *On the Town* wafted through my mind. A duet. The man regrets he's not had the time to wake up and see his girl without her make-up. She regrets not having seen him dry the dishes. It's sad, but—

Oh, well, they console each other, *we'll catch up Some other time.*

Nice music, Leonard Bernstein had never done better; nice words, Betty Comden and her partner, Adolph Green, had never done better either. They'd all been friends of Harry's, and I used to see Betty occasionally, at her Bridgehampton house, when I stayed with Harry. Only for Kerry and me there'd never be some other time. Abner Brown had taken care of that.

Heidi took my arm. We retraced our steps and continued

to the house. I felt heavy, more weighed down than anytime during Corps Infantry training. She sensed my mood and didn't speak. I offered her another double espresso, which I succeeded in making in Harry's machine.

She went upstairs to wash her face. When she came back, she announced she was ready for her coffee and even East Hampton.

We were again sitting in the kitchen.

Heidi, I can't help it, I blurted, there is something I need to know. Are you in therapy? Are you on meds? Do you do drugs?

Tears ran down my face.

Hush, Jack, she said, hush! What kinds of questions are these to ask Mrs. Jonathan Krohn's talented deviant daughter? Yes, I've been in therapy. I'd guess that any girl like me—I mean generally of my background, class, et cetera—would be if she discovered she liked girls. I'm not in therapy now, and I'm off meds. In fact, I feel very good, except when you stand me up. And no, I don't do drugs. I tried to smoke pot in senior year of high school—I went to one of those super snotty jobs on the Upper East Side—and in college, and it never did anything for me. I'm scared of the hard stuff. It may be the only thing I'm really scared of. So I stick to martinis and red wine. Oh, white wine is all right too! And now, Jack, really hush, or I'll get cross.

One more stupid question, Heidi, after which you can bop me with any one of those cast-iron pans. Do you have somebody? I mean a girlfriend, you know, or something like it.

Why should I bop you? It's a legitimate question. I don't. I did. Sometimes I wish I still did. I pick up people sometimes. Like a lawyer outside my firm—I don't believe in firm romances even for straights—some lawyer I meet on some case if we're not adversaries, girls I meet when I travel. In bars. I haven't gone online or stuff like that. Those bars, yes, sometimes they're lesbian bars. And now, Captain, I've got to get going. When's dinner? Seven-thirty? I'll be back in plenty of time.

Drive carefully, I said. It doesn't matter if you're late. As you look at this house, Sasha's is the first house on the left, in case you are late and I've already gone over there.

Don't worry, I'll be on time, but I'll call if I'm late. Hey, is there a gas station on Route 114 between here and East Hampton, other than the one on the right-hand side, soon after Division Street?

I don't think so, I said. What's wrong with that one? I'm pretty sure it's open.

It's one of Father's crazy quarrels. Years ago, I don't know how many, the people over there did something or other that pissed him off when he wanted to get one of our cars inspected. So he forbade me, my mother, and my brother ever to get gas there. He's the sweetest of men, but once he gets a bee in his bonnet it's like forget it. This was before he hired the guy who takes care of everything now, like New York State inspections, the upkeep of the property, whatever.

And you can't just get your car filled up and say nothing?

It would make me feel bad.

Well, I said, there's a gas station on the Bridgehampton–Sag Harbor Turnpike, just as you're leaving town. Turn left on Main Street, keep going, and you'll get there.

That's out of my way. In that case I might as well go to

Route 27. Shit, I'm really not sure I've enough gas for the round-trip. I should have stopped and gotten gas, but I wanted to get here ahead of you! What about your car? How much gas have you got in it?

More than half a tank.

Would you lend it to me? I'm a careful driver!

All right. I laughed. Just this once.

Great! Here are the keys to the Mini, in case you want to go to a bar and pick up boys. Just make sure they're out of here by the time I come back.

We went into the garage, she got in behind the wheel, I pressed the button to open the door, and off she went, not exactly peeling rubber but almost. Harry's precepts and force of habit: I pressed the button again and closed the door. Then I called Sasha, and explained I had a houseguest, Kerry's best friend.

Bring her, she said, of course bring her.

Now I had no excuse. I had to prepare for Jovan's visit and, once that was done, get down to work. I'd work in the studio, I supposed, where Harry was murdered and where I killed Slobo. It's where the curse still lay heaviest on the house. Very fitting, I said to myself; if I'm lucky, that's where I'll also take care of Jovan.

If I were alone I think I'd have followed the tactics that had served me so well with Slobo: leave the front door unlocked, oil the hinges of the other doors downstairs so they don't squeak, make it as easy as possible for the fucker to get in. Then, once he's in, go for him and hope for the best. I got the WD-40 and did the doors very carefully. Yes, that might still be the way, when Heidi got back and she and I were coming home from Sasha's dinner. I would have left just enough lights on in the house to confuse him. Was I out? Was I there? What was the Mini doing outside? He'd try the door, find it unlocked, go in, and wait. Meanwhile, on the assumption he was there, I'd put Heidi in her Mini, for a quick getaway if necessary, with her phone fired up, and enter the house alone, also through the front door. I wasn't going to play games. If he was there, I'd find him and kill him. Cut his stomach open, that would be the preferred way, so he could still talk. I hadn't brought the curare darts or the dart pistol I had on hand for Slobo. Just my Colt, the Ka-Bar, and the switchblade. If he wasn't in the house, I'd get Heidi from the Mini. When we were ready to retire, I'd leave the front door open and count on the creaky stairs and my light sleep. She'd be in Harry's room; I'd be in the guest room across the hall, and I'd have my .45 with me. If Jovan managed to get in and come upstairs, I'd shoot the bastard. Period. In the knees, if possible, again so he could talk. If for any reason he stayed downstairs, I'd go and get him.

I unpacked rapidly upstairs, brought my laptop into the studio, turned on the electric heat to take the chill off, and sat down to write. For less than an hour, I suppose, I was so deep in my text that I wonder whether an aura would have warned me of Jovan's approach.

I was brought back to current reality by the ringing of my iPhone, which I had put on the desk.

A man's voice, a voice I didn't know.

Mr. Dana? Jack Dana?

Yes, this is he.

This is Jonathan Krohn, Heidi's father, Mr. Dana. An awful thing has happened. A truck rammed into Heidi. Practically head-on, on the driver's side. She's at the Southampton Hospital, bruised and badly shaken up, but no other injuries. She told me she'd like you to come over. Your car's been totaled. The truck ran away.

I'll be there in twenty minutes.

XI

Hours later, Sasha said, What do you think? Shall I turn on the TV? We'll catch the nine o'clock news. They should have something to say about what happened. We'll have dessert and coffee afterward. I'll get the Riverhead station. It's the best for local news.

She was right. The platinum-blonde anchor's newscast began with the attempted murder on Route 114.

On the segment of Route 114 between Sag Harbor and East Hampton, she intoned, a stolen white Chevy Silverado rammed a black 2012 Volvo station wagon driven by Heidi Krohn, thirty-one, a prominent New York City attorney and daughter of East Hampton resident and fashion-industry mogul Jonathan Krohn and his wife, Helen Krohn. WLNY-TV has been able to reconstruct the crime scene based on eyewitness interviews. Krohn's station wagon was approaching Stephen Hands Path when the pickup truck, which until then was several vehicles behind her, activated an emergency red light on its roof and a siren, jumped into the left-hand lane, and, going at a speed estimated at ninety to ninety-five

miles per hour, overtook Krohn, did a U-turn, and travel-
ing at even greater speed rammed Krohn's vehicle head-on.
A man jumped out of the truck and, with a firearm in his
hand, ran to the Volvo, looked inside it, shook his head, and
got back into the truck, which did another U-turn and sped
east on Route 114 before turning south on Stephen Hands
Path. WLNY has spoken to Cynthia Mooney, schoolteacher,
of Amagansett, whose Honda was directly behind Krohn's
Volvo.

A video of a thirtyish woman was shown at this point,
speaking into a mike held by a male reporter.

I've never been so scared in my life! she declared. Thank
God the brakes on my Honda held when I hit them. I was
right behind that Volvo, and I had a good look at the guy with
the gun. He was wearing some sort of ski mask. I almost had
a heart attack.

Several eyewitnesses, the anchor continued, had the presence of mind to write down the number on the Silverado's
Florida license plate. According to the East Hampton police,
a quick computer check established that the truck was stolen earlier in the day from the Hertz lot at the Francis S.
Gabreski Airport in Westhampton. After the incident on
Route 114, the Silverado, its left fender and headlight bashed
in, was found abandoned in the vicinity of the East Hampton
Airport. Still according to East Hampton police, Krohn was
saved by the airbags that opened upon impact. She was in
shock when the ambulance arrived and had suffered bruises,
but after a battery of tests and a period of observation was
discharged earlier this evening from the Southampton Hospital. A family spokesman declined to make her or any fam-

ily member available to the press. After this experience, he stated, Heidi and her parents need privacy.

The Volvo that Krohn was driving belongs to Jack C. Dana, bestselling novelist and Sag Harbor resident. Reached at the Southampton Hospital where he was visiting Krohn, Dana stated that he had lent her his car. He declined to make any other comment.

This is pretty much what Heidi said about what she could observe, I told Sasha. She's very clearheaded and very courageous.

Thank God she's courageous, Sasha answered, covering her face with her hands. This is the worst story I've ever heard. Those people wanted to kill. Why her? Who is this person driving the truck? Do you understand what's going on?

I certainly don't know who he is, I said, but I've no doubt whatsoever about what he is. He's a hit man. A professional murderer. He must have been told to make one hundred percent sure that the job had been completed—that's why he was going to shoot the driver of the Volvo if he wasn't already dead. A smart precaution, seeing that Heidi came out of the wreck essentially unscathed! But when the shooter got to my Volvo, he saw he'd followed the wrong car, or for some reason the wrong person was driving it. So, being a real pro, the guy didn't kill Heidi just for the hell of it, just because she happened to be in the car. He hadn't been hired to do that. For all he knew, his employer wouldn't appreciate it.

I wasn't going to tell Sasha—and I hadn't told Mr. Krohn— that the killer was following the right car. My car. Only he expected me to be inside, not some woman he knew nothing about. He would have been worried sick that he'd somehow fucked up and would have to answer to a pissed-off boss. Shaken up though she was, Heidi hadn't missed a beat. She understood completely what had happened. As soon as her father and mother left us to get their car and bring it to the emergency department's entrance, she took my hand and said, The guy driving that truck thought he was going to kill you! He and his buddies will come after you again. Tonight!

They might, I answered, but I'll be ready for them, and if you feel up to it we'll tell war stories tomorrow over dinner in the city.

On Route 114! Sasha wailed. Between Sag Harbor and East Hampton! This sort of thing—gangland murders, gangsters settling accounts—it didn't used to happen here. Not since the Prohibition, when bootleggers ran their launches into Three Mile Harbor. Poor Harry never locked his front door. He didn't think it was necessary. Maybe he should have. I still don't lock mine.

We were back in the dining room. For dessert, she'd gotten from her and Harry's favorite caterer in Sagaponack a prune tart that was by my reckoning big enough for eight. We hardly made a dent in it. She said she'd keep a piece for her dinner tomorrow; the rest I was to take with me. I knew better than to argue.

That poor child! Sasha continued, after she'd put coffee on the table. I'd have so liked to meet her. I don't suppose she's in any shape to stop by tomorrow.

I told her that I'd urged Heidi to stay with her parents overnight and go to the city with them—especially as I'd overheard some talk about taking their helicopter—in which case I'd drive her Mini back and deliver it to her garage.

It's a pleasure to deal with the superrich, I continued.

Once Mr. and Mrs. Krohn decided that Heidi was all right and they could stop worrying about her, Mr. Krohn, all noblesse oblige, shifted his attention to the terrible inconvenience of my car having been wrecked. And right away he found a solution. They have a sort of ancien régime steward by the name of Mahoney who manages their place on Further Lane. Makes sure everything is in perfect condition and runs perfectly. He said he's putting Mahoney on the case, and Mahoney will handle it all, the insurance claim and, this is the best, if I will allow him, buying a new car and delivering it to me. All I have to do is decide whether I still like black or want some other color! And of course, until the new car is delivered, I'm welcome to use one from the Krohn stable—which Mahoney will also be happy to deliver to me. Oh, and he's already had my car towed. I don't know where. He figured it out. What do you think of that?

I like it, she said, they sound like nice people. I'm glad you've found this girl. What happened to Kerry was so dreadful, so unexpected, but in life one has to learn to move on. You're a very young man, you've been through so much, you're really entitled to be happy. You can go on loving Kerry's memory, but don't be like Harry after he lost his Olga.

My uncle had been something of a lady's man. His long love affairs with beautiful and glamorous women had never led to marriage, either because the lady was already married and for one reason or another wouldn't divorce or, in the case of a famous ballerina, because she thought her career made marrying Harry the wrong choice. Then, working on a project for Abner Brown, Harry met a spellbinding Peruvian lawyer proud of her Indian blood. He called her his Inca; she became his obsession. They decided to get married, but less than three months before the wedding date Olga was killed by a bomb attack launched in Lima by the Shining Path insurgency. Harry never stopped mourning her. He told me a wall of ice built up around him, gradually sealing him off from human contact.

Thank you for saying this, Sasha, I answered. I don't want to live in an igloo like Harry, and I do like Heidi a lot. But not like that. She likes me too—but also not like that. That's the situation. We're stuck with it.

Now, now, don't be pessimistic, she told me, and bring her to see me as soon as you can.

I promised I would, kissed her, took the box with the tart, and went through her garden to the gate leading into mine.

The day had been overcast, and it was followed by a pitch-dark night. Nevertheless, I declined Sasha's offer of a flashlight.

Out of the question, I told her, we Force Recon veterans are like cats. No night is black enough for us. I might have added—but didn't—Particularly when we're wearing night-vision goggles.

Instead, before passing through the gate I paused to accustom my eyes to the dark and conscientiously scanned the garden and the house. Nothing. No unwonted shapes lurking among the bushes. No visible change in the house. From the outside, it was as I'd left it, lit dimly so as to confuse, I hoped, anyone trying to guess which room I was in or whether, indeed, I was at home. For the same reason, I'd put the Mini in the garage and shut the garage door. No one could tell from the outside whether the car was there. I'd locked the front door, contrary to my well-advertised habit, and I'd latched all the ground-floor windows. I didn't think that the thug sent to finish the botched job on Route 114 would bother with anything fancy. There would be no attempts to stage an accident, such as Slobo's plan to set fire to the studio while I was asleep in it, or to stage a fake suicide. No cat-and-mouse games, no opportunity for me to take advantage of Felix the Cat's moments of distraction. This would be an old-fashioned Murder, Inc., job: a break-in, followed by a gangland-style shooting. Or he'd use explosives—a satchel charge thrown in through a window, and *poof!*—a typical nineteenth-century Sag Harbor residence is reduced to rubble. Firemen find buried under it the corpse of Jack Dana, cut down before his time. Well, fuckheads, I'd make sure it didn't happen! But for that I needed the use of both hands. The idea of going first to the studio crossed my mind. I dismissed it. The studio was a cul-de-sac. I needed corners, angles, and command of the house. There was a stone bench to the right of the garden door. I set Sasha's tart down on it and drew the .45 from my waistband. I was pretty sure I had a round in the chamber, but this was no time for errors. As silently as possible, I drew the slide back. Yes, the round was there. I sprinted, crouching, to the French doors leading from the garden into the main house.

No sooner was I framed by the lit open door than he fired—and missed. Not by much. The bullet whizzed so close to my head it might have singed my hair. I threw myself on the ground and crawled into the house, keeping my face turned toward the garden and the shooter. *Crack!* This time he got me, in the right thigh. And this time I saw the flash at the end of the barrel. So that was it: a sniper with a high-powered rifle and a night-vision scope sitting in a tree in back of the parking lot of the church to the right of Harry's house! I howled like ten dying banshees. Built up to a big crescendo. Then silence. Let the bastard figure it out. Probably he couldn't. He'd know he hit me because I screamed and perhaps because he could see the sudden movement of my body after the impact, that's all. How he managed to miss me on the first shot, why he fired single rounds, I couldn't figure. Or maybe I could: one of those snipers with a swelled head but not very gifted. Not like Eric, the sniper turned bouncer. Now he was firing again, to make up for lost time. *Crack! Crack!* I felt my thigh. Flesh wound, the bone seemed all right; the bullet had gone straight through. The pain wasn't bad, but I was bleeding like a son of a bitch. I hoped he hadn't gotten the femoral artery. Tourniquet, tourniquet! I didn't have time for games. Just a few precious minutes to take care of the wound and get ready for the fucker's visit. The silence could mean one thing only: he'd climbed down from the tree and was on his way to check out the house.

Getting up was the easy part. Grabbing furniture for support and leaving a trail of blood on Mary's beautifully polished floor, I made my way toward the front door. On the way I snatched from the tote hanging in the hall my Ka-Bar and some extra rounds of ammo, and from the umbrella stand one of Harry's canes. The cane was a big help. I unlocked the front door. Welcome! Welcome! On to the kitchen. Once there, I cut off my trouser leg, made bandage strips out of a dishtowel, and applied a tourniquet. Fortunately the wound wasn't too high on the leg, and the blood wasn't spurting. He hadn't cut an artery, probably only a big vein, and the tourniquet slowed down the bleeding a lot. Now if only the bastard—I hoped he didn't have a colleague—would get over here, we could finish our business. I wasn't sure how long I could wait. The cell phone was in my pocket. I checked: it was charged and I had coverage. Prudence—common sense—told me to call 911. But Captain Dana the warrior said, Fuck! Don't want cops barging in and scaring this bastard off. If they do we'll never see him again. And if they arrive the same time as he does and catch him, what's next? He'll be up for what? Attempted murder? Not good enough for me. I made it to the dining room, from where I had an unobstructed view of the front door. Crouching on the floor was hell. I took a chair, dragged it over to the wall right next to the door, and sat down in it. He wouldn't be able to see me when he came in, but I would see him perfectly in the big horizontal mirror hanging over the sideboard.

Toc toc toc . . . It wasn't the grandfather clock; it wasn't my heart; it was the pulse above the tourniquet. Move it, goon! The minutes passed slowly. Finally, I heard it: someone very cautiously turning the doorknob.

The mirror reflected all I needed to see. The door opened bit by bit and then entirely. In it stood a man dressed in a black running suit, a black ski mask, and black lace-up boots. The same size and shape as my most recent running mate in Central Park. No rifle—he must have left it somewhere outside, perhaps in his car, perhaps outside the door—but in his hand he had what looked to me like a Glock. He remained motionless. Listening? Thinking? A step forward. He closed the door behind him and shouted, OK, asshole—you say you want meet Jovan? Jovan's here, asshole! Come out here, piece of shit! This time I kill. No fuck around.

No fucking around! The bastard took the words out of my mouth. I remained silent and let him advance.

He yelled again, Come out here, dead piece of shit! Come out here, make it easy for Jovan!

The adrenaline flow helped, but I was beginning to feel weak and less and less sure of my aim.

As if on cue, he advanced again still yelling. You're roadkill, asshole.

Now he was in my reduced range. I swiveled in my chair, braced the pistol, called out to him, You're wrong, Jovan, and fired. Bingo! I got him where I wanted, in the right kneecap. The bastard was on the floor on his good side writhing with pain but managed to squeeze off a burst from the Glock in my general direction.

You're wasting ammo, Jovan, I told him. If you want to live, slide that Glock along the floor in my direction. You won't be needing it anymore. I'll count to three. If you don't do it, I'll kill you. ONE—TWO—

Somehow he struggled to his knees and fired again, two rounds this time, more accurately but still missing me. I fired too, one round. Bingo again. I got him in the belly.

All right, Jovan baby, I said, stomach wounds are bad. You're going to die. So talk to me. You're the asshole who makes telephone calls?

So what!

So nothing. You've got a nice sense of humor. You're also the prick who beat up my housekeeper?

The nigger? Yeah, I beat her. Stupid bitch, yelling and screaming.

I don't know how he mustered the strength, but he sat up and fired again. I'd gotten too confident, exposing my left shoulder, and that's where his bullet struck. He gave a weird whoop and fired again. So did I. This time he missed. I didn't. Smack between the eyes. R.I.P., Jovan.

The landline telephone rang. I staggered over, picked up the receiver, and said, Hi Sasha, sorry for the fireworks. Everything's under control. . . .

The next day, when she came to see me at the hospital, she told me that after I'd said those words the telephone went dead on my end. She didn't dare to rush over. Instead, she called the police. It was lucky that she did and that, it being nighttime, the ambulance was able to get there not long after the cruiser. I was unconscious from loss of blood. Jovan, of course, was dead.

The shootout at my house—I was getting used to calling it mine rather than Harry's now that I'd killed in it twice—made an even bigger splash on WLNY than the crash on Route 114, and it made the *New York Times* online Breaking News. Both Heidi and my agent told me later that it was all over the media, *Wall Street Journal,* tabloids, the *Daily Beast,* and TV talk shows included. The themes were what you'd expect: a gangland attack on a bestselling novelist and war hero in the normally quiet and crimeless village of Sag Harbor, speculations about a possible motive and the connection between the attack and my car being rammed on Route 114 some hours earlier, and, in some accounts but not all, questions about a possible link between these attacks and the assault on me at the same Sag Harbor house in the spring of 2012. Some featured more or less florid encomia to my courage and martial skills honed in the U.S. Marine Corps and deployments to Iraq and Afghanistan. The police had hardly any questions for me after I killed Slobo. This time I received in my Southampton Hospital room an afternoon visit of two detectives, one with the town of Southampton and the other with the Suffolk County police, accompanied by a young Suffolk County assistant district attorney. Beyond describing the attack, I told them, feeling Martin Sweeney's virtual presence at my elbow, that whether there was a connection between the incident on Route 114 and the attack at my house was a matter of conjecture, my own belief being that there was, that yes, I had received threats—I repeated almost verbatim what I had told Detective Walker after Jeanette was attacked—and no, I hadn't asked for police protection. Why? I felt I could take care of myself. That gave the three representatives of the forces of law and order an occasion for unrestrained hilarity and put an end to what might be thought of as a formal interrogation. Would I get in touch with them if any information came to me that could cast light on the reason for the attack and identify Jovan's employer or employers? I assured them I most certainly would. They in turn told me that a check of Jovan's fingerprints against various databases revealed his full name—Jovan Babić—and an extensive Serbian and Interpol file. He was wanted, with warrants outstanding for his arrest, on a rich assortment of charges, murder, drug dealing, illegal sale of organs for transplants, and human trafficking. A dossier not dissimilar to

Goran's. Jovan entered the United States on a tourist visa in 2009. That detail reminded me of Slobo, that other Serbian tourist. I expressed surprise at criminals' finding access to the U.S. so easy. Fucking Homeland Security, proffered the Suffolk County detective. Their screening isn't worth shit.

But Heidi had been to see me hours before that, right after I was moved from the recovery room to the room I was to occupy until discharge. She'd called my cell phone and landline numbers as soon as she woke up and was wondering whether she should next try the Southampton police, when her father, who was watching WLNY—I wouldn't have thought that local news was of great interest to people like the Krohns, but I was wrong—came into her room and told her what he'd just heard.

You're providing my parents with the most excitement they've had since Bibi Netanyahu came to lunch in East Hampton three years ago—he and a truckload of Mossad gorillas. They're so worked up that Father wouldn't let me borrow his car unless his chief of security drove me. What's going on, Captain? Two gunshot wounds? I thought you were invulnerable, that bullets just bounced off you!

When she lay on a gurney in this very hospital less than twenty-four hours earlier I thought that a lot of squeak had gone out of her. Obviously, she'd gotten it back and hadn't neglected her toilette in the rush to visit the wounded soldier.

I did better than that, I said. I used to catch them on the fly and throw them back at the towelheads. This time I tried it, but it didn't work. I must be out of practice. But this way I get to see you first thing in the morning in a glamorous red sweater that matches your running shoes!

Tsk, tsk, she replied. If those friends of yours hadn't run me off the road you'd have seen me this morning at your own house in my white silk pajamas! I might even have brought you breakfast in bed.

Can I have a guaranteed rain check on that?

Yes, as many as you like. But when will they let you out of here, Captain, and what are the next steps?

The easy question first. The surgeon, who served with the army in Iraq and actually treated bullet wounds and knows what he's doing, wants to keep me here till Wednesday. Both wounds are flesh wounds, there are no injuries to the bone, but he did have to dig out the bullet that hit me in the shoulder. Then I go home and follow up with a colleague of his at New York–Presbyterian. No problem. I'll have Feng come out and drive me back to the city. But I'm afraid it can't be in the Mini. The surgeon said the choice is between an ambulance and a car in which I can push the seat way back and stretch out.

Don't worry about the Mini, she said. Mr. Mahoney will take care of it. If Feng takes the Jitney or the train to East Hampton, Mr. Mahoney will also lend him Mom's station wagon that's in the garage here. Feng doesn't have to return it. The all-powerful Mahoney will provide. He'll have it picked up.

I want to meet Mr. Mahoney. Can we put him on Abner's case? Other steps. Once I get to New York, I can pretty much lead a normal life, except for running, which will have to wait some weeks, work with weights, and Krav Maga. No limits on martinis or pasta *aglio e olio*! More serious matters. Jovan is the guy who attacked Jeanette and the stand-up comic who used to call me. He won't bother anyone anymore. I'll be sure to offer my condolences to Abner, even though I'm not sure he'll really miss Jovan. Something tells me he has other boys in reserve. I'll call Martin Sweeney and see whether he and Lee have any news about Lena and Boris. If we nail Boris that will be mission accomplished so far as lowlife goons are concerned. That leaves us with the big decision: Do we keep looking for Kerry's other file—and how long do we keep looking—before we take what you've got to Ed Flanagan? Or do we take what we've got to him on the assumption that it will be enough to bury Abner without more?

She'd been nodding as I spoke and remained silent for a moment after I stopped. Then she said, Let's give ourselves a week or perhaps ten days to see whether we can deliver the coup de grâce. I haven't tried hard enough to find the other file. I guess I've tried to think logically about where it might be when I should have been free-associating.

I'll do the same, I said. Apropos of free association, I'm overcome by the feeling that you should come to dinner at the apartment on Thursday and sample Feng's Cantonese cuisine. It's good. Your cover—if you ever had one—has been blown. They know you and I are connected, so there's no more reason for you to stay away from Fifth Avenue.

Miss Krohn likes your instincts and accepts with pleasure, she told me, and put her hand on mine. It's too bad you've lost the knack of catching bullets on the fly, but I'm so happy that the ones you missed haven't done more harm.

Good, I answered. Then we have a date. And there is one more step to be mentioned. That's security for you. I hope your father will have his people on the job from the moment you arrive at your apartment. Abner is a murderous thug.

He will. I promise.

The floor nurse stuck her head in the door and said, Mr. Dana, the doctor was very clear. Short visits only. I'm very sorry, young lady, but the patient needs an injection and some rest.

Demerol is an old friend. I welcomed him. The wounds had begun to throb and hurt. Later that day Mary and Sasha came to see me.

You saved my life, I said to Sasha. I didn't call the police after taking the first bullet because I didn't want that goon to get away. But I was cutting it too close.

I'm glad for once I followed my instincts, she replied. If only I had the night when Harry was killed. . . .

I telephoned Scott and Martin. They both offered to come to Southampton. I said it might be better to plan to get together after I returned to the city. I also spoke with Feng and could tell that he had no doubt I wouldn't have come to harm if he had been at my side.

I saved Abner for dessert and called him right after the two policemen and the assistant D.A. departed. The only number I had was his office number, but what the hell! Don't tycoons sometimes work at their private offices late on Sunday afternoon, especially tycoons who are elbows deep in crime? If he wasn't there I'd leave a message. Wouldn't bother me any if the honey-tongued Eileen listened to it before telling her boss there was a voice message he should hear.

By golly! The southern belle came on. For the first time, I heard a tremor in her voice when she heard mine.

I'll see whether Abner is available, she cooed, Captain Dana.

He was, and greeted me pleasantly: How do I get rid of you, asshole? Do you spend your life calling people who don't want to hear from you? Who wish you'd never been born?

It's easy, I answered. Hire killers who can shoot straight. Not like the late regretted Jovan. But you're on the right track. You gave me Jovan, and I give you my condolences. Now give me Boris.

I can't, asshole, nobody on earth can. Now fuck off!

XII

The dinner to which I invited Heidi at my apartment had to be postponed. The doctors suspected deep vein thrombosis, put me on heparin, and it wasn't until Tuesday of the following week that Feng treated us to a feast that began with three kinds of dumplings and progressed through lemon chicken and spicy pork to a small but entire steamed bass in black-bean sauce and, finally, hot-and-sour soup. We drank martinis, prepared by Feng—I was obeying doctor's orders and mostly keeping my leg up—and a dry Alsatian Riesling, a case of which Feng found in Harry's wine cellar down in the building's basement, a treasure trove that, to my shame, I'd left unexplored.

While I was still at the hospital, Sasha and Mary, and, during the weekend, Heidi had come to visit and brought smoked salmon and roast beef sandwiches as relief from Southampton Hospital fare, and I had been in all-too-frequent telephone contact with Martin Sweeney. Still, sitting in my own library before an open fire, sipping martini number two and admiring, as I did each time I saw her, Heidi's good looks and chic—that evening she wore black patent-leather pumps, black velvet trousers, and an ivory silk shirt, pleated like a man's dress shirt, that she said had been made for her in Hong Kong while she was conducting the defense in a construction arbitration—I succumbed shamelessly to that most banal of self-congratulatory feelings. They made me want to postpone beyond that evening the inevitable discussion with Heidi of a new development. Let it wait, let it wait, I kept thinking, none of it can be repaired. Concentrate on remembering that it's good to be alive, to know that my wounds will leave scars but no other trace, and to spar with that young woman, alternately so effervescent and acerbic.

Feng had just served the fish when I told Heidi how happy I felt to be with her, at home, over dinner.

I like you too, Captain, she replied, and Kerry was the sister I had always wanted. That's why we have to talk about her even as we try not to swallow a fish bone.

You're right, I said. So I might as well give you the news. Martin and Lee were here yesterday afternoon, late; they marched in perhaps an hour after I arrived and told me about Lena. It's not good. The cell-phone number Johnnie the Rat gave me was a good lead. Calling in various IOUs at the Bureau—Lee is also a retired special agent—they were able to get Lena's last name. Radetska. A Russian immigrant, legal, green-card status. Presumably Jewish. They found her address, a studio apartment way east on Ninety-Seventh Street. The super told them he hadn't seen her in a month. That makes it the beginning of this month—you see the significance—but he was unable to pinpoint the specific date on which he had last seen her. Pressed about her private life—was she, as Lee put it to him, a hooker?—the super said, A working girl. Masseuse or maybe manicurist. He was able, however, to direct them to her place of employment, a spa on East Forty-Seventh Street. The sort of establishment you'd expect. Up on the third and fourth floors, massage and bath and sex. Actually quite clean. There the owner—or perhaps manager—was more precise. The last time she saw Lena was on Thursday, October third. You see also the significance of that. Kerry was killed the following evening. The reason the manager was positive about the date is that Lena was owed money for Thursday's work and did not turn up to claim it. Incidentally, she didn't work on weekends, so that she was free on Fridays and Saturdays, the big nights at the Rat. Any knowledge of Lena's family? None. Never heard the family referred to. The manager is Hispanic. Among the masseuses there are a few Asians. The rest are a potpourri of Eastern and Central Europeans. A couple of Moldovans, a Czech, a couple of Romanians. Lee went back there several times and talked to the girls. The idea that Lena might be Jewish provoked varying degrees of surprise or acquiescence. Yes, one of the Moldovans said, there is an aunt or maybe an aunt and an uncle living somewhere in Brooklyn. But she didn't know the names. Didn't think it was Radetska. On top of that, a check of White Pages or whatever else Martin and Lee consulted did not produce any Radetskas or Radetskys of interest. This much I knew already last week.

That's certainly a dead end, said Heidi.

You're making an unintended pun, I told her. That's where they stopped, but, having listened to them I asked whether there wasn't some sort of lost and found for corpses. You know, unknown and unclaimed civilians. People who are found dead, without ID, victims of attacks or dead from other causes. Yeah, they both answered, the morgue. Usually there's something about it in the tabloid local news. So I said since we've gotten nowhere with the leads the super gave you, do you think it would be worthwhile to check on unclaimed dead? Our bad, Martin told me. We'll get right on it. Well, I'm beginning to think I should have been a cop. Through their sources they discovered that on Saturday morning—the day after Kerry was killed—the body of a white woman in her twenties or early thirties, fully clothed, was found slumped in a doorway of a building on West Thirty-Eighth Street. Guess what! Overdose. Heroin. Now kudos to Martin and Lee. They slipped the super a hundred and drove him over to the morgue. There's not the slightest doubt. They keep the bodies on ice for ninety days, you know. It's Lena Radetska. Lena Radetska, whose face, Martin thinks, had been slapped hard.

Whoa, the police didn't do a fingerprint search? Heidi asked. If she was here on a green card her fingerprints must be in a thousand files. What's going on here?

I'll tell you Martin's view. There's a huge flow of heroin into the city, and the price has fallen. Obviously use has picked up, and so have overdose deaths. Lena was dressed like a hooker, looked like a hooker. That she had no ID, in fact no pocketbook, means a companion or companions robbed her. Perhaps moved her from where she died to that doorway. Incidentally, that building houses no fewer than three spas that are more like brothels. So—says Martin—a dime-a-dozen case that didn't call for the investigative effort of New York's finest. And, continues Martin, what do you know? Who was in charge of the case and called it closed? Yes, your friend Detective Rod Walker. No doubt a coincidence, but still . . .

Do you know what will happen to Lena now?

You mean her earthly remains? After I don't know how many weeks—I forgot to ask Martin—unless someone claims her, it's Potter's Field. Hart Island Cemetery, out in Pelham Bay.

Poor thing. She came here from wherever it was . . .

Ukraine, I interjected.

Why not? Of course she came from Ukraine, like some of my ancestors, expecting better things. It's awful.

The tough white-collar-crime defense attorney and former prosecutor has a sweet, tender side, I said to myself, and poured her some more Riesling.

Yes please, keep going, she told me. I feel sick. The kind of sick that gets better with good wine. And what do we do about Boris, Captain? Isn't he next on our list?

He is, I replied, and quite frankly I don't know. Neither do Martin and Lee. All we have is the first name, which can be Ukrainian, Russian, Bulgarian—in fact, it fits all over the non-Greek Balkans. Or he could be an Argentinean tango instructor as well as a pimp! Assuming that Boris is his real first name! Anyway, Martin and Lee are searching arrest records, and obviously convictions, involving anyone with that first name. Anyone, not just pimps and pushers. But they're discouraged. Have you any bright ideas?

She looked gloomy and shook her head.

I don't either, I said, but I haven't tried yet free-associating.

Apropos of that, any progress breaking into Kerry's email account?

Again she shook her head. I try a different password every morning, hoping that one attempt a day isn't enough for Google to lower the boom, but I haven't hit the jackpot. Besides, I'm beginning to doubt that Kerry would have tucked the file away in her mail account. That was probably a silly idea. She would have come up with something more inventive and more secure. I don't think we'll ever find that file. We should just go to Ed Flanagan with what I've got, if only to end this nightmare, to stop that son of a bitch in Texas from doing more harm. I'd rather he didn't kill you. You know that so long as he thinks you're the one who has the file, he'll keep trying.

I agree, and I know it's crazy, but that's in part the reason why I'd like to wait a little longer. I'd like him to send another hit man. I'd like the chance to kill him. Particularly if he sent Boris!

You are seriously crazy, she told me, especially considering your current condition. But let's give ourselves another week. No more than that, because there is another side to this problem: Abner is a one-man crime wave. As citizens we have a duty to stop him. Now I have a question: how badly damaged are you?

I couldn't help laughing. If you're buying, it depends on the intended use. I wouldn't want to deal with Abner's hit men tonight or tomorrow or the next day, unless I can do it sitting down. But there are better days ahead. The blood clot was caught so early, it was so fresh, that the doctors think it's been dissolved or absorbed or whatever it is they call it.

That part should be cleared up by the end of the week. The wounds are flesh wounds. I heal very well. In a very few weeks they'll be just a memory.

Will you give them a chance to heal, so you'll be as good as new?

I nodded. Don't worry! Just like a certified preowned Mercedes.

We finished our coffee. She turned down my offer of a cognac or single-malt scotch, saying she had to go home to prepare for a deposition first thing the next morning.

Are you walking? I asked.

Yes, but Dad's security guy will have my back, and I'll call you when I get home. Though I've got to say I'm cross, she added, all evening I've waited for an invitation to another dinner that never came, and yet here I am, not going out of town, and free every evening!

During the rest of that week I went to the hospital for checkups, received reports from increasingly frustrated Martin and Lee, lunched at home with Simon Lathrop, wrote as much as five hours a day, and, of course—a warrior's reward—had nightly dinner with Heidi. Don't be fooled, Captain, she'd tell me. I'm really coming for Feng's soups and dumplings, not your conversation. An unspoken question was seldom far from my mind. Is it possible that I'm falling in love—let's not kid ourselves, have fallen in love—with this beguiling little witch? Even though it's clear that she can't and won't love me? At the edge of that question, which I didn't care to answer, I reasoned with myself. Of course, she likes you. She's well intentioned and good-natured, and you're an interesting and not-unattractive sort of fellow. But the teasing and flirting mean nothing. She can't help casting her spells any more than she can help being beautiful and elegant. Enjoy being with her as much and as long as she'll let you, but don't be a knucklehead, don't take any of it seriously.

The result was work so concentrated that four days later, on Saturday morning, I completed my draft and was able to tell Heidi, when she called shortly afterward to confirm our dinner date at eight, that we'd have martinis as usual, but after the meal we'd drink a bottle of very good champagne. It's the least we can do, I said. I have trouble believing it, but I've actually finished the goddamn book! All that's left is revisions. I'm getting right on them.

Unless, I added, you want to come over right now!

How I wish I could, she told me, but I'm at the office working and when I finish I have to hit the gym.

All right, I said. I'll revise. Might as well keep going.

That's what I did. A lot of what's involved in correcting the text of a true story like my account of Harry's murder and the revenge that followed is mechanical. You have to make sure that you haven't screwed up the chronology and that you've got right the places where you say you've been and the events that occurred there. I try to pay attention to such details as I go along, and each day, when I sit down to write, I first go over and correct what I wrote the day before, then write my obligatory thirteen hundred words, and, before I quit, I take a first crack at correcting that chunk of text as well. Like everyone who writes on a computer, I keep saving my text probably more often than is absolutely necessary. At the end

of the day I take an extra precaution: I send the new text
to myself as an attachment to a separate email account that
I use for no other purpose: jdanatexts@gmail.com. Having
lost several thumb drives that I used as backstops in the past,
I've settled on this method as the surest. Yes, one can imagine Armageddon in which all of Google's servers would per-
ish, but if they did is it likely that, even if I were among the
survivors, I would have nothing more urgent to worry about
than my drafts? Or that there would still be readers eager for
my new book? I never visit the jdanatexts account until I've
completed the draft of a book unless, as has happened once,
my laptop crashed and I plunged into jdanatexts to fish out
and download the still current drafts to my new machine.
But, when the draft is complete, I find immense satisfaction
in opening the account and deleting the daily accretion of
documents: chapter 1 as of such and such date, chapter 1 two
days later, and on and on. It's like cleaning out your closet
and throwing out running shoes you've worn so long and so
hard they have holes in them. During a pause in revising, I
was happily deleting away, whistling off-key "It's been a hard
day's night," when suddenly I was brought up short. All those
emails I sent to myself showed up as jackdanany with the
subject line below. This one was different: kerryblack22 —
Kerry's Gmail address that, before she left me, I'd see pop up
on my G-chat screen whenever she had a free moment and
could send a message, often just a few words followed by a
smiley, to tell me she loved me, that she was thinking of our
embraces. The subject line was URGENT-PLEASE READ.
I realized that my hands were trembling. I leaned hard on
my desk, controlled the tremor, and opened the email. The

date jumped out at me: October 3, 2013, the day before she died. There were two attachments. I read the message with a mixture of elation and horror:

Dearest Jack,

Please believe me. I've never stopped loving you. I should have understood that you couldn't stop yourself from killing that awful man—Slobo the Voice—not after having heard the recording of how he murdered Harry. Lord knows, you gave me fair warning that that was what you would do. But I got myself stuck in a groove of self-righteous indignation and once in it I didn't know how to escape until it was too late, until I had sunk into such ignominious degradation that once you had understood it you would have had to reject me. Even if you had wanted to take me back, I wouldn't have let you. You are honorable and good. Far too good for trash like me.

Jack, my love, I hid so much from you. I thought I had to, if I was to have a chance to keep you. Now I think I made a mistake. If you had known from the beginning who I really was, you might have—because you are so generous and strong—taken me as I really am. You might have helped me. It's too late for that.

I have the file that swine Will Hobson and his sidekick Fred Minot tried so hard to find in Harry's papers. It's far more detailed than the road map he hid in your great-grandfather's Bible. There is ten times more than enough in it to put Abner Brown behind bars for life without possibility of parole. Since his crimes gave support to terrorist organiza-

tions, perhaps he's fodder for the capital punishment machine. I haven't researched that point. Harry must have had a premonition of what would happen: the murderer sent to kill him, the frantic search through his papers at Jones & Whetstone, at his homes. The file was too bulky to conceal in a Bible or a similar hiding place, and he must have known that his safe wasn't secure. They'd get it opened. So he came up with an astonishingly nutty solution. He placed the file in the Jones & Whetstone vault maintained at the firm's principal bank and marked the envelope "Kerry Black Personal—Last Will and Testament and Estate Planning." That's something partners are allowed to do with their important personal papers. But without telling me about it! So as not to expose me to danger, I'm sure. What he didn't think through is that the file might have lain there forever—well, not forever but almost—since not knowing that it existed I would have never called for it.

Except for a weird coincidence. Last week, I received a notice from the firm's archives manager listing the files existing under my name in the firm's vault and asking whether they should continue to be maintained there or otherwise disposed of. There are limitations of space. The only file with my name on it was this file that Harry created. Since I had no memory of any such thing, I asked for it to be brought to my office and, inside the double sealed envelope, I found the documents and a note from Harry to me, dated 11/1/12, or, as we now know, a few weeks after Hobson threw him out of the firm and started spreading the lie that Harry was demented. The note, which you'll find with the documents, said: "Kerry, forgive me for making you the temporary custodian of this file. I'm too distraught right now to think of another way *of protecting it. As you will see, it's office documents, documents taken by me from Abner Brown's file, my own analysis of his criminal business. All of it is clearly covered by the attorney-client privilege. I have decided, however, that I will turn this material over to the government, and have given Abner one last chance to come clean before I do. I told him over the telephone that he has until January 15 of next year to meet with the U.S. attorney in Houston, or with the Justice Department—whichever his new lawyer Will Hobson advises—and bargain for a reduced sentence on the basis that he has come forward voluntarily. If he does not do that, I warned him, I will deliver the file personally to the Criminal Division of the Department of Justice. I hope to God he will do the right thing."*

Poor Harry! You know what happened in reality.

Next week, I am scheduled to appear before the grand jury sitting in Alexandria that's finally digging deep into Abner's personal involvement in the crimes committed by his companies. I will take with me Harry's file and another one I have myself assembled, and give them to the government. If I am alive.

I'm scared, Jack, very scared. Two days after I withdrew Harry's file from the safe, I got a call from Hobson. You know that he's now with the Houston law firm, doing Abner's dirty work and raking in cash. "Listen you little bitch," he told me, "you've stolen a shitload of Abner Brown's documents from Jones & Whetstone and want to present them to that Mickey Mouse grand jury in Alexandria. You do that and I'll have you disbarred. As Abner Brown's attorney, I hereby order you to surrender them to me. I knew we should never have

*made you a partner." As you see, he's learned Abnerspeak. I'd
never heard anything like it coming out of his mouth before.
I replied in kind—up yours, Will. And I hung up. Then I
cried and cried because I know they will kill me. My darling
Jack, if they do it, it will probably be just as well. Let them.
I deserve it for the way I've lived since I left you. There is no
other way out of the hole I'm in, and I'm too chicken to do it
myself.*

*There was a leak at Jones & Whetstone—certainly about
the documents I've culled from the files and perhaps, although
I can't imagine how, about Harry's file that had been in the
vault, and a leak at Justice or the U.S. Attorney's Office in
Alexandria. Those swine have their fingers in every pie.*

*Give Harry's file to Ed Flanagan—you remember him, the
U.S. attorney in New York. Don't try to avenge me. They'll
just kill you. There is no need for you to die as well.*

*Scanned images of Harry's file are attached. I've sent them
with this letter to your jdanatexts account because no one will
think to look for it there. The original is in your name at Mail
Boxes, Etc., corner of 86th Street and Third Avenue, in a box
I've rented in your name.*

*My own file, the one I assembled while combing through
the office files of the associates who did due diligence on the
aborted public offering of Abner's holding company, I'm
sending to my closest friend, Heidi Krohn. Next to you, she's
the best person in the world. If something happens to me—as
I know it will—she'll get in touch with you. Please trust her
as you would trust me. Standing alone, the file she has should
be enough to put Abner Brown away. Put it together with
Harry's, and he hasn't got a chance.*

This letter is for you only. Also attached to this email is an "official" letter you will be able to show to the U.S. attorney.

Goodbye, my darling, try not to think of me too harshly even when you'll know everything. Remember instead how much I loved you—from the first moment I saw you.

She signed—Kerry. And inserted a little smiley.

I got up from my desk, staggered to the liquor cabinet in the pantry, and poured myself a stiff bourbon. Having gulped it down, I poured another, added two ice cubes, and went back to my laptop. The other letter was short. Dear Jack, she wrote,

The attached electronic file consists of scanned images of documents prepared and assembled by your uncle, Harold C. Dana, in order to show the extent of the criminal enterprises engaged in by companies owned or controlled by Abner Brown, and Brown's own personal involvement in such activities. The originals I have sent to a box opened in your name at Mail Boxes, Etc.—

Here she gave the address.

I am taking these precautions because, having been threatened by William S. Hobson, formerly chairman of Jones & Whetstone and now Abner Brown's principal lawyer at Lindsey & Graham, Houston, I am in fear of my life.

This file supplements, of course, the memorandum as to the functioning of Abner Brown's criminal enterprises found in Harold Dana's library shortly after his death last year and

delivered to Edward X. Flanagan, Esq., U.S. attorney for the Southern District of New York, at a meeting attended by you, myself, and certain others. It is my hope that you will now deliver this file as well to Mr. Flanagan or such persons as he may designate.

Your friend,
Kerry Black

I opened the second attachment, the file for the possession of which Kerry was murdered, and scrolled down it feverishly. Although I was reading much too fast about subjects and transactions I understood incompletely or not at all, enough of the sense got through to convince me that this was it. Once the government had these documents, Abner's goose was cooked.

Must go for a run, I whispered. Old automatism. Running was my remedy for acute distress, as well as a way to keep fit. Then the throbbing in my thigh reminded me of my gimpy leg and the arm that the surgeon suggested I keep quiet for a while, in a sling, as much as possible. Feng was in the kitchen when I reached the pantry. I poured myself another drink. Heidi was due for dinner at eight-thirty. It was a few minutes before six. I told Feng I would lie down and asked him to wake me if I wasn't stirring by eight.

She arrived exactly on time, wearing a knee-length black velvet dress with long sleeves and a little white collar—I teased her about the new habit of punctuality, due entirely, I claimed, to respect for Feng's culinary prowess—and said she was starved. I made our customary martinis and let her demolish a good two-thirds of the plate of canapés before speaking of Kerry's email. My laptop was in the library. I had brought it there on purpose, opened my texts account, and said, Please read. I've told Feng to hold the dinner. He's sure it's not a problem. She read Kerry's letters quickly and started to cry, more and more uncontrollably. The sons of bitches, she muttered, the fucking sons of bitches.

Yes, I said, now stop crying, we're on to the thing that Kerry wanted us to have. Please look at the file and see whether it's the dynamite she thought it was.

Just like Kerry, half the time she didn't have a handkerchief in her handbag, and I had become fond of giving her mine. She wiped her eyes, blew her nose, put on her reading glasses—which I had never seen her use before—and started to read with intense concentration.

After about fifteen minutes, she put down her glasses, shook her head as though to chase a headache, and said, Yes, this is it. Kerry wasn't fooling herself. This is enough to hang Abner and take down a bunch of his cronies. I must say I don't understand your uncle. What possessed him? Why didn't he take this stuff and whatever else he had to the U.S. attorney?

I wish I could give you a convincing answer. Simon Lathrop, his best friend at the law firm and classmate at law school, would say that this was pure Harry, the incredible straight arrow and stickler for rules. I guess given the enormity of what he found he thought he ought to remonstrate, or whatever you call it, with that bastard once again before violating the privilege, and give him that chance to come clean. There is another possible reason that I don't like. I wouldn't mention it to anyone other than you. Harry sometimes lacked resolution. His nerve failed him. He's paid dearly for it. For being such a straight arrow and for the irresolution.

That's right, Heidi answered. So has Kerry. And so has that poor Jeanette.

Stop, I said. I can't bear to hear this.

We had another martini, mostly in silence.

Over dinner, finally Heidi said, Look, Jack, there is no do-over. We better follow Kerry's instructions. Take her file and my file to Ed Flanagan, and let him take it from there. If you like, I'll come with you to authenticate the file Kerry sent to me. You should probably tell your friend Scott what we have and what we're doing. From what I've seen, the Agency will go ape over this stuff.

You're right, I replied. Give me a few days, though. I want to hear whether Martin and Lee have made any progress on Boris. And I would like to see Simon Lathrop once again. An idea is taking shape in my mind. To carry it out I will need his help.

Yup, she said. Boys will be boys! Is Feng off on Sunday night?

He should be, I said, but he won't take time off.

Then may I come to dinner? I'll start paying for my board. Thank God, given the chic of this place, I don't have to pay for my room.

I'd give it to you free, I told her. Yes, definitely come to dinner. But tell me one thing: what kind of security do you have during the weekend or, for that matter, when you're at home? My new idea may make Abner more dangerous in the short term than ever.

I'm embarrassed to tell you. She laughed. There's someone

from Father's security following me all day. Then I discovered there was also a guy sitting in the lobby of my building all night. I told Father that was intolerable, really a cruel way to treat someone, so he said there were two solutions. I could move in with you, in which case you'd be my bodyguard, or the guy has to be in my place. I told Father he should be ashamed of himself, pushing me into the arms of a goy! So there's a series of Mossad types who spend the night in my apartment. In the spare room! So that's the deal. It's worse than a chastity belt.

XIII

The following Tuesday was Election Day. I lunched with Simon Lathrop at his grand club. We'd both voted for Christine Quinn and had the unpleasant feeling that Bill de Blasio would be our next mayor. I didn't want to tell this extremely proper old man the sordid story of Lena's and Boris's end and thought there was no real need for it. So after we'd exchanged brief expressions of regret that Mike Bloomberg couldn't be New York's mayor for life, I came straight to the point.

Simon, I said, what with one thing and another—I pointed to my left arm, which I had just slipped out of the sling, and then in the direction of my thigh—I haven't kept in touch the way I should have. But I need your help.

Of course, dear boy, and don't worry about not lunching more often with this old body. I know you've been writing and have had an unscheduled adventure.

I thanked him and reminded him about Kerry's file that was in Heidi's possession and told him about my discovery of

Kerry's other file in my text email account and, to the extent I could, described what the file contained.

I should tell you, I continued, that Kerry clearly thought that the material in the file she sent to me was covered by the attorney-client privilege. Probably she thought the same was true of what she sent to Heidi Krohn. Nevertheless, she'd decided that she was taking all those files with her to Alexandria in order to deliver them to the grand jury. I've determined that I'm going to give that file, which I now have in my possession, as well as Heidi's file—she's completely on board with that—to Ed Flanagan. I thought I should tell you that. I realize it creates a problem for Jones & Whetstone, but I believe it can't be helped. Abner Brown belongs behind bars for life. For many lives, if only that were possible!

Simon covered his face with his hands and was silent for a long moment. When he spoke he said, Yes, it will be a problem for the firm. Incidentally, I think it's not just a matter of attorney-client privilege, which was an issue when you took Harry's road map to Flanagan. This time, Kerry appears to have stolen law-firm property. The poor thing is dead, so that's probably irrelevant. Certainly the firm can have no recourse against her. But there is a different and serious problem. Could the firm have criminal liability by reason of having constructive—or perhaps actual—knowledge of what Abner was doing? Part of me wants to examine your and Heidi's files. The part of me that's like an ostrich and wants to stick its head in the sand says: Leave it alone. If there's a living culprit it's our disgraced former presiding partner, Hobson. He's in Houston, and if they go after him, so much the better. If poor Harry was in some way culpable, he's in a place Flanagan and his colleagues can't reach him. So I think the ostriches have it! I don't want to look at your files.

Thank you! The last thing I want, I told him, is to cause trouble for you or more pain. But I do need your help. I want to confront Abner; in fact I want to show him the goods we have on him. I'd like to time it so that we see each other the day before I'm scheduled to meet with Flanagan. Of course, I'd make sure that the files will get to Flanagan on the appointed day whatever happens to me. If possible, I'd like to see Abner in New York, perhaps when he's here for a board meeting. Is there a way you could find out when that might be?

Simon laughed and said, That's easy. We're both still on the board of the museum; in fact we're on the executive committee. Why I haven't strangled him at one of our sessions is a mystery. Or rather a proof of my senescence. Let's see when we meet next.

Simon must be one of the last men alive in the industrialized world not to keep his appointments on a computer and a smartphone. He extracted from the inside pocket of his beautifully tailored navy-blue suit coat a carmine Smythson pocket calendar, adjusted his reading glasses, and turned pages.

You're in luck. He chuckled. Next Wednesday morning, a week from tomorrow, executive committee, followed by a full board meeting on Thursday. He's bound to attend and spend at least Wednesday night in the city. In fact, he might spend the weekend. Linda—that's his wife—likes the theater.

How convenient, I said. According to gossip columns—

I've Googled the bastard—he lives on Fifth Avenue, right across the street from the zoo.

Simon nodded. In an apartment full of armor! Don't yield to temptation and beat him into a pulp with a mace!

That will be hard to resist, I answered, but I'll do my best.

As we were leaving the club I told him that instead of accompanying him to his office on foot as usual, I'd have to take a cab.

Doctor's orders!

God bless you, my boy, he answered. I'll walk. If you go, as I had to, to the trouble of getting an artificial hip, you feel duty bound to use it.

What happened to Boris, to the extent we could verify it, was indeed sordid and terrifying. I am certain I was right to spare Simon the account. The leads—there were hardly any except more chatter among the masseuses at the spa where Lena had worked—about her being picked up after work or being brought to the spa occasionally by a big black-haired guy whom they thought they heard her call Boris, but to whom she never introduced them, were useless. How many big black-haired men were there in the five boroughs and the greater metropolitan area? And if you narrowed it down to the subset among them that frequented girls like Lena, where were you?

Zilch, said Martin. The bastard's disappeared. Gone back to Lower Slobbovia. Joined the marines. Jack, I'm genuinely sorry to be wasting your money looking for him. If he turns up, it'll be exactly when we're not looking for him and when we least want to find him.

Of course he and Lee checked the morgue. Lena's case taught them that. Nada.

So matters stood until Sunday, two days ago. Martin called me first thing in the morning and said, Jack, I bet you haven't read the *News*.

You know I don't read it, I answered. Why?

Why? Listen to this. I'll read you a short item that appeared this morning. Are you sitting down?

MUTILATED BODY FOUND BY BIRD-WATCHERS

Sunday, November 3, 2013. A party of bird-watchers, led by Joshua Phillips, a Columbia history professor and noted ornithologist, made a grisly discovery while hiking yesterday in the Norton Basin Natural Resource Area. Lying on its back in the immediate vicinity of multi-family homes on Bay 32nd Street, Queens, was the mutilated body of a white male. According to the Police Department's spokesman, the body had been beheaded and the fingers of both hands had been chopped off. None of these remains could be seen in the vicinity of the body, and the spokesman speculated that they had been disposed of somewhere else. No papers of any sort were found in the corpse's clothing. Based on the condition of the corpse, the murder occurred between four and eight weeks ago. The police are investigating.

Holy shit! I exclaimed. Do you suppose that's Boris? Abner's an accurate son of a bitch. He told me, when I called him from the hospital after killing Jovan, that neither he nor anyone on earth could send Boris to me. That must be Boris. They killed him after he killed Lena, or they killed them both—perhaps the same day.

Could be, replied Martin. We're on our way to the morgue. That's real cute, cutting off a guy's fingers to get rid of his fingerprints.

Martin has a soft side you'd never suspect, I said to myself, remembering the nameless archer on Torcello whose finger I'd cut off to send to Scott so his fingerprints could be studied. A useless undertaking, as it turned out.

He called me late that afternoon. I'd gotten impatient, wondering what had held him up. He and Lee were together, and he had conferenced Lee in on his cell phone so they could both speak to me. The body was a horrific sight, they said, the neck severed as though with a dull saw.

I hope they shot the guy before they did it, Lee interjected. I saw a guy decapitated in Pakistan, but never anything like this.

I wouldn't count on it, was Martin's comment. They sawed the fingers too. Didn't use a knife or a cleaver. Sawed. Fucking sadists.

Anyway, he continued, there was a tattoo on the right forearm. A weird sort of cross—above the regular beam, you know, to which Christ's hands were nailed, there's another short beam parallel to it, and way under the regular beam another short beam slanting from left to right. I took a picture and I'll send it to you.

That's OK, I interrupted, it's an Orthodox cross. Used in Russia and Ukraine and all over the Balkans. Keep going, please!

The bastards didn't see it, Martin said, because they didn't bother to strip the body. They missed something else that's really weird too. The guy had a tiny letter *b* in Cyrillic tattooed on his prick! I know it's a *b* and the morgue attendant who's Russian confirmed it!

Holy shit! I practically screamed into the telephone, I didn't know you could have your prick tattooed.

Believe me, it's not frequent, Martin replied, but it does happen. This guy must have been real proud of his dick. Like his Stradivarius.

I winced when he said that.

Anyway, after that Lee and I got on the phone to Pablo, you know, the bartender at the club. He lives in Washington Heights. Our call woke him up. I told him I thought we'd found Boris—murdered—and would he get over to the morgue to identify him. He went into a song and dance about how he was tired and his wife would kill him if he went downtown. To make a long story short, I offered him five hundred. Jack, I hope you don't mind?

Good God, no!

Well, that got him into a taxi in a flash. We waited for him outside the building and brought him in. Bingo. Same arm, same cross, he said. I saw the cross real clear at the club. Then he rushed to the toilet and vomited.

You and Lee certainly have the run of the morgue, I said stupidly.

Captain Jack—Martin laughed—Lee and I combined have fifty-plus years in the Bureau. If that didn't give us an entrée or two, there'd be something seriously wrong. All kidding aside, I think we've got what's left of Boris. We'll never be able to prove it forensically, of course, unless his DNA's in the database. The chances of that aren't high.

The news that Boris—or the man we called by the name, who I had no doubt killed Kerry—was now most probably dead too, murdered, I had to believe, by Abner's thugs, left me speechless and drained. I couldn't rejoice; I couldn't even bring myself to say anything grotesquely banal like He had it coming or It couldn't have happened to a nicer guy. I was numb.

Finally I said, Since we're not going to look for whoever murdered Boris, I guess we've run out of the killers who actually do Abner's dirty work. That leaves us with the master puppeteer himself, Mr. Abner Brown.

No, Simon had no need to hear this ghastly story. But I could now hope to get thoughts about Boris out of my head and concentrate on the final task before me. I had a week to lay the ground. A lot of time, but not too much. But while resolving to forget Boris seemed easy enough, making good on the resolution turned out to be no more possible than to forget Kerry. Horribly, obscenely, the two were intertwined. Pimps are like catnip, Johnnie had said. The vigorous although not necessarily violent sex, including anal. Now the images of his tattooed prick and forearm. Did she draw her finger over the cross when they sat at the bar? Did she suck the monogrammed prick, when she lay down on the bed at that hotel? What kind of idiot are you, I screamed at myself, how can there be any doubt she sucked? But she wasn't lying on the bed. She was on her knees, gagging and sucking and gagging. He would have told her: Suck big little Boris, bitch. Or filth worse than that.

It was ten o'clock. Heidi didn't come to dinner; she went instead with her parents to a nephew's bar mitzvah, having told them that she invited me but really with my bum leg I couldn't go to a service where I would have to sit more than twenty minutes without taking a few steps and certainly couldn't stand up at a reception. I put on a sweater and the blazer I'd worn when I went down to Le Raton and had a taxi take me to Hotel Leblon, a block west from the Rat. Two old wrecks, the canes of the fatter one and the walker belonging to the other at their side, were sprawled catatonically in adjoining armchairs. Nylons rolled down to the ankles. Feet in orthopedic shoes that once were black. Band-Aids covering sores on knees and calves. Wearing something like housedresses. The fatter one almost bald. No one else in the lobby. I knew from Martin that the night man who was on duty on Friday nights was there through Tuesday. Besides, the description matched: Golden Gloves–boxer type gone to seed, cauliflower ear.

Technology hadn't caught up with Leblon. Behind the night man was a board with room keys hanging off little hooks. All that was missing were pigeon holes for the guests' messages and bills.

Speak to me, I said, putting on my best Sam Spade growl, and dropped two C notes on the desk.

What do you want, he replied, palming the bills and putting them in his pocket.

Tell me what happened the night Kerry Black overdosed in 522.

You a cop? I've talked to you guys. Show me your badge.

I'm not. I was her boyfriend before she dumped me.

Sorry, chum. It was good riddance.

Maybe it was, I replied, but I want to know. Tell me what happened.

Nothing happened. I told the cops all there's to tell. There was a fucking detective, pushy son of a bitch, Walker or Dork or something like that, went on and on threatening me.

Threatening you about what?

Cop stuff. Running a whorehouse, pimping, usual shit. I had nothing to tell him.

Well, what did happen? Tell me from the time she arrived.

Be my guest. You paid for it. The broad—I mean your girlfriend—walks in and asks if I have a room. Yeah, I do. $250, payable in advance. All right, she says, and pays with a credit card. That's how I knew her name was Kerry Black. Then she says there's a man—Boris—big guy with black hair, will ask for her. Please tell him I'm in 522. She gave me a twenty and went into the elevator.

He gestured toward a scuffed door across the hall.

How did she seem?

How did she seem? Excuse me, but just like all those broads. Shit out of her mind, real high heels, some kind of black outfit unzipped to her belly button, you could see her tits.

And then?

And then? This guy Boris came, asked for her, and went upstairs. Later he came back down and left.

How much later?

An hour? Probably less.

Did you notice anything unusual?

Shit no! How do you know a guy got laid or didn't?

I thanked him.

So long, he replied.

The Rat was closed. The street was empty. Perhaps Abner had given up on having me tailed. Too bad. This was as good an opportunity to put me out of my misery as any you could imagine. I had the .45 in my waistband, my left arm was almost back to normal, and, contrary to the white lie Heidi told, my leg wasn't so bad. But all the energy, all alertness, had drained out of me, replaced by a vast fatigue. Or was it sadness? Standing before the door of the Rat I thought I could draw the pistol, blast open the locks, take over, and devastate the place. I'd be gone before the cops or the Rat's security service arrived—or maybe I wouldn't. What difference did it make? Was the Rat more to blame than I?

I waited until Friday. No use, I said to myself, giving the son of a bitch too much time to work the problem and come up with one of his ploys. First thing in the morning Texas time, I called him. On my landline.

Hi, Eileen!

Oh, Captain Dana, sir, she cooed, I was so sorry to hear about your accident on TV and to read about it too.

It was no accident, sweet Eileen. Just someone's plan that didn't pan out. You know what the poet said: "The best laid schemes o' mice an' men gang aft agley, an' lea'e us nought but grief an' pain. . . ." Is the head mouse in?

You're so funny, Captain! You're killing me! I'll see if Abner can take you.

No preliminaries; no I'm putting you right through, sir; no treacly charm wafted by ether. Perhaps the bastard was listening in from the start.

What's on your mind, fuckhead, if you have a mind?

Hello, Abner! Just a couple of things I want to tell you. Item one: I have Kerry's file, you know which one. Remember? You had Boris murder her so she wouldn't give it to the grand jury. Item two: I have another file, that's even better. They're both going to the government next week. And that will be the end of you. You'll spend the rest of your life behind bars. Or maybe you'll hit the jackpot: lethal injection for being a whore for terrorists. Your family will disown you. Out of shame. Linda will divorce you. Those nice sons of yours might kill themselves, like the Madoff kid. Or perhaps they'll go to jail too.

You haven't got dick on me, fuckhead. What is it you want this time?

Now that I know you've murdered Boris? Nothing. Nothing except the pleasure of seeing your shit-eating face when you browse through the files. I want to bring them to you and let you read them. Oh, and don't bother having me killed except for the fun of it. The files are going to Uncle Sam whatever happens to me. And they're going even if I change my mind. And don't bother trying to get hold of the files. I'll give you copies myself. The originals are in a place neither you nor your goons can reach.

I swear I could hear the bastard breathing hard. Like someone gasping for air. I wondered whether he was having a stroke.

You want to come down here? he asked after a moment.

No, I told him, I want to see you in New York. You have meetings at the museum Wednesday and Thursday. I'll see you at your apartment on Wednesday afternoon, at four.

Silence. The son of a bitch must have been looking at his calendar.

Can't do four. Be there at four-thirty.
Click.

It was time to bring Scott and Heidi on board with what
I had done and what I was planning to do. I called Scott.
Susie was just fine, there was no problem with the pregnancy,
but real pressures at work. There was no chance of his getting to New York over the weekend or any time the following week before Thursday. Thursday was too late. I had my
date with Abner on Wednesday, and I wasn't about to change
it. We could have a telephone conference over the weekend.
Late Saturday afternoon worked for him.

I checked with Heidi. She was staying in town. She'd come
over at six-thirty, she told me, only if she could stay for dinner. In that case, I said, I have no choice, so I'm inviting
you—very reluctantly—and will ask Feng to whip up something you might like.

Duck, she replied, any style at all, provided it's duck!

Then I called Scott back to tell him the six-thirty call was
on, and that Heidi would be there.

Have you and she gotten together, brother? he asked. It
would make Susie and me very happy to know that you're
with someone you love and who loves you.

No, old friend, no and no. She's terrific, sometimes I think
I've really fallen for her, but on her end it can't go anywhere.
That's something I've had to resign myself to. We just spend
a lot of time together. For instance, she's staying to dinner after our call. She'd probably be having dinner with me
tonight as well, but her parents are taking her to the opera.
I've begged off doing that.

It beats me why she won't go for you. I've got to meet her

and figure it out. Maybe straighten her out. I know you're a monster and all that, but you're an attractive and rich monster. A lot of women would be happy to overlook your faults.

Poor Scott! I wasn't about to help him. Why it couldn't go anywhere with Heidi was a subject I wasn't going to discuss even with my best friend, the brother I would have wished to have, the man who had become my brother.

Let's talk about something else that's almost as important, Scott continued, your staying alive. I don't know what you have up your sleeve, and I'm willing to wait until tomorrow to find out. It doesn't matter what you've told Abner. Don't start thinking that there is anything you can do that will stop him from wanting you dead. He doesn't need to have a practical reason to kill you. He'll do it for the hell of it, because that's what he likes to do, and because he hates your guts, just the way he got to hate Harry's guts.

Realizing he couldn't see me nod, I said, I'm afraid you're right.

Then don't take any chances. Stay at home. Have Feng answer the door when the doorbell rings. If you must go out, don't get into the first cab that stops when your doorman is hailing one for you. That may be Abner's taxi. Take the third or fourth taxi that goes by. That's what our people do when they're on a mission in sensitive territory. Better yet, let Feng get your car out of the garage and drive. You've got a replacement car now?

I had to laugh. Yes, Mr. Mahoney, the Krohn factotum, has seen to that. It's exactly like the old car only new.

Then use it! I've already told you once: my son won't need a dead godfather.

Hey, I said, when I called Scott the next day from the library of my apartment, I've put you on the speakerphone and I'm using my landline. The beautiful, elegant, and exceedingly intelligent Heidi is here. Heidi and Scott, say hello.

He's gone out of his mind, Heidi observed. He thinks he's running a preschool class. Hello, Scott, this is Heidi.

Hi, Heidi! This is Scott.

Well done, children, I told them. Now I'm going to expose you to the new, superefficient, and possibly lawbreaking Jack Dana. As you both know, I called my friend Abner yesterday. What you don't know, and what I'm pretty sure he doesn't know, unless he's got some technology that detects it, is that I recorded the conversation. Heidi, was I breaking the law?

It depends on where he was when you called. If he was in New York or Texas, you weren't. But if he was in another state, you may have been. But even if you were, I wouldn't let it upset you. An estimated fifty million American men commit at least one felony per day, and most of them don't realize it.

No kidding! said Scott.

I don't give a shit, I continued. And I don't give a shit who listens to this conversation. NSA, CIA, FBI, ABC, NBC, or CBS. Or Fox News. So here goes.

I'd figured out how to reconnect the device on which I'd recorded Abner and me, and pressed PLAY. The quality of the recording was damn good. We came through loud and clear. Heidi listened enraptured, occasionally giggling.

When we came to the end, Scott said, This is great, brother, and I renew my warning. This prick won't care whether it's useful to kill you. He'll want to do it, as you put it yourself, for fun. Heidi, he continued, this goes back to a conversation Captain Dana there and I had yesterday: I want him to stay alive.

I vote for that, said Heidi. Motion carried.

All right, I replied. I want to stay alive too, and I want Abner dead or locked up.

Amen, said Heidi. If we can nail him for Harry's and Kerry's murders, you might see him on a gurney, getting the long-goodbye injection. Commissioning murders through the use of interstate methods of communication happens to be a federal felony, subject to capital punishment.

And aiding terrorism? I asked hopefully.

Tough, said Scott.

Heidi chimed in, Tough but potentially possible.

To see him dead would restore my faith in the criminal justice system, I told her.

We all fell silent. Worried that Scott might leave us, I said, Let's talk quickly about some logistics. Here is what I would like to do, subject to your agreement. I'd like to email to each of you, at your private addresses, Kerry's file and her letter to me. The idea is obviously that if I'm not around, either one of you will be able to deliver this stuff to Ed Flanagan. *D'accord?*

Yes, said Scott.

Yes, except I count on you to be here.

Heidi gave me a dig in the ribs as she said that.

It would be good to meet with Ed Flanagan on Thursday, I continued. Can you arrange that, Heidi? I'm sure you can get through to him more easily than I. And will you attend the meeting and bring the file you have?

Certainly, she said. I'll let you both know what I work out.

How about you, Scott? OK to send the file to your private email address? Will you attend the meeting?

Yes, but I can only be at the meeting with the U.S. attorney if it's after two p.m.

Noted, said Heidi.

Finally, I'm going to make sure that each of you can have access to Mail Boxes, Etc., on East Eighty-Sixth Street and take possession of the original of Kerry's file. I'll get that done tomorrow.

They say you were a hell of a good platoon commander, said Scott. I see what they mean. I'll keep my fingers crossed. Susie will pray for you—I'll tell her that once more you're putting yourself in harm's way.

XIV

've got a couple of guys downstairs, Abner said. All I have to do is whistle, and they'll come up and kill you. While I watch, fuckhead. Then they'll put you in a body bag, and, believe me, nobody'll ever find you. *Whoosh!* Fucking war hero, third-rate novelist, and pain in the ass. But it's too easy. You'll be dead by the end of the day, fuckhead, that I guarantee, but first you'll have a surprise. Ha! Ha! Ha!

The laughter sounded at once insane and genuine, with nothing forced about it.

Suddenly he sang: I'll be glad when you're dead, you fuck-head you! Dead, dead, dead. Killed by you'll never guess who.

Simon Lathrop was right. This son of a bitch's library was like the Met's medieval armor section. Dummies in full suits of armor, their visors lowered. In the corners, and displayed cunningly on the walls, were maces, flails, halberds, cross-bows, daggers, estocs, and two-handed swords. Grab a flail, I thought, and beat the bastard to death. Crush his bones and don't spare his face. Then bring them all in: the fucking body-guards and the secretary outside the door, platinum-blond

Mrs. Abner Brown, the sons if they're in the house, the cook, the butler, and whoever, and say, Look, here he is, the Lord of Evil, look at him, beaten into a pulp. Then let them call the cops or call them yourself. Unless the bodyguards decide to take you out. With a flail in one hand and an estoc in the other, even in your condition, you'll do some real damage before they shoot you. And afterward? With his crimes documented by Kerry, and by Harry before her, with the murders he's commissioned, let them try to get a New York jury to convict me. And if they do convict me, if that's the price of turning him into a bloody pulp, so be it! The price is right.

The temptation was strong, my hands were sweating, but I controlled myself.

Don't worry about me, I told him. I had fun killing Slobo and Jovan and the nice fellow with a crossbow on Torcello, and I'll have fun with your surprise. Hey, you want to do some reading? I promised to let you see Kerry's files. Here they are. Nuts, I should have brought copies for your wife and sons too. They'll love reading about you. You know what? It's I who will see you dead. You won't survive this stuff.

Brown hadn't moved from behind his huge mahogany partner's desk since I was ushered in. I walked over and dumped the contents of the two Redrope file folders I'd brought with me on the desk. It was as though he hadn't noticed, sitting there seemingly frozen. Then something must have stirred inside him. He reached for the thicker file—the one Kerry had sent to me—put on his reading glasses, and began going through it. Almost immediately, a flush came over his normally pale face. Except for the motion of his fingers turning pages, he was perfectly immobile. Since it didn't look as though he'd interrupt his reading to ask me to sit down, I plunked myself down on the leather sofa placed to the right of his desk against the library bookshelves. There were magazines on the chinoiserie lacquer coffee table — *Weekly Standard, Human Events,* and the *American Conservative,* and off to the left *ARTnews.*

Expressionless, Abner's face was turning a deeper red. Would the bastard really have a stroke? None of the endless garbage extolling his good works that I'd plowed through on Google mentioned heart disease. He'd thrown his money at cancer and diabetes, but no mention of Abner and Linda Brown cardiology clinics. There was always the first time. If he just kept reading!

I didn't think there was any immediate likelihood of his stopping. That's all right; I was in no hurry. Feng was parked a couple of doors up from Abner's building, just in case, he said, I was too tired to walk home. I'd left Harry's huge beat-up leather briefcase made for him by I couldn't remember who in London with Abner's doorman, a florid Irishman who I decided — based on nothing other than his fine brogue and the way he said, Brown, penthouse apartment, sir, but please see first those fellows over there who'll check you out — wasn't one of Abner's goons. I'd better be right, since at the bottom of the briefcase were my .45 and my iPhone. The "fellows over there," exact replicas of the security guys I'd met at Abner's building in Houston when I visited him a year and a half ago, led me into a room off the lobby equipped with a metal detector, asked for my name, checked it against a paper, and then asked for the last four digits of my social security number. When I told them I didn't know it, they looked at each other unsmilingly.

Jeez, said the taller one, who had about an inch on me. Please wait here.

"Sir" apparently was not part of their lingo, not for types marked on their document for careful vetting.

After what must have been a telephone consultation, the taller one reappeared from an inner room and asked for my birth date and year of graduation from college. As I was able to supply those, he invited me to pass through the metal detector and patted me down.

What's in these files, he asked, pointing to the Redropes I'd put on the table next to the metal detector.

Dynamite, I told him.

Is this supposed to be a joke? he asked.

Find out for yourself, I answered, don't you have an explosives detector?

The guy had no sense of humor. He passed his gizmo over the files, and asked, OK to open them?

Sure, I said, I'm bringing them for your boss's amusement.

Clearly, the guy didn't like me. He opened the files, passed them through the metal detector, and said, Good to go.

The shorter guy took me to the elevator, which, it turned out, served only the penthouse, and told me not to touch any of the buttons. We're sending you up.

Yup, sending me up. Or setting me up. Or preparing to put me down. I now wondered whether these clean-cut former noncoms were the guys who'd kill and bag me if he whistled. Why not? It takes all kinds to field this man's army. I hoped they wouldn't take it too hard if I deprived them of this choice bit of fun.

Abner was past crimson. He'd reached the color of a rich burgundy. I saw that he'd worked his way through the file Kerry had sent to me and started on the one she'd sent to Heidi. That one was prefaced by Kerry's analysis of the underlying documents with references to the sections of the U.S. criminal code Abner and his companies had violated and applicable penalties.

When he spoke to me, the words—Fuck you!—came out as weird loud rales.

Cool it, Abner! I laughed. You should know that when I talk to the prosecutors tomorrow and deliver these files I'll mention something neither poor Harry nor Kerry knew about: your Amazon venture! The perfect channel for distribution of everything that's illegal, from cash through drugs through counterfeit medicines. And ten dozen other rackets I can't think of. You put the guys who operated Silk Road on the darknet to shame. Compared with you, they're real pikers!

Abner didn't respond at first. Just sat there glowering, making those funny crackling noises as though he were gasping for breath. But perhaps that was my imagination. After a few minutes, he got up, crossed the large room to where I was sitting, and lowered himself into a club armchair kitty-corner from me. By some miracle of his physiology, his face returned to its normal pasty pale.

I should have fired that pansy uncle of yours the moment I saw he was too big for his britches. Stopped doing what I said. Started telling me what to do. That's not what I was paying him to do. Nothing's worse than a lawyer with a swollen head and loose lips. I don't need people to tell me what I should or shouldn't do. The great ideas, the concepts, are mine. Nobody else's. There isn't my equal in this whole country, perhaps in the whole world. Only I have the genius of invention, the clarity of vision, and the will to make my vision the reality. I inherited money and a small business from my father. He had inherited from his father, and so on back to the beginning of nineteenth century, when my people came over from the Midlands and Sussex. They worked hard and saved. They didn't ask for alms. They didn't wait for the government to bail them out. What they wanted, they took. They kept the bloodline pure. No fucking Irish or Jews. Only good English and German stock. With what my father left me, I built a fortune second to none in this country—*Forbes* and Bloomberg get it wrong—I'm richer than Buffett, smart guy by the way, and that clown Bill Gates. Only Carlos Slim is in my league. Steve Jobs? An appliance salesman. Did I accomplish that by listening to Harry Dana? Hell no! I listened to my demon, my own genius.

He paused, perhaps waiting for me to comment. I said nothing. While he spoke, I wondered what had happened to Abner's foul mouth and then realized that I was for the first time hearing him such as he must be at innumerable board of directors' and trustees' meetings and when he stirs the poisonous brew of his politics. A minor Texan orator!

He spoke again. There's more I will tell you, Dana, but perhaps you'd like tea and cake. Or my favorite, pecan pie. My chef makes the best pastry in the world.

Yes, thank you, I answered.

First intelligent thing I've heard you say.

He picked up the telephone on the side table next to his armchair and spoke into it. Eileen, Mr. Dana here and I will take tea. We'll want pecan pie and pound cake.

Bang. Abner hung up.

Harry Dana and that Jew girl sidekick of his had the presumption to think they discovered a criminal empire I was running and Lord knows what else. In your ignorance, you've taken the bait. It's no criminal empire they came across but a paradigm for liberty, for raising the mighty structure of a capitalist enterprise to an empyrean height, for the exercise by a great man of his divine creative will. Iranian or North Korean sanctions! The stifling skein of regulations that Lilliputian legislators, regulators, and bureaucrats wind around our banking and financial systems, the Luddite imbecile environmental regulations, the metastasizing cancer of our tax system—I could go on—is it criminal to shake off their shackles? On the contrary, it is the exercise of virtue, the duty of the great free individual—the complement to my political action, which has only one goal: restore the free rein of the great individual! But could your pansy uncle or his Jewess acolyte grasp even for a split second the grandeur and rightness of my actions? They couldn't. With their pismires' view of the world, they deserved only one fate: to be crushed beneath the foot of a great man. Such was their fate, and so it was accomplished.

You know, Abner, I said mildly, I've actually read Ayn Rand's *Atlas Shrugged*. At prep school. When I was fifteen. I thought then she was preaching nonsense and I think so now. Only fools and teenagers take that stuff seriously.

Are you stupid enough to think I was ever taken in by that Jew commie? I am talking to you about American freedom. The freedom of our forefathers. The freedom of a man like me to build and to create, to brush aside with indignation the bonds fashioned by the Lilliputians in government, in

Congress—and to live! To take the best the world has to offer. Look around you! The armor and arms you see here are the finest in the world. The books on the shelves are all the rarest of first editions—but I don't collect first editions for bindings and rarity. The books themselves must be masterpieces. At the summit of intellectual and literary attainment. You've seen my bronzes in Houston. They're good, but that's only a hobby. On the walls of this apartment, and in my homes in Houston, in Dark Harbor, and in Cap Ferrat are paintings by the greatest masters. They are their finest paintings, ground-breaking, seminal, coveted by the most important museums. My taste is unerring, and my passion for art has never abated. When a work brought into my presence meets my exalted standards, a tremor passes through my body, and I get a hard-on. It tells me to buy, and it has never failed me. Perhaps you are beginning to appreciate, you deranged and misguided fool, the stature and the quality of the man you have tried so hard to destroy.

I don't know how much longer he would have harangued me in this manner if the door had not opened. Eileen entered followed by a butler in a black suit wheeling in the tea table.

Shall I pour the tea for you, Abner, and for Captain Dana? she asked in her sweetest tones.

He nodded, whereupon Eileen, having ascertained that I take my tea plain—no milk, no lemon, and no sugar—handed me my cup.

Staffordshire bone china, she pointed out helpfully. The entire service was in the family of the dukes of Devonshire, Captain Dana. Abner bought it from the estate of the eleventh duke. He does love and understand fine china!

Very lovely, I told her.

Meanwhile the butler served the cakes.

Have a piece of each, Dana, Abner told me. Myself, I'll have two pieces of pecan pie—that's my favorite—and one slice of lemon cake. Large pieces, Ralph, he added, addressing the butler.

That'll be all, he continued, dismissing both Eileen and Ralph. If we want more tea, Dana here will pour it.

He waited until they were out the door and said, Sweets are strictly verboten! I suffer from type 1 diabetes. Since kindergarten, and it's not been getting any better. But this is such an occasion, and you're such a guest, that I've decided to indulge. You should too. These are the last sweets you will get to eat.

I don't think so, I answered. Fortunately, I'm not on any sort of diet. I look forward to a long life of eating desserts.

Your remaining lifespan can be measured in hours, Dana. But as sweets go, you've been undeservedly lucky. My sweet blood—no amount of willpower, no amount of exercise, no asinine treatment, has helped. Measuring the blood-sugar level after every meal, the injections, doctors fiddling with doses . . . misery. Can you imagine what it was like when I was a schoolboy? In prep school? This has been my one defeat. Until now, until you've come along. You're a lemming, Dana, a good-looking moron. That nincompoop George W. attacks Afghanistan and Iraq—hop, you jump in. Did you ever ask yourself whether Americans, American arms, American treasure, had any business doing that? Oh no, your lemming instinct was enough. Fruitcake Harry gets the idea he has to stop me—can you imagine such a thing, that limp-wristed fairy pitting himself against me, like a mouse blocking the path of a lion—and what do you know, his stupid nephew takes up the cause. To your everlasting shame.

You're out of your mind, Abner, I said quietly. That's a possibility I should have been considering. Until now, I've thought you were evil, evil through and through. But now I think you're also seriously crazy. How do the murders—the only ones I know, of course, are of Harry and Kerry, of your own hit man Boris and his tootsie Lena, but there must be many others—fit into your superman will-to-power model? Collecting masterpieces with one hand, paying hit men with the other?

How can you expect me to concern myself with trivia at a time like this? The simple answer is: I kill because I can. When it suits me to do so. It suits me to kill you, and when this capital scene ends, I will have sent you to your death.

He said all this very calmly.

In the meantime, he said, you have succeeded where your homo uncle failed. When these despicable files are made public, when I stand naked and bound before the jeering Lilliputians, your fellow moral dwarfs, much of what I have built will crumble. And what will you have achieved?

The end of you, I answered.

This made him laugh. The same unforced laugh. There is no end of me. I've seen to that! There never will be. Another piece of cake?

I shook my head.

Very well.

Eileen, he spoke into the telephone, please bring my insulin kit.

I've no idea how you've been brought up, Dana. No doubt

badly. Had your education not been neglected you would have been raised, just as I, reading *The Swiss Family Robinson,* that too-little-read classic. An immortal phrase from it, one you surely don't know, although it is pregnant with profound meaning—"In the midst of this, Fritz did not neglect the training of his young eagle"—encapsulates much of what will follow here. Not everything is metaphor, Dana! Reality, above all, reality! Even so I, Abner Brown, have never neglected my diet. Except just now, for a short while. Wasting my time. Talking to you. Or my insulin. Meanwhile, only the Lord knows where my glucose level has gone to. No, I know. Sky-high! Oh, Eileen, thank you. Please set the insulin box on the coffee table. A Renaissance object, Dana, not that I think you would care!

It's lovely, I said with sincere admiration, studying the inlay that showed Actaeon already transformed into a deer and pursued by his own hounds.

If you only knew what you're looking at you would understand that it's singularly apposite. Long-toothed and merciless hounds pursuing a noble hind.

He opened the box and examined the contents.

Eileen, he said to the rose of Texas, who was waiting by his side, this being a special occasion I will want a full vial of this wonderful life-preserving stuff and a real syringe. Would you mind bringing them?

Right away, Abner.

She returned with the two objects on a silver tray I recognized as Georgian, and asked whether he would like her to administer the insulin.

No, Eileen, thank you, he replied, I will do the injection

myself. But I would first like to dictate a short memo to Will Hobson.

Yes, Abner, she simpered, I'm ready.

It was pure prestidigitation. Somehow, from some hidden pocket, she produced a stenographer's pad and a ballpoint pen.

Then take this down:

Will—

In the lowest circle of hell are punished traitors. There, locked for eternity in a frozen lake, lie Lucifer himself and Judas Iscariot and, of late, Harry Dana. His nephew is delivering to prosecutors tomorrow a set of the documents I'm sending to you herewith, all stolen from the files of your former law firm, Jones & Whetstone, or prepared in shameless breach of the attorney-client privilege and the sacred duty of loyalty.

Be forewarned!

That will be all, Eileen. Finish the memo with "Dictated but not read by Abner Brown" and get it and these files to Hobson by messenger.

He pointed to the files I'd brought, which were still on his desk.

Have the fellow take the plane this evening, he continued, and call Hobson to tell him that a package is arriving and will be delivered to his home even if the hour is late.

Yes, Abner, I will, she said. As she turned to leave the room she shot in my direction a look of undiluted hatred.

Well, well, said Abner, opening the Renaissance box, do

you see these strips and related gizmos? They're for measuring the sugar level. Pain in the ass, we know it's high and I'm about to make it higher.

The tea table was still there. Without getting up from his armchair, he reached, grabbed a slice of pecan pie, and ate it, dispensing with plate and fork. When he finished, he licked his lips, belched, and wiped his hands on the tablecloth.

Time for the injection, he told me, and unbuttoned his suit jacket, took off his necktie, unbuttoned his shirt, and opened his trousers. He wore suspenders, without a belt. Flabby stomach, I observed, although he isn't a fat man.

Now I prepare the syringe. A small man, planning what I have planned, would have eaten no pie and no cake or at most a crumb. Made the job easy for the old insulin. My actions are large, just as I am large and my accomplishment is gigantic. Therefore, here is how we do it.

He took the fresh vial into his left hand and with the right drew its contents into the syringe Eileen had brought.

Full size, he told me, not one of those midget syringes for regular doses. This is a fine afternoon, neither the pie nor the cake disappointed me, so I'm quintupling the dose. Let's do it after the high Roman fashion. We don't want to be on a Sunny von Bülow roller coaster, do we? There, this should do it. Do you wish to administer the injection, Dana? It's simple. Subcutaneous. You make a tent of the flab on my stomach with your index finger and thumb, push in the needle, and zoom. That's all there is to it.

I think I'll just watch, I answered. It's your show.

Chicken, he said, here's how. Your end won't be so painless or easy.

I remained silent. He stuck the needle in and pushed in the plunger, showing no hesitation. A big smile spread over his face. I don't know how many minutes passed until he slumped deeper in his armchair and his head drooped down on his chest.

I picked up the telephone, told Eileen that her boss passed out or was dead, and left the apartment, without anyone attempting to stop me. On the way out of the building I retrieved my briefcase from the Irish doorman and gave him a tenner. A quick look inside reassured me. The iPhone and .45 had not been disturbed.

Shall we go home, sir? asked Feng.

Yes, I replied, but I'll walk. I'll go in through the zoo entrance and head uptown and should be home in twenty minutes.

Feng looked troubled. It's cold, sir, and getting dark, wouldn't it be better to go back in the car and have a nice hot bath?

Don't worry so much about me, I told him. I need to clear my head and a walk will do me good. Really, I'll be fine. Here, hold my briefcase open for a moment, I'll just grab my pistol and stick it in my waistband. The briefcase can go into the car.

I walked slowly to the zoo, which was already closed, looked longingly at the pool where the seals and sea lions were all surely asleep, resolved to visit them soon at feeding time, and headed uptown, walking toward the arcade between the zoo proper and the Children's Zoo. The Delacorte music clock was striking six and began to play "Row,

Row, Row Your Boat." I paused, never having been able to resist the parade of animals. My head was absolutely empty. So that was the evil genius, the murderer by remote control, the quiet fanatic working to subvert the republic! Mad. Mad as a hatter. Feng was right. I should have let him drive me home. There was a chill in the air. The park was deserted, the wind chasing dead leaves and ice-cream sandwich wrappers along the path. My leg was doing its throbbing act, but I wasn't about to baby it. Instead, I picked up the pace and began humming a marine cadence: There's travel and adventure and loads of fun, and we'll even teach you how to shoot a gun. I broke into a smile—like Abner, it seemed to me—but I couldn't help it. So this is how it all ended!

There was a choice between a path that went up some rocks and one that avoided them. I wasn't in a mood to climb. Instead I turned left. How to shoot the gun, how to shoot the gun. I thought I'd left all that in Afghanistan. That turned out to be an illusion. What lay before me now? Abner's threat. But the guy was dead. Dead men don't kill. I started up the cadence again and wished I could break into double time. Memories, that the distance had made fond, of drills and marches occupied me until I became aware of the figure of a man of about my build, dressed in camo, who appeared from the bushes on the right, about twenty feet ahead of me, reached the asphalt path, and began to walk in my direction. Peering through the rapidly falling dusk, I recognized him. Eric! What a strange world: once a noncom in my platoon, now a bouncer at the Rat. I waved to him and he waved back.

Hello, Eric, I said. What brings you to Central Park at this hour of the evening?

You're not as quick on the uptake as you used to be, Captain Dana, he answered. You brought me here. I'm here to kill you. The only question is how I do it. The Ka-Bar or a bullet? I'd rather see you bleed. It'll be the knife.

You're insane, I said. This is on account of Helmand? I saved your ass from a court-martial and the brig. Many years in the brig. You know that. Anyway, if you wanted to kill me, why didn't you do it then? Why did you take out the sniper who would have done the job for you?

Two reasons, Captain. One, back there we were both marines. That's over. Now nothing stops me from settling our score. Paying you for the rank, wife, and kid I lost. Because of you. Two, you're going to make me able to quit my fucking job. There's a serious price on your head.

I've got news for you, Eric, I replied, Abner Brown died just about half an hour ago. If I were you, I wouldn't count on being paid. Anyway, what the hell are you doing working for him?

Why do I work for him? To save this fucking country from assholes like you—and make good money on the side. Got it?

The Ka-Bar flashed. I reached for the .45, knowing I was hopelessly late. It was a hell of a way to die.

He cut my good arm which held the pistol and was going for my throat when I heard the crack of a gunshot. Eric stopped in midmotion. Part of his cranium was no longer there. He stood there perplexed and sank to the ground. Whoever had shot him must have used a hollow-point bullet. Who the fuck was it? I turned around, looking for the shooter.

Running toward me was Feng, a Glock 17 in his hand.

Are you badly hurt, sir? he asked.

Just a cut. Nothing serious. You got here in the nick of time, man! How did you know?

I didn't, sir. Just being cautious. It's an old habit.

He looked at Eric and said, This fellow is quite dead. Do you believe, sir, that we must call the police? If that's not absolutely necessary, we could cut over to the avenue. You might sit down on a bench and rest while I get the car.

Epilogue

A couple of Goldman Sachs traders out on their early dawn run found him. The report of the discovery, only a short distance north of the entrance to the Children's Zoo, of the body of a white male in camouflage fatigues, armed with a combat knife and a handgun, the top of his head blown off, took over morning TV shows and online breaking news posts of major papers. It made the late editions of the *Daily News* and *NY Post,* and for a few days distracted attention from Police Commissioner Kelly and his stop-and-frisk policy. Already the next day it was known that the victim was Eric King, a former Marine Corps NCO, working as a security guard at an entertainment space in Chelsea. Taking decidedly the second place—although it rated a below-the-fold first-page obituary in the *New York Times*—was the report of the sudden and unexpected death at his Fifth Avenue triplex of Abner Brown, the multibillionaire Texas investor, noted philanthropist, and principal backer of right-wing candidates and policies. The apparent cause was an injection of insulin for his type 1 diabetes condition that, as was his custom, he administered himself.

I was no more eager to take my knife wound to the emergency room and face the inevitable questions it would provoke than was Feng to call the police after he shot Eric. How could you blame him? His firearm was unregistered. He bandaged my arm expertly and, deciding that the cut would benefit from a few stitches, called his friend Dr. Yan, whose office on Mulberry Street was just closing. The doctor jumped into a taxi, was at my apartment within the half hour, and within another twenty minutes had me sewed up and rebandaged. Afterward, assuring me it was just a formality, he asked how I got hurt. Feng, hovering in the background, made a face so sour you'd think he'd eaten an ice-cold egg roll. I sighed and said, It was so stupid of me, I cut myself shaving.

The bandaged arm fit neatly into the sleeve of my suit jacket. For the first time since I returned to the city from Torcello, I did not spoil the hang of my clothes by sticking the .45 into my waistband or the switchblade into the pocket of my jacket. I doubted that Abner had yet another surprise waiting for me. Besides, I was on the way to the U.S. Attorney's Office, where I was meeting Heidi and Scott. The hardware would make the wrong impression, I told Feng, who drove me there, having first pointed out, politely but firmly, that it would be prudent to stay out of the subway for a while. I had with me the file Kerry had sent to me at Mail Boxes, Etc. Heidi had her own "Kerry file." Flanagan received us with considerable solemnity in his conference room, flanked by FBI agents from the New York office and D.C., the chief of his criminal division, a couple of younger assistant U.S. attorneys, and an emissary of the U.S. attorney for the Eastern District of Virginia presenting the case against Abner and his enterprises to the grand jury in Alexandria. We handed over the files with equal solemnity. High-speed copiers are a great invention. Within minutes copies of the files were distributed to the assembled jurists. They read and read in complete silence.

Ed Flanagan was the first to speak. This is it, he said, there's more than enough here to indict just about every one of the Brown companies and a dozen of their executives. Too bad that Abner bailed out.

Prompted by Scott, I raised my hand and gave an account of the Amazon packages I'd received, courtesy—I was certain—of Abner Brown, and Scott completed my narration by telling of the effort to track the sender. The news drew a prolonged collective whistle from the assembled forces of law and order, the FBI representative from D.C. stating that he would recommend to the director the start of an intensive and accelerated investigation.

We'll want you, Miss Krohn, and you, Mr. Dana, to authenticate these files and tell the grand jury how they came into your possession, as well as, of course, the Amazon story, said the Virginia assistant U.S. attorney. Could you be in Alexandria for instance next Wednesday, in the early afternoon?

It turned out that she could. Of course I was free. We both accepted Scott's invitation to have dinner with Susie and him and spend the night at their house.

The indictments handed down after Heidi's and my appearances before the grand jury provided grist for the media mills for weeks afterward and were accompanied by howls of outrage at yet another political witch hunt from conservative radio talk-show hosts, Fox News, and the *Wall Street Journal*'s editorial board, on the one hand this and on the other hand that news analysis by the *New York Times* and the *Washington Post,* and a mixture of jeremiads and jubilation from left-leaning blogs and publications including, months later, a five-thousand-word article in the *New York Review of Books.* The untimely disappearance of Abner Brown himself did not go unnoticed, regretted on the right (he would have vindicated himself against these jackals) and on the left (he should have lived to a ripe old age in jail).

For weeks I waited for the other shoe to drop, for my presence in Abner Brown's library when he gave himself the fatal injection to come to light and draw the interest of the New York district attorney or perhaps Ed Flanagan himself. I did not think that a great leap of imagination was required to see Abner's hand in the attempts to murder me of which I was twice the target in Sag Harbor, a year and a half ago, when I killed Slobo and lost forever the love of Kerry, and just recently, when Jovan came close to killing me before I killed him. Abner was dead. His punishment for those crimes and so many others of which he was guilty would have to come in another place, if there was one. For my part, I preferred to leave those matters just as they were—closed. Never far from my mind was Goran Petrović and his unfortunate fall down the 103rd Street subway station stairs. That too was an adventure I didn't wish to revisit, and I particularly didn't want to renew my acquaintance with Detective Walker.

The following week, on Tuesday, I had lunch with Martin and Lee. Their engagement was at an end, and I wanted to thank them and exchange another round of war stories. I had already settled our financial accounts and pretty much forced Martin to accept an advance contribution to his daughter Nora's college and graduate-school scholarship fund.

Jack, he protested, we were just kidding when we talked about that. I've earned good money with you, very good money. She's just started high school! A couple more clients like you and by the time she goes to college I'll be rich.

You may have been kidding, I told him. I wasn't. All I ask is to meet Nora when she's in Manhattan with time on her hands and to be kept up-to-date on her studies.

Instead of the neighborhood joint that was the venue of my previous meals with Martin, I took him and Lee to Harry's favorite French restaurant, where he was still remembered with great affection, and talked them into trying braised oxtail, the restaurant's signature meat dish. I had no secrets from these two honorable men. They knew we wouldn't be at table together sipping the burgundy recommended by the headwaiter, to whom Harry had always left such matters, if Feng had not followed me unseen into the park. And if his aim had not been so deadly sure.

I owe him my life, I told them, and since I owe Feng to you guys, indirectly I owe my life to you.

He's happy, said Martin. You don't know it, but he calls me every few days to say he's happy and hopes you'll keep him on.

Do you know the Chinese expression "He has an iron rice bowl"? I asked. They mean by it that the person's job is secure. No one's going to break the bowl from which he eats. You can tell Feng that and much more.

That is happy news, Martin replied, and Lee and I have some news for you that we've been saving up. Do you remember Detective Rod "Tannenbaum" Walker? He's off the force.

I can't believe it, I said. It's too good to be true. What happened? How did you guys find out?

This made them laugh. Lee, who habitually let Martin do their talking, spoke up.

It's like Martin told you. When he and I were still with the Bureau, we worked on a joint task force with the NYPD for more years than I can or want to remember. Mostly on major drug investigations. It so happens that our contact at the Drug Enforcement Agency there now heads the department's Internal Affairs. They're the folks who are supposed to make sure everyone on the force stays on the straight and narrow. It also happens that we belong to the same social club in Maspeth. You know, we get together over the weekend, go bowling and stuff. Well, we talked to Gerry, that's the name of our pal, strictly on the QT of course, about Walker's peculiar behavior—like his knowing about the telephone call Jovan made to you when you met this guy Goran in Central Park—and the way he handled or didn't handle the murders of Lena and Boris. Gerry thought this was pretty strange stuff. And wearing that little Tannenbaum on his lapel . . . So Gerry did some poking around, and he and Walker had a few talks, and Walker realized he had enough time in service to retire. Which was a good move. You know, before something could prejudice his pension. So that's what he did, and you know what? Immediately he got another job. Of course, he had to relocate to Houston. A job with Abner Brown Enterprises security. What do you think of that?

I'll be goddamned, I said. I just hope that in spite of the recent events he's got job security!

An iron rice bowl! they both cried out. Guaranteed lifetime employment!

My book was waiting. To use one of my mother's favorite expressions, the wounds, however inconsequential in the long run, had made me a lot less bushy tailed, and teaming up with the sequence of events that brought the nightmare that began with Harry's murder to an end—the attempt to run Heidi off the road, the attack later that day directed at me, Abner's suicide, and the bitter confrontation with Eric—had brought my work to a halt. I resorted to the one remedy that in my experience never fails: I slept. Three or four long nights' sleep crowded with agitated and bizarre dreams followed by lazy mornings, lunch with wine, and dreamless naps in the afternoon. The record of success remained unbroken. I completed the draft, gave it what I call the first manicure, and sent it to my agent. Two days later, the beautiful Jane sent an email saying: Bull's-eye. Keep revising if you wish, but I'll submit the manuscript to Holly Gibson—the name of my editor—as is.

I wish, though, your manners were as good as your storytelling, Jane wrote to me. How many weeks have passed since you said you'd invite me to dinner?

What was I to do? I fired off a three-word message: *Mea maxima culpa!* But I didn't propose a dinner date. How could I? I was having dinner with Heidi practically every evening.

Apparently Jane wasn't too cross to recommend the draft with her usual vigor. A week later I got a letter advising me with real or feigned enthusiasm that the house would be honored to publish my new novel. A telephone call the next day from Holly Gibson advised me that the in-house lawyers were relieved. With the man I called Abner Brown dead, the chance of being sued for libel had been reduced to the neighborhood of zero. They're so happy. My editor laughed. They keep telling me it's all right, you can't libel a dead man!

Feng was surely laughing up his sleeve too, because Heidi told him the only reason for my having her company at dinner was his cuisine, which of late included Hunan tripe and sliced lamb in hot scallion sauce. She'd arrive promptly at eight every night, unless she was out of town on a case or was summoned by her parents to the opera or a family function that she couldn't finesse without bringing down on herself what she called the ire of Jupiter. The wrath of Juno she could handle, her mother being, she said, a 24-7 nag. Her father, she explained, was something else. He'd stay mad. I didn't care why she came, so long as I knew she'd be there. More than once it was on the tip of my tongue to tell her that we were like one of those new couples, a working wife and a house husband. Only in our couple there was no sex. I never did tell her. I didn't want to break the spell.

The Krohns would spend the Thanksgiving weekend in East Hampton, Heidi announced. Would I like to come to their Thanksgiving Day lunch? It'll be great fun. All the families! When I looked blank, she explained, New York real estate families, you dummy, my brother and his new trophy wife my parents can't stand, and the guy who built a replica of Palazzo Pitti on the Water Mill beach. He's a peach. She laughed at the rhyme. And his wife's a lapsed hairdresser. Excuse me, stylist!

The thing about Heidi was that everything amused her, and she saw each thing coming before it rounded the corner.

My thigh. I groaned. My arm. Both my arms. I can't cut my meat. Or shake hands. The only thing I can do is type! And even that's over. I won't do revisions until Christmas.

At ease, Captain! I've told them that. But you're going to have to come up with something new for the New Year. Credibility! You're going to lose, if not your good name, then surely your credibility.

I've thought ahead, I assured her. It's my anxiety attacks. Ever since that night in Anbar Province.

The upshot was that I agreed to go to the Krohn parents' for tea, in return for which she volunteered to have her dinners with me in Sag Harbor over the holiday weekend and to come with me to White Plains to visit Jeanette and her sister the preceding Sunday afternoon. It was Jeanette's first weekend out of the Burke facility and at her sister's apartment. Harry had done well by Jeanette. The apartment was larger than I had imagined, and sunny. She was in the living room, in a wheelchair, slurring her words but intelligible and bright, with the old affectionate light in her eyes. Astonishingly, she remembered Heidi's one visit to Fifth Avenue and the sauté of chicken that she, Jeanette, had cooked for dinner, and was able to talk about the assault that awaited her on the way to her sister's. Did they ever catch that guy? she asked.

Not exactly, I told her, but he went after someone else a few weeks later; there was some shooting and he was killed. He was a very bad man.

I'll still feel sorry for him, replied Jeanette, and I'll say a prayer for him.

According to Heidi, I sailed through the tea with Mr. and

Mrs. Krohn, or Jon and Helen, as I now called them. My success was crowned by an on-the-spot invitation to a pre-Christmas party at their New York apartment. Pre-Christmas, Helen explained, because the day before Christmas Eve they would leave for Palm Beach. I accepted gratefully, a look from Heidi telling me that I had better keep my PTSD in reserve for another occasion. I tooled home happily. Heidi would be over at eight.

As Christmas and the Krohns' pre-Christmas party approached, I invited Heidi to dinner at our usual Madison Avenue restaurant. I toyed with the thought of the French restaurant and decided against it. Better to stick to what I knew we both liked. There's no longer a reason we can't go out to dinner, I told her. We can give Feng a night off.

But not having Feng on hand to put the fear of God or of overcooked baby pork ribs into her pushed her right back into bad habits. We were to meet at eight-thirty. By the time she arrived thirty-seven minutes late, I had ordered my second martini and asked for a piece of bread to still my rumbling stomach. Was this to be again our theme song? I took a cab home from the office, she announced, took a bath, got dressed, and then decided I'd walk here. You don't mind, do you.

How could I?

We drank a Refosco, which made her wrinkle her nose. I offered to have the waiter bring the Pinot Nero she liked, but she said, No, it's not the wine, it's me. Somewhere between the *vitello tonnato* and my new favorite, spaghetti *neri,* which she agreed to try, I asked her the question that had been waking me up at night. Was she going to Palm Beach with her parents for Christmas?

Is it possible that she guffawed?

No, she said, laughing so hard she had tears in her eyes. Guess what? I've bought two pairs of silk pajamas, one black and one very red. Like this.

She pointed to the belt she wore over her black trousers.

And you know why? Because, if Feng will be around, I'm going to spend Christmas, and the week between Christmas and New Year's, in Sag Harbor. Will your master chef and nanny be there?

He will, I said, and so will I.

Well, that's good, she said, I was sort of counting on it. And will I get to have the master bedroom?

I nodded.

In that case, she told me, in that case, Captain, you will be able to share it with me. But remember, we'll only cuddle!

ACKNOWLEDGMENTS

Once again, the author wishes to express his profound gratitude for advice and comments of inestimable value proffered by his friends Matthew Blumenthal, Mark P. Goodman, Dr. Jonathan L. Jacobs, and Dr. Daniel I. Richman.

Kill and Be Killed

LOUIS BEGLEY

 A READER'S GUIDE

An Essay by the Author

There are many reasons why novelists are not content to leave a novel they have finished alone and, instead, write one or more sequels. Sometimes the reason is that the subject matter is too vast to be contained in one tome. Marcel Proust's *In Search of Lost Time* is such a case. More often, the novelist becomes so attached to one or more characters in his novel that he doesn't want to take leave of them. Writing a sequel, in which some of those characters reappear, makes it possible to go on living in their company. Anthony Trollope's Barchester and Palliser novels illustrate this point. Trollope didn't want to let go of the admirable and lovable Mr. Septimus Harding and his daughters, or Archdeacon Grantly, or Bishop Proudie and his terrible wife. Or, when his focus moved from Barchester to London, his other splendid creations: Phineas Finn, Lady Glencora Palliser, Madame Max, the Duke of Omnium, Plantagenet Palliser. He returned to them in volume after volume. Crime novels and thrillers offer abundant examples of the creator of a great detective, charming criminal, or avenger allowing him to continue his work. Sherlock Holmes, Hercule Poirot, Sam Spade, Commissaire Maigret, Arsène Lupin, and Jack Reacher come immediately to mind. In my own novels, there has been Albert Schmidt, Esq., the retired lawyer known to his friends as Schmidtie. I became so fond of him, of Carrie and Alice, the women he has loved, and his friends Gil Blackman and Mike Mansour, that I came back to him three times, in *About Schmidt*, *Schmidt Delivered*, and *Schmidt Steps Back*. Occasionally, I dream of revisiting him one more time.

And then there is my new friend, Jack Dana, the heroic former Marine Corps Infantry captain and Force Recon platoon leader, who becomes a successful novelist after injuries sustained in Afghanistan preclude his continuing in active service. He finds himself locked in a life-and-death struggle with Abner Brown, a quintessentially evil extreme right-wing billionaire, who stands at the head of twin fortunes, one of which is legitimate, and the other a vast criminal enterprise engaged in drug trade, human trafficking, an evasion of North Korea and Iran sanctions, and money laundering. In the first Jack Dana novel, *Killer, Come Hither*, Jack discovers that the apparent suicide of his beloved uncle Harry, who is found hanged in his Sag Harbor weekend house, was in fact murder committed by a hitman sent by Abner. Harry, a leading New York City lawyer, was Abner's principal legal counsel and came upon evidence of his crimes in the course of preparing the public offering of one of Abner's top holding companies. He confronted Abner, and Abner's riposte was to have him killed, lest he turn the evidence over to the authorities.

Jack's helper in *Killer, Come Hither* is Kerry, Harry's protégée and favorite young partner. He and Kerry fall deeply in love, but Kerry is ultimately revolted by the way Jack kills the hitman who murdered his uncle. She thinks Jack crossed the line that separates justifiable homicide committed in self-defense from murder. She tells him she smells blood on his hands and throws him over. Disconsolate, Jack retreats to Torcello, an island in the Venetian Lagoon, to try to forget Kerry and concentrate on writing his new book.

I could have left Jack there and turned to other matters. But I really didn't want to. I had enjoyed writing *Killer, Come Hither* and found I didn't want to lose touch with Jack or, for that matter, with Abner, who had turned out to be a grimly satisfactory villain. There was only one way out—I had to write a sequel. That sequel is *Kill and Be Killed,* and, I may as well admit it: I had an even better time writing it. *Killer, Come Hither* had at its origin my own deep-rooted fear of intruders and violence, thus the murder of elderly, honorable Harry by a brutal criminal who invades his house, and also in my hope that there are some young Americans of a background as privileged as Jack's who decided to get into the fight after 9/11, not because they thought invading Afghanistan or Iraq was a good idea or because they fell for George W. Bush's warmongering rhetoric, but because they thought it was their duty. They would stand up for their country, whether it was right or wrong. *Kill and Be Killed* has identifiable roots, too: my desire to have Jack confront Abner and discover what lies in that heart of darkness, my preoccupation, which Jack shares, with the corruption rampant in our society, made evident by the influence of the money that floods our political system, and our coarse indifference to the suffering of some of those who most deserve our compassion: returning veterans, the long-term unemployed, segments of our population stuck in stubborn, ingrained poverty. Finally, I wanted to explore the gulf of misunderstanding that separated Jack and Kerry that results in his failure to recognize her vulnerabilities. Those vulnerabilities, and the vortex of self-destructive behavior into which she is dragged by them, prevent her from calling out to Jack for help when Abner decides it is her turn to be eliminated. Like Harry, she knows too much. Ignorant of Damocles' sword hanging over her head, Jack is unable to save her. But he will avenge her.

As I followed the ensuing struggle I gave Jack a new teammate determined to do her share in bringing Abner to account. She is Heidi, Kerry's best friend and another super-bright lawyer. Unflinchingly courageous, she is also irresistibly beautiful, elegant, and clever. I consider her one of my finer creations and am happy to know she is at Jack's side.

Questions and Topics
for Discussion

1. In this chapter of the Jack Dana series, Jack allows the justice system to take its course when dealing with Abner Brown. Compare and contrast the outcomes of Jack's behavior in this novel with what happened when Jack took justice into his own hands in *Killer, Come Hither*.

2. Kerry and Jack's relationship ended primarily because of their starkly different views of justice. Does Kerry's death make you reconsider their respective positions on the issue?

3. Did you believe, at any point, that Kerry's death was actually a suicide, or did you share Heidi and Jack's conviction of foul play throughout?

4. Do you think that being with Jack kept Kerry away from doing drugs and that she started doing them after their breakup, or do you think she kept it a secret from Jack while they were dating?

5. With Kerry's death, Jack realizes how much he didn't know about her. Do you think it's possible to love someone to that extent without knowing him or her?

6. If Jack had known that Kerry would leave him if he killed Slobo, do you think he would've gone ahead with it? Would Kerry still be alive if he hadn't?

7. Do you agree with Jack's vague suspicions that Heidi and Kerry were romantically involved, or do you think that they were just close friends?

8. Kerry, Jeanette, and Heidi all get attacked as a result of their relationships with Jack in some way. Does Jack bear any responsibility for these attacks? Do you think he could've done more to protect them?

9. Throughout the novel, Jack refuses the protections offered by Scott, Martin, and Feng, knowing that Abner is trying to kill him. What do you make of his behavior? Do you think that he's trying to tempt fate? Do you perceive this behavior as arrogant?

10. Eric greets Jack with warmth and enthusiasm at The Rat. Were you surprised by the encounter between Jack and Eric in the park at the end of the novel?

11. At the end of the novel, Abner has killed himself and his legacy is tainted. Is this morally satisfying, or would you have preferred a different outcome?

12. What do you make of Heidi and Jack's relationship? Do you believe it will continue to be platonic? If they are eventually to be together, is this disrespectful to Kerry?

13. In the same way that Harry's death brought Jack and Kerry together, Kerry's death brought Heidi and Jack together. How much of their relationship can be attributed to their loss?

LOUIS BEGLEY's previous novels are *Killer, Come Hither; Memories of a Marriage; Schmidt Steps Back; Matters of Honor; Shipwreck; Schmidt Delivered; Mistler's Exit; About Schmidt; As Max Saw It; The Man Who Was Late;* and *Wartime Lies,* which won the PEN/Hemingway Award and the Irish Times/Aer Lingus International Fiction Prize. His work has been translated into fourteen languages. He is a member of the American Academy of Arts and Letters.

louisbegley.com

ABOUT THE TYPE

This book was set in Hoefler Text, a family of fonts designed by Jonathan Hoefler, who was born in 1970. First designed in 1991, Hoefler Text looks to the old-style fonts of the seventeenth century, but it is wholly of its time, employing a precision and sophistication available only to the late twentieth century.

Chat.
Comment.
Connect.

Visit our online book club community at
Facebook.com/RHReadersCircle

Chat
Meet fellow book lovers and discuss what you're reading.

Comment
Post reviews of books, ask—and answer—thought-provoking
questions, or give and receive book club ideas.

Connect
Find an author on tour, visit our author blog, or invite one of
our 150 available authors to chat with your group on the phone.

Explore
Also visit our site for discussion questions, excerpts, author
interviews, videos, free books, news on the latest releases,
and more.

Books are better with buddies.
Facebook.com/RHReadersCircle